WITHOUT SHADOWS

A Novel

Kathryn Horsley

Vendera Publishing

Published by Vendera Publishing | www.venderapublishing.com

Edited by Carolyn Pinard

Interior design and typesetting by interiorbookdesigns.com

ISBN 13 Digit: 978-1-936307-33-3

ISBN 10 Digit: 1-936307-33-2

Published in the United States of America

To my girls, who keep me in constant supply of glitter, drama, and loving support

They say that time changes you, but they would be wrong. If time alone had a way of altering people, then I would have changed since Claire's death. But my sorrows could not bring me closer to the human I once was. Thirty-four years may seem like a long time for the humans, but it passes quickly for a vampire.

Perhaps that is why Luther acts so infantile. Why he can't be here on time... why he cannot track his own prey... and why I am waiting for him in the cold, yet again.

Sitting on the ground, I rest my forearms on my knees. The snow beneath me saturates my pants making them stick to my skin uncomfortably. And yes, I do blame Luther for that.

Quietly, I watch the silhouette of a woman with her kitchen light behind her. I have seen her numerous times before, with her chestnut hair and baby blue eyes. Alone and timid, she keeps to herself – which is good for me and what I want to do.

I can sense him before I hear his footsteps.

"About time," I grumble to Luther.

He skids to a halt beside me. "What? Do you have something better to do?" he says sarcastically.

Even after more than a hundred years, his vile tone grates on my nerves. "Well, I could be learning how to juggle or holding my breath or anything else. Hell, I'd rather be confessing my sins to a priest right now." Standing up, I continue, "But instead, I am here trying to help you. And wasting my time."

And I mean that. If it were not for Marcella's persistence, I would not be training Luther at all. Instead, I would be enjoying my time with Kate by my side. But Marcella wanted me out of the house, though I am not sure why. Perhaps, she is secretly hoping that tonight will be the night that I remove Luther from our family once and for all.

He huffs, "Wasting your time? You're immortal, Nick. You have time to waste."

Dusting off the seat of my pants, I tell him, "That's true. Everyone has time to waste until one day they don't."

He knows I am right. Tomorrow is not guaranteed, even for immortals. Just ask the werewolves I have killed. They thought they had a firm grasp on forever. They thought wrong.

I, on the other hand, am not hoping for an eternity. I am merely biding my time in this world, not quite ready to disappear completely. But not really finding much reason to stay, either.

"Come on," I start. "I would rather not be here when the sun comes up."

I turn my attention back to the small house nearby and watch the woman wash her dishes for the last time.

"What's her name?" Luther asks.

Looking sharply at him, I reply, "Don't confuse the situation, Luther. We are not here for social hour over a spot of tea. She is a sheep. It would help if you started thinking of her in that light."

I know my words did not settle into him when he shrugs. "What now? We just wait until she comes out?"

His inexperience is mindboggling. How has he survived this long? Oh, wait, we all keep saving him, that's how.

"You can wait." I smile slyly, "I'm going inside." Reaching into my pocket, I take out a pair of glasses. With one glass cracked and chipped, they would not help anyone to see better. Not that I would use them for that anyway.

I slide them on and see the curiosity cover Luther's face. Letting my fingernails grow out, I slice a cut along my hairline and let the blood trickle down my forehead.

"What are you doing?" Luther asks as the laceration begins to heal.

Glancing up at him, I say, "Putting on a show." I smear the blood across my forehead and down to my cheek. And though I know he does not understand what I mean, I do not clarify. He will see soon enough.

Leaving him in the snow, I sprint across the yard and walk onto the porch. So much of being a good vampire is about knowing how to lie. And lie well. It is about playing a part that has nothing to do with the real you. Only showing the world the things that they want to see and know.

Slumping against the doorframe, I knock weakly. Making a pained expression, I place my hand against my head.

I hear Luther scoff to himself. "No way this works," he mumbles quietly.

Of course it may not work for him. He is oppressive, which women can sense. But me? I am confident and exude a tenderness that he simply does not possess. So, that being said, I will have no trouble monopolizing her naïveté.

It only takes a moment for her to open the door, and I look up at her with vulnerable eyes. "I'm sorry to bother you, but I just wrecked my truck," I say, pointing behind me and moving my hand enough to expose the blood on my forehead. "And I was wondering if I could use your phone."

Half stunned, she steps aside. "Of course, come in." And that's how it is done.

I step inside and she closes the door behind me. "Are you all right?" she asks, looking at my bloody forehead.

Smiling a nearly bashful smile, I tell her, "I'm better now."

Not only am I inside her house, but I have a few moments away from Luther. So yes, I am better now. But that is not what she hears.

She smiles softly at me. "Are you flirting with me while you're getting blood on my carpet?" she asks, though I know I am not truly bleeding still.

My smile becomes lopsided as though I am embarrassed, "Seems that way." Of course, it only seems that way to her.

Taking my hand gently, she pulls me toward the kitchen. "Come on. Let's get you cleaned up."

Her causal touch makes me almost wish that she was not intended to become a sheep, that there was another way to take what we need. That maybe, if things were different, if humans knew about creatures like us, some would volunteer for the life of thralldom we subject them to. But wishing for things only gets you so far, and the world is not ready for that amount of change.

She leads me to a chair beside a small oval table, and as she starts toward the sink, she tells me, "Go ahead and have a seat."

I let the chair creak under my weight as I sit down and watch her wet a cloth.

Letting the water warm, she keeps her fingers under the faucet, making it splatter into the bottom of the sink loudly. Her light brown hair falls forward but I can still make out the profile of her face. With a small, pert nose and wide, bright eyes, she looks even more beautiful close up than she had from far away, and I cannot help but second-guess giving her to Luther.

With one hand, she pushes back her feathered locks as she turns and walks to me. "So where did you wreck your truck?" she asks, reminding me of my purpose here.

It takes me a moment to answer her as she removes my glasses and lays them on the table. Then she presses the towel to my cheek and wipes the blood away gently. Such a tender touch, one that I do not deserve.

"About a mile from here," I tell her.

Her eyes meet mine with kindness. "There are closer homes. Why did you walk all the way to my house?"

 I shrug. "Your lights were on," I say simply. And what else could I say? Because her loner lifestyle makes her an easy target? I doubt that would have a very nice effect.

"Besides," I start, "you're the one I was looking for, Lindsey."

Her heart picks up a beat as she asks, "How do you know my name?"

She pulls her hand away but I grab her wrist. And just like that, I am locked on to her. Her will belongs to me. "Stay calm," I tell her.

And as her body relaxes, the towel falls to the floor with a plop.

I have often wondered what it would be like to be enthralled. Whether you hear your own thoughts as clearly as my voice. Whether your body resists it at all. Whether you could stop it if you knew to try.

"Come with me," I say as I lead her toward the living room. I do not say anything to her as I open the front door. There is really nothing to say. Not unless I want to lie, which I don't. Not if it can be helped.

Glancing up at Luther, I nod at him. He hurries across the yard and onto the porch. Stopping in front of the door as though there is a wall preventing him from going further, he says, "Let me in, Nick."

I smile. "You know what you need to say," I whisper to him, keeping Lindsey from hearing my voice and mistaking my comments to be her own thoughts.

He grimaces. "You can burn in hell," he says, crossing his arms.

"And you can starve," I remind him with a smirk.

He looks up at the top of the door for a moment, considering his next words. Sure, I could make this easy for the both of us, but where is the fun in that?

Sighing, he drops his arms. "Please," he says through gritted teeth.

"Well, that was not convincing," I start sarcastically. "But come in," I tell him with a certain satisfaction that only comes from winning even the smallest battles with him.

He pushes past me, knocking my shoulder back with his. His childish pouting makes me chuckle lightly to myself before I close the door.

Standing near Lindsey, he looks her over. "This is it?" he asks unpleasantly.

His smug tone annoys me to no end, and I step between him and Lindsey. "Yes," I tell him quietly so she does not hear me, "and when I let go of her, she will be scared. She will scream. She will run. But you cannot let your severely pathetic amount of control get the best of you. Keep your eyes from changing to black and don't finish your meal. For once."

He purses his lips for a moment, then asks with heavy sarcasm, "Is that an order, your majesty?"

Perhaps, if his attitude was not so abrasive, I would be inclined to keep my hand on Lindsey's wrist; keep her quiet and still, make this easier for him. But his tone does little to encourage me to help him more than required. I know that her struggling and screaming will only increase his need to fill his belly with her blood.

And honestly, a small part of me is hoping he will fall short of stopping so that his position in this family does not change. His position being: the failure.

I slide my hand away from Lindsey and she blinks her eyes a few times as her thoughts begin to clear. Her eyes meet Luther's. "Who are you?" she stammers out nervously. "What are you doing here?"

Valid questions that will soon be answered. "Try not to kill this one," I tell Luther matter-of-factly.

Hearing my words causes her breathing to become chaotic and her heart to pound against her ribs as panic sets in. She backs away from us, knocking a lamp over with her hand. It smashes to the floor and scatters its pieces across the hardwood.

"Nice going, Nick," Luther says sharply. Though, it is not the lamp that he is referring to. Sure, I could have kept her calm but, realistically, he needs to be able to do this, despite a human's fear.

Besides, what more does he want? "I basically delivered her to you on a plate. I suppose you want me to spoon-feed you, too? Maybe hold your hand when you cross the street?" I step closer to him. "Be serious, Luther. It's time to be more than a man. It's time to start being a vampire."

I realize that it may be difficult for him since he is not much of a man to begin with. But he has to try.

I nod my head toward Lindsey, who is picking up a sliver of the broken lamp. "Go fetch."

His eyes narrow on me but still he starts across the room. Lindsey swings the shard wildly at him while she moves around the coffee table.

"Stay away from me," she orders through erratic breaths.

Luther follows her. Not rushing, he tries to keep himself calm, which is good. He will need to focus.

But after several minutes of watching them essentially dance around the small table, I say, "I hope you don't plan on buying her dinner, too."

Even though he does not look over at me, I know he is listening, so I continue, "I hate to be pushy, and patience is a nice thing to have. But speed is a virtue, too. So let's move this along."

No sooner than the words leave my lips, Luther reaches for Lindsey. She swings the piece of lamp at him, cutting his arm. Although it does not even slow him, I am slightly impressed that she has enough fight in her to at least try.

Grabbing a handful of hair just behind her ear, he keeps her at a distance. Her fear takes over and she struggles against him as tears begin to roll down her cheek.

His fangs grow out and his fingernails dig into her scalp, causing her let out a scream, one of more fear than pain. Little does she know that her terror only makes my heartbeat quicken and my senses heighten as my body yearns for a kill.

I inhale deeply, trying to focus. But tasting her cold sweat hanging in the air only makes me hunger for her blood more.

As Luther leans close to her neck, despite the way she pushes away from him, I place my hand on his shoulder. "Keep your eyes soft," I remind him quietly.

I remember being here. Remember feeling as though keeping my human eyes while feeding would be impossible. Feeling the fire in my throat and knowing that my instincts are to take lives.

Feeling too weak to complete the task at hand, too weak to successfully enthrall a sheep. But I did it. That night, I found my control. That night, I found a part of myself again.

Although, this part is difficult for us, calling your sheep can be just as problematic. To let yourself be so vulnerable, so distracted, for even a moment, feels unnatural. Some vampires refuse to keep humans simply for that reason. And Luther may refuse it, too. However, his reason will be more about skill than comfort, even if he does not admit to that.

Luther places his lips to her skin and bites into her neck. Her arms fold into his chest, pinning them, while she cries out painfully. Somewhere between her sobbing and jagged whimpering, her eyes meet mine. Fearful and pleading, they pierce through me, bringing with them a pity that I hold for very few humans.

My guilt urges me to look away, but don't. I let myself feel the pain I am causing her. Let myself be swayed by the sadness in her blue eyes, the understanding that this is the end, along with her patience for death to find her.

She fights to keep her eyes open as they begin to haze over and her body slumps against Luther.

"That's enough," I tell him.

But the possessiveness in him makes him tighten his grip on her waist, pulling her closer. Without seeing his face, I know that his eyes are black and he has failed again.

"I said, enough," I order sharply.

Still, he does not listen. His hand slides up her back, supporting her weight, as his hunger rages. I can hear his heart pounding in his chest and his quick breaths between drinking.

I grab her limp body and rip her from his arms, causing his teeth to slice through her tender skin. "Stop!" I tell him abruptly as I let her fall to the floor.

Without his touch, she regains her consciousness and clutches her neck as the blood pours from between her fingers. Gasping and sputtering blood from the gnashes in her neck, she attempts to stand but finds that she is much too weak for that. She tumbles over again, smearing blood across the floor.

Ignoring her, I keep my eyes fixed on Luther. "Are you really that weak?" I say, not attempting to soften my harsh tone.

He shrugs. "I have a lousy teacher," he says as his eyes change back to brown.

Is he really putting this on me? I scoff at his remark. "It's called *self*-control, Luther. And you have had over a hundred years to gain some and haven't yet. That's my fault too, I suppose?"

I feel a hand grab my ankle. Knowing that it is Lindsey, I shake my leg, making her lose her grip on me.

"I think it is funny that you blame others for your problems," I continue to Luther.

Wiping the blood from his lips with his sleeve, he asks, "Why is that funny?"

"Because you learned from me," I smirk, "your lousy teacher."

He smiles, laughing lightly to himself. And I admit, when he is not being obnoxious, he is somewhat likeable. Though, I would never say that to him.

His eyes find their way to Lindsey lying on the floor in a puddle of her own blood and his smile fades. "What do we do with her?"

I look down at her scared eyes and blood-soaked hair, and let out a heavy sigh. "I guess I could try to enthrall her myself. But after your feeding, I'm not sure if there is enough blood left in her to keep her alive."

He crosses his arms, more insecurely than defensively. "We just kill her then? Why even stop me?"

What should I say here? It's not over? He has not failed yet? There is a chance he could save her? Those are all lies.

Pushing my hand through my hair, I exhale forcefully. "Just let me think."

We cannot come home empty-handed. Marcella has made it very clear that if we do not bring someone back with us tonight, she will find her own sheep. And Marcella on the hunt is never a good thing. Slaughtering and feasting her way through a town until she finds someone pleasing to the eyes. Someone who will tempt her in more ways than one. Though, she would never use the sheep for more than sustenance. She simply happens to be vain – like most vampires – which is why most vampires only turn attractive people. I suppose that also explains why vampires tend to be conceited.

Only moments into thinking of a plan, we hear someone sloshing through the snow and coming toward the house.

My head jerks up quickly. This could be the answer. "Pick her up," I order, keeping my voice low.

Luther pulls her from the floor and follows me into the hallway.

The person outside steps onto the porch and knocks.

Even with Luther's hand over her mouth, Lindsey manages to attempt to scream for help. Even though her muffled cries are not very loud, I whisper, "Keep her quiet." "I'm trying," Luther insists.

There is another knock then someone calls, "Lindsey?"

A man's voice. Not my favorite choice for a sheep, but anything will do at this point.

She struggles against Luther's unmoving arms and I am surprised by how much power she is still able to muster, despite the significant blood loss. His hand only subdues her wailing so much and I tire of his incompetence.

"Keep her quiet," I say through gritted teeth. If she were in my arms, she would be relaxed, calm, even peaceful. But because he is so incapable of the most basic of skills, she is resisting.

"I'm trying," Luther says again but this time, more sternly. And I think, *obviously not.* "What else would you have me do?" "Lindsey?" the man yells again.

Frustrated with Luther, I tell him, "If she is going to scream then let her scream."

I can tell by the look on his face that he does not understand. But in all reality, doing something is more natural for a vampire than hiding in a hallway is.

As he slides his hand away from her mouth slowly, I let my fangs grow out. Standing still, she stares at me for a moment before I lean close to her face. "Scream," I say coldly.

"James!" she shouts fearfully.

The front door swings open quickly, slamming into the wall. Without hesitation, I grab her head and jerk her chin around, breaking her neck. Her head drops forward as her body slumps in Luther's arms.

There is a brief pause in the man's steps when, I assume, he is stopped by the sight of blood pooled on the floor. "Lindsey!" he calls with worry lacing his voice.

He rushes unknowingly toward us. It only takes a split second for the sound of his footsteps to grow close. Only a split second for me to run from the hallway and grab him by the neck. Before he even sees my face, I slam him into the wall hard enough to leave an indentation outlining his shape. My teeth are in his carotid before a scream escapes his lips.

His smooth blood cools the fire in my throat. For a moment, I tease myself with the idea of letting my eyes change to black and gorge myself with this simple meal, but I know how to control this better than that.

A strength surges through me with every swallow. Alluring and enticing, it beckons me to drain him, invites me to feel the power behind taking a life, provoking me to give in to my thirst just this once.

He begins to lean his weight against me and his ragged breaths grow calm and even. I pull my mouth away, letting my fangs recede.

Holding his limp body, I listen to the slow beating of his heart, trying to talk myself out of finishing him. Then, removing my hands, I let his body slide along the wall and onto the floor. Sliding my tongue over my lower lip, I lick the blood off it as Luther steps into the room, still holding Lindsey's dead body.

I smile at him. "You can drop her now."

He looks down at her as though he had forgotten she was there at all. Tossing her aside, her body lands on the floor with a thump. Her hair drapes across her face and her hands clasp together like she praying. Which, deep down, I hope she has already done tonight.

"What are we going to do about this?" Luther asks.

We? Last time I looked, this is his mess. Not mine. "Nothing. Let the police sort it out."

I know what they will think. A man comes in and kills, what I assume is, his girlfriend then runs away. It happens every day.

"Leave her," I continue. "We take James."

He does not need to ask who I am referring to. It is quite clear to both of us that even if she was not screaming for this man, it does not matter much. A name for a sheep is as good any other.

"Let's go," I tell him before anything else can happen tonight.

Listening, he picks up James's body and lays him over his shoulder. Closing the door, we leave the house in shambles and hurry to the truck, which is parked nearly a mile away.

Luther slides James into the middle of the bench seat and hops in the driver's side. I am not very happy about riding in the passenger seat for such a long trip, but at least James is between us.

The road is rough but that does not bother me. I stare out of the window, quietly. There is nothing much to say to Luther. Nothing nice, anyway.

I will never understand how someone so pretentious can be so pathetic. He has such potential to be a great vampire but he squanders it with stubbornness and selfishness. Of course, he would never be better than me. But he should try to be.

He does not deserve to still be alive without contributing to this family even a little. And he never deserved Kate's affection. Nor did I ever understand what she saw in him.

"What are you thinking about?" Luther asks, breaking my concentration.

I could tell him that I was thinking about Kate, but I know how that would hurt him; remind him of the way she loves me but never has loved him. The way she still clings to me. Still waiting for me to want her, too.

I have no reason to be kind to him so I respond, "Kate will know that a male sheep was not my first choice." I look over at him. "She'll like James, though." She always picks men. I smirk. "Guess someone will be happy that you are still a terrible vampire."

His eyebrows draw close together but he says nothing.

My eyes find their way back to the window. "Just make sure you get him home alive," I say sharply.

"What do you mean?"

I look over at him, irritable. "I mean, there is not a chance in hell that I am riding for five hundred miles next to you."

Not in a million years will I ever enjoy sitting so close to Luther for even half as long. "When we reach the safe house to exchange trucks and meet the plane, I am going to run the rest of the way. You can fly home by yourself."

"Good," he says, shrugging. "I hope the sun comes up on you."

I laugh to myself. Even walking, I would not run the risk of being caught in the few hours of daylight Fairbanks has to offer at this time of the year. "I will be home before you." There isn't a doubt in my mind.

"Want to bet?" he taunts.

Intrigued, I sit up straighter in the seat and tell him, "Alright."

I smile at the thought of winning so easily, "When you lose, you have to talk Marcella into teaching you herself. I don't want to have to come out with you again."

He looks over at me instead of watching the road, but never comes close to wrecking. "You're the best at enthralling, Nick." That's true. "That's why I asked for you."

No, it isn't. He asked for me so that he would not be stuck with Kate, who broke his heart. And knowing that is why I answer, "You could always ask Kate instead."

There is a pause before he says, "Fine. I'll ask Marcella. But *only* if I lose." Rest assured, he will lose. "And if I win," he adds, "I get to pick the next sheep."

I stop for a moment. I always pick the sheep. Stalking the prey is an essential part of the hunt. A part I happen to enjoy. If I let him take that away from me, there is nothing left in these trips for me. These lessons will be even more painfully boring than they are now.

But I do not intend on losing. I reach my hand around James and say, "Deal."

My *legs carry me over* the snow-dusted tundra. Moving quickly, I ignore the way my body aches for another feeding. The way my throat burns with

desire for more blood and the distraction of my senses picking up on every stray human around me.

I keep my focus on beating Luther home. It is the only thing that matters to me now. It is fair to say that I am a bit competitive, especially when it comes to Luther. Not that I feel threatened by him; merely that I enjoy watching him lose at everything.

Without realizing the pleasure it brings me, he mopes around the house for days, pouting and whining about even the smallest of things, like a child would.

Having avoided town to keep from slowing my progression, I can see the house in the distance. Small but adequate, it serves as our vacation home here within the Arctic Circle. After all, why would we not spend the majority of our winters where there is no daylight to hide from? The humans here have not seen the sun for weeks. When it does reappear, the days will be short at first. And when there is more daylight than nighttime hours, we will leave. It's that simple.

The blue-gray paint on the house is fresh but frigid-looking, and the narrow porch only serves as a place to dust off your boots before coming inside.

I know the others hear me coming, but I only hope Luther is not one of them as I bound onto the porch. I rush through the door and see Kate standing near the couch with wide eyes.

"Is Luther here?" I ask in a hurry.

Kate steps around me and closes the door. "Not yet. What happened?"

That is all I needed to hear. I won.

Grabbing her around the waist, I lift her up above me. She laughs lightly as I spin her in a circle. Her happy cries only make me hold her tighter and my smile grow more lopsided. Stopping, I set her down in front of me but keep my hold on her.

Draping her arms around my neck, she asks, "What was that for?"

I do not attempt to hide the excitement in my voice. "I'm free!"

That is – as long as Luther keeps up his end of the bargain.

"What are you talking about?" she asks, slightly concerned. "Where is Luther?"

I drop my arms. "I didn't kill him, Kate." Though, I wish I had. "We made a bet, that's all." A bet that he will stand by, or he will be answering to me.

"I didn't say that you killed him, Nick." She leans close and kisses my cheek. Keeping her face next to mine, she whispers, "I only thought it."

I can hear the smile in her tone and it makes me laugh to myself quietly.

"Well, well, well," I hear from an all-too familiar voice that makes my heart stop. "As I live and breathe."

I pull away from Kate quickly, though I am not sure why. There is nothing happening between Kate and me to be ashamed of, so why do I feel so guilty all of a sudden?

Standing across the room is a beauty unlike any other. The most tempting vampire I have ever laid eyes on. With her high cheekbones, straight nose, and dark eyes, she is a Chinese jewel with a Mia Farrow crop. Stunning. Absolutely stunning.

And I cannot hide my smile for her. "Yen."

She holds her arms out to me. It is an invitation that I cannot turn down. I hurry to her, wrapping my arms around her and squeeze just hard enough to make her squeal.

I press my lips to her cheek gently and then step back from her, taking her hands in mine. "Look at you," I say, looking her over. "The past hundred years have been kind."

Smiling, she rolls her eyes. "I look exactly the same, Nicolas."

That is true. Mostly. "I like your hair," I tell her as I run my fingers through the short locks.

She places her hand on her head. "Really?" I nod. "You don't think I look like boy?"

I do not think she could ever look like a boy. I do not think she could ever look any less irresistible. "No. Not at all." Jokingly, I continue, "I do think you look like you lost a bet, though." Hitting my arm playfully, she huffs.

"In a good way," I add, smiling.

Knowing that I am not serious, she takes my hand again. Her ease around me almost makes me forget how much time has passed since I last saw her. It is almost as though she has always been here with me. But she was gone. And for a very long time, too.

"What are you doing here?" I ask her softly.

Yen looks up at me as though she is hiding something. "Do I need a reason to visit my favorite vampires?" She looks around me. "And Kate?" she adds.

Behind me, I hear Kate snicker a noticeably fake laugh, making Yen smirk.

Long ago, I realized that Yen and Kate would never be great friends, but I have always hoped they could at least try to be amiable to each other. However, that has not happened yet, despite my attempts.

"Hey," I tell her, regaining her attention. "Why don't we go to my room to talk? I need to get ready for work anyway."

Looking at me, Yen raises an eyebrow. "Asking me to your room already?" she says is sultry voice. Then she loops her arm through mine, "What took you so long?"

Ignoring the feeling of Kate's eyes burning into me, and the sound of her clothes swishing as she crosses her arms, I lead Yen out of the living room and down the hallway.

"I thought you were in Mexico?" I start.

Sighing lightly, she answers, "As it turns out, a three-day sex stint with a man who doesn't know he has a heart condition isn't the best idea I've ever had."

I laugh to myself. Yen does have a way of picking men for all the wrong reasons. Very much like the way I choose women – purely physical. We seek the short-term pleasures another can provide.

"You need someone who can keep up with you then," I tell her as we walk past the first two bedrooms.

"Like you?" she asks with a smile in her voice.

Reaching for the doorknob to my room, I look over at her. "Not this time."

And though I did not mean it as a joke, she laughs just the same. Stepping past me, she walks to my bed and sits on the edge. "When have you ever said no to me?"

Not often enough. Closing the door, I walk toward her. With two beds along the wall, the room is more crowded than our other homes, but we cannot afford to stand out with an ostentatious house in this town. Drawing attention to vampires would only be detrimental for us.

Besides, sharing a room with the sheep is not as bad as sleeping next to Luther, so it suits me just fine.

Placing my hand next to her on the bed, I bend over her, making her lean back toward the bed. With my nose close to hers, I can smell the sweetness of her skin and iron-rich blood. It makes my mouth water, but I am in control.

I rub my fingers across her cheek, feeling her delicate flesh. "No," I whisper. Dropping my hand, I stand up straight and smile. "That's once."

She laughs to herself as though she does not believe in my resistance to her. And if I am honest with myself, I have my doubts, too. In the past, I have never been strong around her, but then again, I have never tried to be, either.

"Don't look," I tell her, "I need to change clothes."

As I walk to the closet, I hear her say, "It's not like I haven't seen it before." She crosses her legs, laying her hand on her knee. "I doubt much has changed."

She is right. My body has not changed in nearly six hundred years. Not since I was turned by that thing; that vampire who so callously took everything from me. The one vampire I hope to meet again before I die.

Opening my closet, I take out my orderly uniform. Solid white is not my favorite color to wear, probably because white tends to show blood too easily for comfort. I will need to be aware of my actions in this attire before I take a life.

"Why do you work? I thought you were a writer?" Yen asks without looking at me.

I am a writer. But so much about writing is knowing about humans and the way they live. I could say that I am working beside the humans for research proposes, but truthfully, I am doing this for redemptive reasons. Trying to right the wrongs I have committed against man. Trying to prove to myself that I am not as cold as I truly am. But so far, I am falling short.

I pull on my clothes quickly. "Being around the humans makes me feel more alive," I tell her.

If anyone understands that, it is Yen. She spends more time with the humans than with her own kind, only coming to visit us once every fifty to one hundred years. And not having much contact with any other vampires in between.

There is something to be said about the way the two of us enjoy living a lie more than being who we are.

"What are you really doing here?" I ask her as I button up my shirt.

Alone with me, the one she has always opened up to, she can be honest. I can hear in her sigh that she knows it, too.

"Marcella called me." She turns to face me. "She's worried about Kate," she says softly.

I smile. Since when has Yen cared about Kate? But my smile fades quickly as I consider what Marcella could have been referring to.

As I walk over to the bed, she continues, "She thought you could use a distraction."

Of course Marcella thought that. She knows how Kate feels about me, and that I don't feel the same. Though, truly, I think I could. Kate is beautiful and smart. She is fun and determined. She is my best friend and knows me better than anyone else, which is also why I cannot love her. My relationships always end badly, and I do not want that for her.

Marcella obviously does not trust me to keep an appropriate distant from Kate. And I am not that surprised that it was Yen she called for help with me – especially considering our past.

I sit on the edge of the bed. "And you agreed to that?"

She slides closer to me. "Say what you want about us, but we always have fun."

That is true. The way her eyes sparkle when she talks about us makes her alluring, but I decided the last time I saw her that what I have with Yen needs to end.

"I don't need you to babysit me. I know exactly what I am doing," I tell her.

"Maybe you don't," she starts as she takes my hand. "Maybe you don't realize how charming you are." The softness of her voice draws me in, and I struggle to not fall back into my old role with her.

It would be so easy to let myself enjoy her tender touch, to run my fingers through her short locks, to feel her lips against mine. It's a familiar position to put myself in with her, one that is comfortable and safe. Nobody gets too close. Nobody gets hurt.

Rubbing her fingers over the back of my hand, she continues, "If I remember correctly, you charmed my pants off. Literally."

I laugh to myself and pull my hand away. "Then you don't remember correctly. It was you who seduced me," I remind her. But in reality, she didn't have to try very hard. I was such a young vampire that I did not have much control over my desires at that point. "And after you left, I went through three weeks of a bloodlust that made me think I was dying. Or at least, wished I was."

It set my progression back a year. And at the time, I could think of nothing but getting out of that basement and hunting a human the way my instincts were begging me to. I resented Marcella for keeping me beyond the time that I believed I was ready to roam the night. But she was right; I wasn't ready. "Yeah," Yen says causally, "But I was worth it." I smile. She definitely was.

Standing up, I tell her, "I have to go to work now. Try to be nice to Kate while I'm gone."

Rolling her eyes, she makes an X over her heart with her finger.

Cradling her face in my hands, I kiss her forehead gently. "It's good to see you again, Yen. I hope you're here when I get back."

I walk to the door, and as I open it, I hear her say, "You say it's over between us," I turn as she walks over to me, "but I know you, Nick. As soon as something goes wrong, it's my arms you'll run to."

Grabbing my face firmly, she presses her lips to mine. There is a force behind her desire that makes me crave her. She slides her hand to the base of my skull as she pulls her lips away. Placing her cheek against mine, she whispers, "And rest assured, I'll be here for that."

Telling myself to let her go, I do not stop her from leaving my room. As soon as she is gone, I begin to breathe again. This might be more difficult that I thought. But I cannot focus on that now.

Sighing, I run my fingers through my hair and start down the hallway.

I find Marcella in the kitchen alone. She has not changed much in all of these years. She still has the same short blond hair, the same bright red lips, and the same sharp eyes. She smiles when she sees my uniform. "You look so human in that."

Although I am not sure if she meant it as a compliment or not, I smile. "Just so you know, your plan isn't going to work."

She looks at me confused, though she knows what I am speaking of. So I continue, "I am not getting close to Yen just to put some distance between Kate and me. In fact, your plan is backfiring because I'll be sleeping in Kate's bed tonight so Yen can have mine. It's the only logical place for her to sleep."

Logical because in this small of a house, there are not enough bedrooms for guests to have their own. Plus, vampires do not often trust each other to sleep in the same beds. But luckily, Kate trusts me. And sure, I could sleep on the couch, but I am not going to.

By the look on her face, I can tell Marcella never considered that Yen would not be sleeping with me. I press Marcella's hand in mine. "I'll see you later."

Gently, I kiss her cheek and start into the living room just as Luther and James, who is now awake but still disoriented, come through the door.

I cannot hide the contentment Luther's look of frustration brings me. "What took you so long, sweetheart?" I tease. "Did you stop off to do your nails? I understand you have to look pretty for second place."

He tosses a set of truck keys into a blue bowl that is resting on the small table beside the door. "You cheated," he accuses sharply.

Excuse me? I do not need to cheat. "I did not," I snap, "Do not blame me for your incompetence, Luther. I can't help it if you are terrible at everything."

He steps toward me. "You told the pilot to delay takeoff. It's the only way into the city." Of course it is the only way into the city. There are no roads past Deadhorse.

He leans his face close to mine just to provoke me. "You are a liar, Nick. It's not that much of a stretch to make you a cheat, too."

My pulse quickens. How dare he call me a cheat. A liar, sure. But a cheat? Never. "If I had cheated, it wouldn't have been such a narrow race." A heat rolls through me and my English accent begins to weigh heavy on my tone as I say coldly, "Now step aside. You reek of failure."

Using the back of my hand, I push him away from me. I go to the door and grab the doorknob.

Sighing, I drop my accent and yell, "Marcella, Luther has something he wants to ask you."

Luther huffs, letting me know that he did not forget our bet. Losing means he must convince Marcella to take him out for training herself.

I look at Luther and smirk. "Pitch it to her well, Luther. Because if I go out with you again, it will be your last night alive," I say matter-of-factly – and part of me does mean it.

"Feed my sheep while I'm gone," I order him. "After all, of the two of you, he is the more difficult one to replace."

His eyes narrow on me. "Go to hell."

As if I have never heard that before. I believe he already said something to the same effect earlier in the night even. I laugh to myself just to rile him. "No one ever accused you of being an original thinker, that's for sure."

No wonder Kate loves him. Oh wait, she doesn't. And I could tell him that. I want to say it to him. But I fight back the words and instead say, "Tell you what; I'll be gone for about nine hours, so you think of a really good comeback for that. But pace yourself; I wouldn't want you to get hurt."

I do not wait for his droll response. Do not pay any mind to his grumbling and huffing. Grabbing my coat, I walk out of the house and back into the dark day, glad to be rid of him for a few more hours.

The snow, that never seems to melt, crunches beneath me as I walk toward the small hospital across town. Sure, most humans would drive the distance, but the cold does not bother me much and the occasional shivers these frigid temperatures bring makes me feel more human, which I need to feel since I work around so many vulnerable humans.

I kick a clump of snow with my boot and watch it disperse into a fine powder around me. The air is much too dry to make the snow heavy and wet. Not really suitable for packing into snowballs, which is a shame for the children here.

The town is quiet for now, as it's too early for most of its inhabitants to be awake. But every once in a while, there is a random light on in the window of one of the cold-looking houses.

I pass by the bank with frost on the windows and leave my footprints in the snow as I walk through the parking lot of the sleepy grocery store. Letting my fingers trail over the bars of a lone shopping cart in the lot, I feel the frigid metal threatening to cling to my skin. Like the moon on the tide, there is a gentle pull to it, reminding me of just how cold the darkness is here.

Just past the tavern, I see a truck parked in the road, still idling. A stream of hot air escapes the exhaust. The quiet murmuring of the engine disrupts the still morning.

I walk up to the driver's side window, knowing what I will find inside. Sure enough, the young man inside has his head leaning against the window as drool runs down his chin. His shaggy blond hair is smashed on the glass, parting his hair in an unnatural way, and his hot breath fogs up the window, making it difficult to see his face clearly. But I already know who it is.

Tapping on the window, I watch him stir, struggling to blink his eyes and wiping his face with his sleeve. Disoriented, he looks around the cab, smacking his lips together and trying to alleviate, what I am sure is, an extremely dry mouth.

After a brief moment, he gathers himself enough to roll down the window. "Hey, Nick," he says with half-opened eyes.

The smell of whiskey is strong enough to make me turn my head and take a step back slightly. "Hey, Luke." I turn my eyes back to him.

Although, physically, he is nearly the same age as me, he seems so much younger. With baby features and a soft voice, one might assume him to be only sixteen. And I am sure that if he lived in a bigger town, he would have a hard time getting into the bars that he frequents.

"You do realize that you have to be at work in about fifteen minutes, right?" I ask him.

As he rubs his hands over his face, I believe I hear him cuss under his breath. Then looking up at me with his still-sleepy eyes, he says, "I can make it on time."

I cannot help the smile that forms on my face. Very rarely does he ever make it on time for his shift. And that's when he is sober.

"I hope so," I tell him. "They're going to fire you if you don't watch it." Which would be a shame since he is one of the few humans that I enjoy working with.

He scoffs at my comment. "Sure they will," he says sarcastically. "Like they can find someone else who wants to mop up puke for a living."

I could remind him that orderlies and janitors, like us, are a dime a dozen, but instead I laugh causally. "Just be there," I tell him. Then I turn to start toward the hospital again.

Quietly I hear, "Thanks, man." And then mumble quietly to himself, "You saved my ass."

I do not stop walking since I am sure he did not intend for me to hear him. But still, I smile to myself.

Luke is a good kid. Just a little mixed up. Too young to have his priorities straightened out yet. And without any real goals for himself, he has simply coasted through his life so far. But I feel confident that he will be able to turn it around, sooner or later.

Surely, a human's fingers would be numb by now, so I shove my hands in my pockets, just to look the part, and start across the parking lot of the small hospital.

Surrounded by snow, the building looks icy, but then, everything here seems cold. Maybe that's because it is. But there is still something about the little hospital that is inviting. Cute and petite, in a cozy sort of way.

I pull one of the heavy glass doors open and stroll inside. Pushing into me, the warm air feels good against my skin, as I imagine it would to a human, as well. As I cross the lobby, I shiver just for show.

"Good morning, Nicolas," the lady behind the desk says without looking up at me. If I didn't know any better, I would assume her to be a werewolf since she has no trouble finding me in a crowd. But she simply happens to be one of the very rare, observant humans.

With her head down, most of her dark hair covers her face, which is a shame since she is one of the more beautiful women that I work with. I watch her as she pushes her locks behind her ear. She glances up at me with only her eyes and bites back a grin, making her seem even lovelier.

From the color to the smoothness, her skin reminds me of Kate's, and the reminiscence makes me smile. "Morning, Grace," I say just as soft as if I were talking to Kate herself.

Without stopping in the lobby, I walk to the locker room and hang my coat on the wall. I take my timesheet from the rack as people shuffle in and out of the room on their way to begin their shifts. Some of them say 'hello' or 'good morning', but most are more concerned with filling out their time cards.

Taking my timesheet, I step away from the crowd around the rack – too many humans, much too close for comfort. I know I could kill them all and get away with it, but what good would that do me?

Pacing myself, I scribble the time on the paper card, trying to occupy as much time as I can in here.

Finally the room begins to clear, and the last human leaves. Alone, I walk back to the rack and place my timesheet back in the holder. As I drop my hand, I stop in front of another time card.

Looking around to ensure that nobody is watching, I take the card down and write in *0500*. Quickly, I place the sheet back in the slot near mine and walk out as though nothing had happened.

I walk upstairs to the inpatient level and approach the nurses' desk where Mary is waiting for me. With her frizzy red hair loosely pulled back, and her freckles splattered across her nose and cheeks, she looks younger than she truly is.

"Well, if it isn't my ray of sunshine in this dark, dark winter," I say as I slide close to her.

She taps her pen on the desk twice before she responds, "You know, it's that kiss-ass attitude that keeps you employed here."

I smile at her sarcasm. "You know you love me."

Fighting a smile, she starts again, "Have you looked at next month's schedule yet?"

As the evening supervisor, it is her job to make out the schedule for the orderlies, like me. Normally, I look at them fairly quickly. But with Christmas and training Luther, I hadn't done it yet, which I know is not the best idea since the first is tomorrow, and I am not sure if I work it or not.

"Am I still on it?" I ask causally.

She rolls her eyes but does not drop her smile. "Be here tomorrow at six a.m. And sometime today, write down what shifts you work."

I open my mouth to response with what, I am sure, will be a sarcastic remark when Doctor Price walks up to us.

Mary's face lights up when she sees him. It is clear to me that their secret affair must have taken a turn for something more serious recently, though I am not sure what the twentysomething Mary sees in the almost-fifty doctor. All I see is a pompous ass with blond hair and smug smile.

"Hello, Mary," he says, making her bite her lip. And I wonder if she realizes how transparent she is being. He points to me. "Nathan, right?"

"Nicolas," I correct him without a hint of kindness in my voice.

"Listen, Norman," he says to me, making me have to hide the snarl I have for him, "why don't you go fetch me some coffee?"

Letting my disdain show, I reply, "That's not exactly my job."

Slightly taken aback, he looks at me in disbelief, though he really shouldn't. This is not the first time I have been blunt with him. But I suppose he does not remember things like that. Or names.

"Nick," Mary scolds softly.

I turn my eyes to Mary, which is a vast improvement of scenery, but it does nothing for the cold tone I have. "Pretty sure the coffeemaker's broken." It's not, "I'll go stock some linens, though."

Before she can say anything else, I walk away from the desk. There are a few things about my job that make it very difficult to spare the humans here. And Doctor Prick, I mean, Price, is one of them.

For most of the day, I busy myself with stocking the linens, taking vitals, and even giving the grouchy old man in room twelve a sponge bath, which I will try to forget as soon as I clock out.

The pretty nurses in white smile at me and treat me like I am one of their longtime friends, easy to converse with – easy as breathing. And for a moment, I forget what I am. I forget the pain I have caused; I forget the hunger inside and the burn that scratches at my throat. For a moment, I catch a glimpse of who I once was.

This is why I work here. To hide from myself. To pay my dues to a weaker species. To feel some atonement for my sins.

And as I stretch the crisp, white sheet over an empty bed, I feel more human than I should. Repeating the mundane tasks of my job everyday should not bring me as much joy as it does, but I know my feeling of humanity will not last.

I slide my hand across the taut sheet, smoothing out the wrinkles. Some would say that I take pride in my work; others would say it is perfectionism. I say wrinkles prevent the blood from smearing across the bed the way it should. And it is those kinds of thoughts that keep my vampire self on standby, constantly waiting for an unsuspecting fool and an adequate opportunity.

In the hall, just outside the door, I hear the sloshing of a mop and squeaking of shoes on the wet floor. I smile to myself. The only person I know who walks behind his mop, leaving his footprints on the clean floor, is Luke. But I think he only does that to annoy his boss.

He starts to pass across the doorway, and when he sees me, he stops. Leaning the mop against the doorframe, he walks over to me with a big smile on his face.

"What's that about?" I ask, referring to his grin as I finish smoothing the sheet.

Pulling a slip of paper from his pocket, he hops on the bed happily. He lays back and props his dirty shoes on end of the bed, making me stand up straight. He is my friend, but still, there are times I consider killing him.

"I got a phone number," he smirks.

Gesturing for him to get up, I tease, "Did you get that from someone in the morgue?"

Huffing, he does not move, but says, "From the ER. She was here with a patient this morning."

Crossing my arms, I tell him only half-seriously, "You have five seconds to get off my bed."

With a smile, he wiggles into the mattress, making himself more comfortable just to spite me.

I do not wait the full five seconds before I shove him off of the bed and let him smack onto the cold tiles.

"Ow," he moans, but I know that he did not actually get hurt. Not severely anyway.

Stripping the sheet from the bed, I continue, "So does this girl know you're a janitor, or did you tell her you were a doctor?"

He stands up stiffly as though he is sore, and I slightly feel sorry for pushing him down. But that does not even begin to register on the list of bad things I have done.

"I may have said 'CEO'," he admits.

Laughing, I toss the dirty sheet at him. He catches it and rolls it into a ball in his arms as he laughs to himself.

"I know," he starts. "Not my best line."

It isn't a good line – especially if he was dressed as a janitor when he said it. Besides, he happens to be much too young to be a CEO. So either she is not that observant or she doesn't care.

As I slip another sheet on the bed, I ask, "Is she pretty?"

But before he can answer, Trish, another nurse, pops her head in. "Nicolas, can you help me for a minute?"

"Sure," I tell her as I slip the final corner of the sheet into place.

She disappears back into the hallway and I start after her. When I am just steps from the door, Luke says, "Thanks for clocking me in this morning. I was about ten minutes late."

I smile at him. Of course he was late. I knew he would be. "I don't know what you're talking about," I lie without attempting to make it sound convincing.

Walking backward into the hallway, I watch him as he half smiles at me. Deep down, he knows that his job is not as secure as he would like it to be; that if he is late many more times, he will be fired. Then there will not be any money for his late nights at the bar. No hope of moving out of his mother's house anytime soon. Just another job search, for just another job.

In the hallway, I catch Trish's scent quickly. The alcohol smell of her cheap perfume is easy to separate from the sickness around me. My eyes look ahead in the direction that her aroma is leading me, and I see her standing outside of a room just down the hallway from me.

I walk to her and look inside at the patient lying in bed. A little girl, no more than eight, lies back, staring at the ceiling. Her hands are wrapped completely in gauze and are resting alongside her. Peeking from under the blanket are the folds of a much too big gown, and at the end of the bed there is an empty space where her feet do not quite reach.

"This is our Jane Doe," Trish says without looking away from the girl. "The Pattersons found her behind their house trying to start a campfire. She burned herself pretty bad."

For the life of me, I cannot fathom why an eight-year-old would be camping outside. Not above the Arctic Circle during the summer, and definitely not this far into winter. It is cold enough here that there are times when even I feel the chill of the air. I can only imagine how that must feel to a human.

"I've already called the sheriff. But we're keeping her for now," Trish continues, looking up at me. "She won't tell us her name. We don't know anything about her. And she is refusing to eat."

Trish grabs my arm lightly. "All I need you to do is feed her. Work your magic."

My magic? I am sure she is referring to the few times I have temporarily enthralled a child to make them hold still for an injection. Something I shouldn't do in front of the humans, but could not help myself when there is a thrashing child and a needle nearby.

I nod. "I'll try."

She pats my arm. "Good," she says softly and glances one more time at the girl.

As she starts to walk away, I ask, "She hasn't said anything at all about who she is?"

Thinking, Trish smiles, "Yes, she did." She laughs to herself for a moment. "She said her name was Rapunzel." "Rapunzel?" I repeat.

Her smile widens enough to show most of her teeth. "Good luck," she says as she walks back down the hallway.

I watch her leave, then I look at the girl again. Her shoulders rise and fall with a quiet sigh. I wonder what could have happened to make a little child not trust us enough to give us her name.

As I start toward her, she sits up straighter. Thin and frail, there is a pallor to her skin, a tiredness to her body, and a dullness to her long blond hair, which is singed along her bangs. Her light blue eyes are directed at the wall in front of her, but when I walk past them, I realize they are not focused on anything.

I approach her slowly, being sure not to make any noises. Silently, I stand beside her as she continues to stare at the wall, listening for me. I wave my hand in front of her face but she does not blink, because she does not see it. She does not see anything.

Knowing that she is blind makes me approach this different. I have to focus more on what I am saying than the expression I make. Though, it is true that people can hear a smile in your voice.

I could still enthrall her, but I do not want to. I don't like to do that to children. Not if I can help it.

I step away from her just as quietly and go to the little table with a tray of food on it. I lift the napkin covering the dish. I look at the pork chop, which surprisingly does not look too bad, and the dry green beans and carrots, then cover it up again.

Grabbing the back of a chair, I drag it over to the bed, letting it loudly scrape the floor as I do. The girl looks over in my direction but still not at me exactly.

I stop close to the bed and sit down. I might as well make myself comfortable.

"So, Punzi," I start, "you have a pretty nice room here. It's bland and boring." Then I mumble, "It's actually kind of miserable."

She fights a small smile back so I continue, "But it has to be better than being outside in the snow, right?" Refusing to answer, she sits very still.

"Oh, you're not talking to me." I begin again, "That's okay. I'm used to that. Usually, though, I do something wrong first." Leaning forward, I continue, "So let me begin. I'm Nicolas. I'm a Gemini, which basically means there are two sides to me." A human-ish side and a more prevalent vampire side. "I'm twenty-two, but I feel like I am a lot older most of the time." All of the time, because I am. "No girlfriend, no kids. I live with my mom and I have a crummy job. So you could say I'm quite a catch. How about you?"

She says nothing, and makes no attempt to, so in the worst little girl voice I can work up, I imitate, "My name is Punzi."

A laugh escapes her lips before she is able to stop it. And as she tries to quiet it, I continue with my childish voice, "I'm eight years old. And I like to catch butterflies with a net."

Then dropping the act, I say, "Actually, I don't know about that last part. You've probably have never even been around a butterfly. Not a live one anyway."

Still trying not to smile at me, she sucks her bottom lip into her mouth. But I can tell that she likes me being here, and knowing that makes me smile, too.

"Let me be really honest with you. My shift ends in about thirty minutes. And if you do not eat for me, they'll just send another errand boy in here to sit with you until you do."

I pause for a moment, letting her process what I am telling her, then start again, "Now, I don't know how hungry you are," From the sound of her grumbling belly, she is pretty hungry, "But I know that you don't want someone babysitting you all day. So this is the first of three times I am going to ask, will you let me feed you?"

Her eyes dart back and forth as she mulls over the idea. Her stomach moans its answer and I watch her slowly yielding to the pain. Somehow, her eyes find me, and though she is blind, it feels as if she can see the real me, as though she isn't afraid of what she finds there. I stare back at her, motionless, until she drops her eyes and nods at me.

Standing up, I walk over to the tray and remove the napkin again. "Looks promising," I tell her. Though honestly, it appears a little too dry, probably from sitting out for so long. But something tells me she is hungry enough that she will not care.

As I slide the table over to her, I ask, "Do you like pork chops?"

Her only answer is the blinking of her eyes, and I realize that she is finished responding to me.

Scooting the chair closer, I sit down near her. I pick up the fork and knife. "I'll cut it into pieces. You let me know if they are too big, okay?" I say, but do not expect for her to tell me so I cut them smaller than I would for anybody else. The knife slices easily through the meat but I still seem slightly more inept at it than I should be. Especially since I enjoy cooking as much as I do. Perhaps it is merely than I am not used to serving children. And to be honest, I am not sure if I am doing it right.

"Okay," I say to myself when I have a few pieces cut up. Setting the knife down, I look for the drink and find two. I pick them up, one in each hand and ask her, "Do you want juice or milk?"

I look over at her sitting quietly, then answer myself, "Milk it is," I set the juice to the side and open the milk. "I know you don't want to talk so if you could just nod or raise your hand when you want a drink, I'd appreciate it."

I press the fork into the meat. "Alright. Open your mouth," I tell her gently. And to my surprise, she does.

Carefully, I lay the pork on her tongue so that she knows where it is. She closes her lips around the fork and I pull it back to me slowly.

As I watch her chew, I cannot help but to wonder if someone is looking for her. Surely, someone is missing such a sweet child. How could they not? Even with her messy hair, she looks like an angel. Kindness radiates from her. There is a tenderness to her that I do not find in very many humans.

But there is something else, too; a fear and uncertainty, as though she does not trust the adults around her. And I do not blame her. She was alone and hungry, left in the snow. Like I was once, when I was turned and my maker left me for dead. But Marcella found me; she took me in and helped me when no one else would. I could do the same for this girl. I could be her savior. I want to be.

She swallows and raises her bandaged hand in the air slightly. Knowing my cue, I give her the milk, placing the straw on her lower lip. She closes her mouth around it and drinks, and do not try to hide the smile it brings me.

I continue to feed her, watching her chew quietly, watching her grimace when I give her the green beans. Each time, I hold back a chuckle and remind her that if she does not want them, all she has to do is say so. And each time, she eats them without uttering a word.

She finishes the milk and we move on to the apple juice. But either she does not like it as well or she is beginning to become full, because she drinks it much slower.

I pull the straw from her lips before she is done, and some of the juice spills onto her chin. "Oops. Sorry," I nearly whisper to her.

Taking the napkin, I wipe her chin gently. As I start to pull my hand back, I stop. "What's this here?" I ask and wipe her cheek, though there is nothing on her. "And here?" I say, rubbing her nose with the napkin. "And here? And here?" I repeat as I quickly run the napkin over her eyes, ears, and forehead until I hear her giggle.

I smile at her just as Elliot pops his head in the doorway. "Hey, Nick, your shift is over. Do you want me to take over in here?"

Looking back at the plate of mostly gone food, I tell him, "No. I'll finish."

"You know Mary doesn't want overtime," he reminds me.

I glance at him with his red hair and freckles splattered across his face and tell him, "This is on my time."

He shrugs his thin shoulders. "Alright. I'll let her know." And just as quickly as he appeared, he leaves.

I turn my eyes back to the girl and see a simple smile on her face. I knew she would not want another stranger in here, but I suppose I did not realize how much me staying would mean to her.

Taking the fork, I pick up another piece of pork. "Okay, Punzi, we are almost finished."

As I start to bring the fork to her mouth, she asks in a soft voice, "Why do you call me Punzi?"

Slightly surprised that she spoke, it takes me a moment to answer. I lower the fork and tell her, "Punzi is short for Rapunzel, isn't it? That's your name, right?"

A big smile spreads across her face. "Right," she agrees. Crossing her legs under the blanket, she continues, "No more green beans, okay?"

A small laugh escapes me. "Okay."

I help her eat the rest of her food before I stand up. Ensuring her that I will see her tomorrow, I leave. Though truly, I would rather stay a little longer.

I go to the locker room and as I take my timesheet out, Mary finds me. "I don't know how you did that." "Did what?" I ask causally.

Placing her hands behind her, she leans against the wall. "Got her to eat. She must like you."

I smile to myself. I like Punzi, too.

"Are you coming to Bradley's tonight?" Mary asks. "Everyone's going to be there."

Oh, right. New Year's Eve. Of course everyone will be at the bar. Everyone – including the local werewolf pack, the ones that frequent the bar owned by their third in command.

"Probably not, I'm not much of a drinker." I fight back the smile I have for that particular lie.

Leaning toward me, she takes my arm. "Come on, Nicolas. You need to get out more."

I write my time in on the card as I say, "I have to work tomorrow."

She smiles. "Yeah, well, you're not much of drinker so that doesn't matter."

She has a point.

"Besides," she continues, "everyone gets a little crazy during a full moon."

Full moon? "It's a full moon tonight?" How did I miss that? I am usually right on top of that. It is the only time the wolves are not littering the town with their presence.

She nods.

The discomfort it causes the wolves to be human during the full moon means that they will not be at the bar tonight, except for maybe Bradley, the owner. And I can handle one distracted wolf.

"I'll think about it," I tell her.

Pushing off of the wall, she says, "I hope you'll be there." Then she walks out, smiling as though she has won.

I grab my coat and start out. I walk through the lobby, waving goodbye to Grace before I leave. I pass through the parking lot that is still fairly empty, since not everyone here owns a car.

The wind whips at me, trying to bite at my nose and ears, so I tuck my head down like a human would and wrap my arms around myself.

I pass where Luke had been parked this morning and the bar he, undoubtedly, had been coming from hours before. Keeping, my eyes on the ground in front of me, I walk past the many houses on my route. This time, however, most of their lights are on.

For the most part, I keep to myself. Trying to ignore most of the people who pass me; trying not to get involved in their lives. Distance is the best way to keep them alive. That is, until I hear a set of muffled voices.

"Don't walk away from me!" a man orders from the alley.

Then a woman says just as sharply, "You don't own me, Jericho."

I peek around the building to see a young brunette woman backed against the side of a house. The man she is with, Jericho, holds her by the wrist with his face close to hers.

Smelling his musky wolf scent, I know I should just keep walking. This is none of my business. Let the pack handle this.

But as she struggles to get away from him and screams, "Let me go!" I feel myself step into the alley.

Very quietly, I walk toward him, unnoticed by both of them, not sure of what I am about to do.

"You leave when I say," he says with a husky tone.

From this distance, I can smell the heavy scent of whiskey pouring off of him. There is nothing I will be able to say to justify coming between a wolf and his human mate. Not to my family, and certainly not to the pack. But that thought does not even begin to cross my mind.

Without hesitation, she brings her knee into his groin fairly hard, which I know was a mistake.

His eyes phase into the bright yellow of his wolf. His fingernails grow, digging into her wrist. Although I can tell that he is fighting the change, he is losing.

Hearing the low rumble of a growl in his chest, I hurry the rest of the way to them. Then, grabbing him by the back of the neck, I pull him away from the woman and slam him into the adjacent building with enough force to leave the impression of his skull in the stone siding.

His body goes limp, but he is not dead, just merely unconscious, which is a shame. But probably better for me in the scheme of things. Better not to give the wolves a reason to chase us out of town.

Letting him fall onto the ground, I look up at the brunette. I can smell the sweetness of her blood where his claws ripped through her wrist as I pulled him away.

Her coat sleeve hangs over the marks but a trail of crimson streams down her fingers and drips into the snow.

"Are you okay?" I ask her softly.

With her rapid breathing fogging up the air between us, she stares at me with wide eyes.

Another drop of red stains the snow at her feet. Then feeling the pain of the cuts on her arm, she pulls her wrist to her chest, smearing the blood across her light pink coat.

"Let me see," I say. My mouth waters with the scent of her blood as I step toward her. As I reach toward her, she bolts into a run, leaving me standing alone.

As I watch her dash out of the alley, I yell after her, "I wasn't going to hurt you." At least I didn't plan on it.

It is strange how I want some humans to trust me but still know that they shouldn't.

Sighing, I look down at the still human man with his face in the snow. The humanity in me says I should get him help. Maybe prop him up, lean him against the trash just to get his face out of the snow some.

But instead, I shrug and walk away. I hope he gets frostbite.

Her *hazelnut hair dances* from side to side as we walk down the narrow road, her warm arm looped around my elbow. Her fingers are pressing into my forearm.

Everything feels so very familiar and comfortable. Everything feels like a fairytale I have read before but cannot remember the ending to.

"Thank you for dancing with my sisters tonight," Ann says with a gentle voice. "They simply adore you."

Looking into her kind eyes, I tell her, "To be honest, I only did it to make you smile." Truthfully though, I would have done it regardless of whether Ann had seen me or not. Her younger sisters are sweet, just like she raised them to be.

I place my hand on her cheek and rub my thumb across her milky skin. "I would do anything to see that smile."

Closing her eyes bashfully, she smiles, biting her lip gently.

"I love you, Ann," I tell her softly, "I can't wait until you are my wife. I can't wait to make you happy every day."

Stopping in the street, I take her hand in mine. "Of all the things I want to do in my lifetime, being with you seems the most important."

A soft smile spreads across her face. "You have such high hopes. I have no practice at being a wife. I only pray that I do not disappoint you."

As if she could ever disappoint me.

"But there is something I do know how to do very well," she continues. "I know how to love you. And I promise that will not change so long as my heart beats."

Leaning in slowly, I kiss her gentle, caressing her lips with mine. My hand slides to the small of her back, pulling her into me. And I can feel her smile at my touch.

Pulling away slightly, I keep my face close to hers, not wanting the moment to be over, but propriety tells me it is.

"Someone could have seen us, Vincent."

Vincent? That is my name. So why does it sound so foreign? Why does it feel wrong? As though I am someone else entirely.

I do not think of this long before I relinquish the concerns with it in favor of the present. "If someone keeps watching, they might see more than just a kiss," I whisper to her.

She laughs and pushes me back lightly. Taking my hand, she tells me, "I think you should walk me home."

Playfully, I sigh loudly. "Fine."

Then smiling at her, I lead her down the dirt road again. She rests her head against my shoulder as we walk. It isn't long before I hear her yawn quietly.

Knowing that she is tired, I say, "Why don't we cut through the alley? It'll be quicker."

Sleepily, she smiles at me as I pull her between the stone buildings. The stacks of rock give the houses a cobbled appearance and the straw roofs hang over, blocking most of the light from the moon that is attempting to shine down on us. Yet, I do not need the light to see her beauty or to feel her warmth beside me.

However, there is something I do see in the shadows ahead. A man, doubled over in pain, clutching at his abdomen.

Letting my fingers slip out of her hand, I go to the man. His dark hair hangs over his face so I cannot tell whether I have seen him before or not. But something inside me says I haven't. That maybe I wasn't supposed to ever see this man.

Kneeling down beside him, I place my hand on his shoulder. "Are you all right?" I wonder out loud.

His head rises and that is when I notice his wickedly satisfied smile. His eyes flash open but all I see is my reflection in their black hollowness.

He thrusts the palm of his hand into my chest before I can even react to the sight of him. My body slams into the house behind me hard enough for me to hear the stones shift and my bones snap.

Dropping to the ground, I gasp for air but only find pain. Inhaling small, sharp breaths, I grasp at the indentation where my breastbone used to be.

That is when I hear her scream – high-pitched and fearful. Piercing, it cuts through me, hurting me worse than the fact that I know I will not survive this.

Like a fish out of water, I suck at the air violently but never really inhale. Still, I manage to push myself up onto my arms.

Just in front of me, the man grabs Ann by the hair. Faster than I can process, he places his hand on her chin and twists, silencing her.

Insignificantly, he tosses her to the ground across from me as my arms give out. Unable to cry out to her, I watch her for movement. Her lifeless eyes stare back at me while I take what I am sure will be my last breath...

Sitting up in bed, I gasp for air, still feeling the crushing pain in my chest. With a firm pressure, I hold my sternum but it is not caved in as it was a moment ago. Still, I cannot catch my breath and I continue to draw limited air, despite my chaotic and rapid breathing.

Beside me, Kate sits up and slides close to me. Placing her warm hands on my cheeks, she turns my face toward hers. "It's okay. It was just a dream."

But it wasn't a dream. It was a memory. And it felt as real as the day it happened.

"Breathe, Nick," she says as though I am not already trying to.

My eyes dart around the room as I search for something to focus on. Something to take my mind off of erratic breathing and my racing heart as it pounds inside me.

Sternly, yet still softly, Kate tells me, "Look at me."

And I do. I have to admit, there is something calming about her.

"Exhale. Nice and slow," she insists. I suppose she thinks I need the example because she breathes out slowly, keeping her eyes locked to mine.

Following her lead, I let out a long, slightly jagged breath and I do feel better. I continue to focus on her as she holds my face gently until I can speak again.

"Thank you," I pant out. Pulling her hands from me, I lay back in the bed. Closing my eyes, I run my hands through my hair and exhale forcefully.

"That must have been some dream," she mutters quietly.

Because Ann was some woman. "Yeah," I say simply. There is no need to explain that my dream was about Ann. They are always about Ann.

Kate shifts and lies down beside me on her stomach. "You need to let her go."

Words that are easier said than done. "I know," But part of me does not want to let go. Part of me knows that without her, I am not even a shadow of the man I once was. Not a hint of the man I want to be again.

"Maybe if you tried, you could learn to love someone new. You might not even have to look that far. They could be right in front of you," Kate nearly whispers to me.

I know who she is speaking of. I know the way she feels about me, what she wants for us. And sometimes, I find myself wanting it, too. But I do not love her, and she would only be hurt by me in the end.

I open my eyes slowly and look over at her, but she is not looking at me. Instead, she keeps her eyes on the mattress, hiding the vulnerability in them.

"You could, too," I tell her gently, but she glances at me sharply.

"I don't need to give up yet. Unlike Ann, you're not dead," she states coldly.

A defensive heat ripples through me, but I bite my tongue to keep from saying anything disrespectful.

Pulling the blanket back, she climbs out of bed. "Now if you will excuse me, I need to get dressed." She points to the door while keeping her irritated expression.

I slide out of bed. "Me too." I walk to the door as I finish saying, "I'm going to Bradley's tonight."

No longer annoyed with me, she drops her arm. "The bar? That's a werewolf hangout, you know."

"I know," I say as I place my hand on the doorknob. "But it's a full moon, which means the wolves won't be there. Besides, a girl from work asked me to. Or should I say, a woman?"

True, I may have said that last part just to watch her roll her eyes. Part of me enjoys her jealousy. Just a little bit.

But I do not let her fret over it too long, however, before I say, "I don't think she meant it as a date, though. It was just Mary."

Knowing that I intended for her to become envious of a mere human, even for just a moment, she smirks at me. And just like that, she is no longer irritated with me.

"Well," she starts, crossing her arms, "I suppose you will need someone to come with you."

I don't. But I do enjoy my time with her. "Don't think I can handle myself?"

She walks toward me. "I think it's New Year's Eve. And I just invited myself to tag along."

Passing me, she goes to her closet. Pulling the doors open, she looks over her options.

"I'll meet you in the living room in ten minutes." I open the door and add, "Nothing too sleazy."

She laughs to herself. "Well that limits my choices," she says under her breath with heavy sarcasm.

Her words make me smile as I go to my room. I open the door quietly and peek in but nobody is there. My bed is still made neatly without the slightest wrinkle, proving to me that Yen has yet to sleep in it. But the folded pile of clothes has been put away. Probably thanks to Marcella.

I make my way to the closet, pulling off my shirt and letting it drop to the floor. As I start to slide my pants off, I feel someone lurking in the doorway and I know exactly who it is by the hint of cherry blooms in the air.

"If you are going to watch you could at least close the door," I say with a smile.

The door creaks shut as she asks, "Modest are we?"

I look back at Yen from over my shoulder. "Catholic, actually."

Laughing lightly, she tosses her head back ever so slightly. Twisting around, she falls gracefully onto my bed.

The way her shirt lays against her accentuating her shape draws my eyes to her. There is always something enticing about a beautiful woman on my bed that makes my heart beat a little quicker. But her words soon end my thoughts from progressing much further.

"A Catholic vampire? That's an oxymoron if I've ever heard one." She rolls onto her stomach so she is facing me. "Kind of like a sober Catholic."

I turn back to the closet to hide my annoyance with her comments but she knows me too well.

I can hear the smile in her voice. "I'm kidding, Nicolas."

Not satisfied with her apology, I jerk a shirt down from the hanger. I should not have to explain myself to her, nor will I. The fact that, like most vampires, she abandoned her beliefs in light of this life proves to me how weak she truly is.

"You know, Yen," I say as I slide my shirt over my head, "sometimes I wonder why I like you so much."

I slip off my pants, letting them drop to the floor.

As I kick them from my feet, I hear her sigh lightly. "I know why I like you," she mumbles quietly.

I pull on a pair of pants. Maybe it is because I like to hear admiration of myself or perhaps I just realize that there is not a chance that I could stay angry with her. Either way, I smile my lopsided grin.

"You like me because I remind you of yourself," she informs me.

Grabbing a pair of boots, I sit on the bed next to her.

She loops her arm around my chest. "And deep down," she whispers in my ear, "that's who you are really in love with."

Glancing back at her, I ask, "Is that right?" Laying my hand on her forearm, I rub my fingers across her skin. "I suppose someone should."

Her eyes light up. "Love you?" she says like a joke as she laughs effortlessly. "You have done nothing to deserve that."

True. I have not done much of anything deserving since I became a vampire. After spending nearly two centuries killing at will, the good I do manage to achieve does not even begin to cover the pain I have caused. Why would anyone choose to be with me? A monster masquerading as a man.

Leaning forward, I pull myself from her loose grip and slide my feet into my shoes. "And yet people still fall for you," I tell her as I stand up.

I hear her mutter, "Silly humans."

Grabbing my coat, I turn just to see the grin she wears… and there it is; sarcastic, yet still very simple. It makes me smile back at her softly.

Suddenly, my door swings open wildly and Luther blurts out quickly, "Nick, you have to come see this."

Slightly annoyed that he continues to call me 'Nick', though I have asked him not to on several occasions – and even more irritated at the sight of him – I snap, "Stop talking." Pointing toward the hallway, I finish, "Get out. Close the door. And knock."

"Nick –" he starts again.

I interrupt him curtly, "Don't come in until I say you can."

"This is important," he pleads.

I could tell him that common courtesies are important, too. Or that I simply do not care what he has to say about anything. But instead, I keep my eyes on him sternly with my finger showing him the way out until he rolls his eyes.

"Fine," he sighs.

Stepping out, he closes the door. Even though he is frustrated with me, which I happen to enjoy, Luther knocks lightly.

But I do not tell him to come in nor do I even acknowledge him. As I pull my coat on, Yen shifts on the bed, letting her feet graze the floor in front of me.

Trailing her finger along the zipper, she asks, "Where are you going?"

There is another knock, this time a little harder.

"To Bradley's. It's a bar in town," I tell her, knowing she is fully aware of what Bradley's is – and that the owner is a werewolf.

"You *are* Catholic," she mutters under her breath but still loud enough for me to hear.

I laugh to myself as she starts again, "I suppose you should let me get dressed then. You can't go to see the wolves alone," she says, though I am sure she has not forgotten about the full moon tonight.

"I don't need protected by a girl," I tease, making her roll her eyes as she shakes her head. "Besides, Kate is already coming with me."

Knocking again, Luther calls to me, "Nick. Open up."

Yen's hand glides down to my belt buckle. "Then I should definitely go. Have to check out my competition, don't I?"

Pushing her hand away, I remind her, "We have a truce with the wolves, you know. No killing any humans within a hundred miles."

She huffs playfully. "What kind of vacation is it when you cannot try the local cuisine?"

I ignore the pounding on the door by Luther and answer her, "A peaceful one."

She smiles at me. "You're not leaving without me."

My eyes dart around the room as though I am thinking, but honestly, there is not a chance I will argue this with her. "You have five minutes."

She stands up, placing her face just inches from mine. "You'll wait as long as I take."

Her assertiveness is alluring. The way her words hang between us thickens the air. The way one eyebrow shoots up suggestively.

There is something about a strong woman that has always sparked my interest. I suppose I like the challenge they offer.

But, infantile Luther manages to ruin the moment by standing too close to the door, pounding and grumbling.

"Come in," I call to him without taking my eyes from Yen.

The door opens slowly. Hearing him sigh heavily, I look over at him. Standing with his arms crossed, he keeps his eyes narrowed on me.

"I think you should see this," he says through gritted teeth.

I can feel the anger toward me rolling off of him. Although his distress does bring me joy, I try not to smirk at him. But that does not stop Yen from smiling at the situation.

As I walk over to him, leaving Yen where she stands beside the bed, I ask, "What is it, Luther?"

His hard eyes follow me as I approach, but they do not intimidate me the way he intends them to. Not that he could do much of anything to daunt me. I have already proven to the both of us that I could kill him if I tried. Actually, I am not sure why he even still attempts to be threatening towards me.

"It's in the living room," he says shortly.

Passing him, I start down the hallway. I would rather not talk to him if it can be helped. But of course, he starts, "That sheep you picked out for me, her name was Lindsey, right?"

"You mean the sheep that you couldn't enthrall and we ended up killing because of your incompetence?" I look over at him, "Yeah."

He smirks at me though I am not sure why. "That's what I thought."

We pass through the kitchen and walk into the living room. The lights are turned off but the room is bright from the luminance of the television. The TV – my least favorite object in the living room. (Aside from Luther, that is.) It serves as more of background noise to me than entertainment. What could be enjoyable about watching a world that does not accept us? It only reminds us of what we cannot have. And I, for one, do not need reminding of that.

Luther lays his hands on my shoulders and pushes me gently through the room. And though his touch makes me cringe, I do not say anything to him. I simply cross my arms over my chest and let him lead me.

"Just watch. It's coming up," Luther says when we stop in front of the television.

Glancing over at Luther, I see him smiling, eager and nervous at the same time, and I cannot help but wonder why. But before I can think of this too long, the commercial ends and the news comes on.

"Welcome back," the reporter says. The beautifully dark woman with black hair and a young face sits beside an older Eskimo man, only looking down at the paper in front of her briefly. "A homicide in Fairbanks leaves neighbors in shock."

Of course it does. I have heard these reports before. It really is not as big of a deal as Luther is making it out to be.

"Lindsey Sparks," she continues, "was found early this morning in her home off of Gaffney Road. The brutal slaying is said to have taken place late last night. Authorities have not released many details of the case, but insiders say that the main suspect is none other than the police chief's own son, James Miller."

And that is when I stop listening. "Oh, shit," I mumble to myself. James? Our James is a police chief's son? This is bad. Really bad. Someone will look for him. A whole station of people will. We do not need people snooping about so close to us.

My thoughts are interrupted by Luther chuckling to himself. "Oh, Nick, how the mighty do fall."

His laugh makes my blood boil. Grabbing him by his shirt collar, I jerk him toward me. "This is your fault," I say with a heavy accent. "If you could have only pulled yourself together for five minutes, the girl would be here and nobody would care."

He pulls away from my grip and I do not fight to keep him there.

"But no," I continue, "you always seem to find a way to drag us down."

I feel Marcella enter the living room but I keep my eyes narrowed on Luther.

Luther, on the other hand, is too irritated with me to even notice her, which is a sad sign of his lack of instincts.

"No," he says sharply. "You do not get to blame me for this. I am not the one who is impotent."

Idiot. "It's 'incompetent', you twit. And yes, everyone here agrees that you are." I step close to him to irk him more. "Why can't you just try to prove us wrong for once?"

"That's enough," Marcella chimes in as she approaches us. She grabs Luther's chin and holds his face toward her. "Luther, you failed once again. I am not surprised, so neither should you be." Jerking his face away, she lets him go. "But ultimately, James belongs to Nicolas, which means it's his problem now." She looks harshly at me. "Fix it."

"Of course," I tell her without my accent.

She starts to walk away as Yen enters. Stopping next to Yen by the door, Marcella looks back at me. "No more mistakes, Nick."

"Yes, ma'am," I say quietly. My respect for her keeps my sarcastic tone hidden.

Marcella looks over at Yen. "And you, you're here for a reason. Start making yourself useful."

Yen leans back against the doorframe causally. "Sounds like someone put a little too much bitch in their coffee this morning," she says smartly.

"Hey," I snap at Yen. Female or not, nobody speaks to my mother with disrespect. "Don't talk to her like that," I say a little calmer.

Yen's eyes meet mine. And where I expected to see contempt, I only find guilt. I admit, I am slightly surprised by her remorse. She is not the type to regret the things she says or does. But I suppose I have never spoken harshly toward her before, and she must not have been prepared for it.

"It's fine, Nicolas," Marcella says without taking her cold eyes off of Yen. "Some people use their quick wit to compensate for their lack of significant combat skills."

That is true. Just look at Luther. He is a dreadful fighter and a pathetic vampire, as well. But the problem is that his quick wit is neither quick nor witty.

Yen looks over at Marcella's smirk, which is only meant as a challenge, and smiles sarcastically. There is nothing for her to say. She is not stronger or faster than Marcella, and has never won a battle against her – despite Yen's adept abilities – and probably never will.

"I'm sure your lack of personality has nothing to do with it," Yen says boldly.

Marcella's chest stops rising with breath as she holds air in, focusing only on her control. Her eyes, cold and distant, pierce through Yen and I can see the hunger in them; the need to kill and the desire to destroy.

I have seen her look at people this way before, but usually only before she tears them to shreds.

Knowing that Marcella would feel sorrow from killing her friend, and to a certain degree, I would too, I say, "Yen," merely as a distraction, "come over here."

Sensing the heat rolling off of Marcella, Yen pushes herself from the doorframe. Gliding across the room, she walks to me, full of unwarranted confidence and smiling as though she has won. Surely, she realizes that Marcella is not one to trifle with. But then, maybe she does not care.

Looping her arm through mine, Yen leans close to me, "Take me outside, won't you?"

All for show, I am sure, she drapes her arms around my neck just to rile Kate, who we both know has stepped into the living room. Even if I could not smell the coconut-laced perfume, I still feel Kate's presence more than the others. Perhaps it is because I am always hoping for her to be close to me.
Or maybe, it is simply that I know her best of all.

I smile at Yen, keeping my eyes soft. "Kate will," I offer her.

From across the room there is a quiet huff and I can practically hear Kate's eyes roll. If I was not already smiling, that would have made me grin. Just a little.

Taking Yen's hands, I slide her arms away from me, "And take Luther with you." Just knowing he is looking at me with those overconfident eyes and flashing a bumptious smile sickens me. As if none of this is his fault. As if he is the only one who is allowed to make mistakes.

I do not need to hear him gloat about this any further. I do not wish to listen to anything else he has to say. But of course, he speaks.

"I don't want –"

Raising my hand to stop him, I interrupt, "Quiet, Luther. The adults are speaking."

Notably irritated, he crosses his arms over his chest, which brings me a slight satisfaction. "Are you going to let him talk to me that way?" he asks Marcella.

"Yes," she says simply then looks at me, waiting.

I run my hands through my hair, thinking. I know what she wants. She wants an answer to this problem; an answer that I do not have. I could kill James. That would be easy, but hopefully not necessary. Starting over to acquire a sheep is time consuming for me. Many hours go into stalking and studying my subject. It sounds easy in theory. You find someone and make them yours. But in actuality, finding the right sheep takes work.

A sheep must be many things. Its blood must be succulent and refreshing – something you would not mind drinking routinely. It must smell appropriate, nothing too tempting, nothing too repugnant. The sheep must be someone who, rightfully, should be missed but will not be.

Needless to say, certain precautions should be taken when attempting to gain something as important as a sheep. Nothing draws attention to us quicker than missing humans and a trail of bodies.

But Luther does not understand this yet, even though he should. And I am tired of trying to teach it to him.

Looking up at Marcella, I tell her, "Just keep James inside for now. I'll think of something."

She lowers her head in a single nod and leaves us, walking away gracefully but not quite satisfied.

"Come on, Yen," Kate says. While she sounds kind and caring, I can tell that she is faking her sentiments, though I may be the only one who notices.

Yen steps away from me, trailing her hand across my chest as she leaves.

They gather their coats and are out the door quickly, perhaps not wanting to be in the room with Luther and myself any longer. Or maybe Kate just wants to give me the opportunity to say what is on my mind. The types of things I will not say in the presence of ladies.

And I do want to say something – tell him he is an inconvenience on everyone. Explain that, though he blames me, it is truly his ineptitude that put us here. But deep down, I know my errors in this too. Although I will never admit them to Luther.

When the door closes and we are alone, I notice the news anchors on the television again. For a moment, I had forgotten it was on.

"The search continues for a missing child in Anchorage…" the female reporter says. Her voice grows quieter and quieter as I turn the knob until it clicks and the screen goes dark.

Biting my tongue on what I want to say, I simply ask, "Are you coming with us?"

Surprised by my question, he stares blankly at me for a moment. I suppose he was expecting me to be less docile and more resentful.

"You want me to go with you?" he finally asks.

No. Not at all. There is not an ounce of me that wants to spend the evening with him, but even he should not have to be alone on New Year's Eve.

"It's just a question. Either you come with us or you stay here. Alone. Marcella is going just outside of Wasilla to hunt tonight," I inform him.

Truly, I hope he decides to stay. That would make my night more enjoyable. But since we are going to a werewolf's bar, perhaps he will be eaten up. That would certainly be very entertaining.

He shrugs. "Okay. I'll come."

I fight my instinct to grimace, and smile instead. "Good. Grab a coat. We're leaving."

Not waiting for him, I walk to the door and step outside while he fumbles at the coatrack.

The sight from the porch makes me smile my lopsided grin. There, standing several feet apart, are Kate and Yen with their backs to each other. Yen stares at the sky, though she is not actually looking at anything. She merely does not want to look at Kate. And Kate is glaring over her shoulder at Yen. Her eyes make their way up and down Yen's body with a slightly confused look on her face. Probably wondering what I ever saw in Yen.

But when they hear the door shut as Luther steps onto the porch, they both turn toward us, eager for the extra company.

I lean toward Luther slightly. "Try to walk between Yen and myself."

The corners of his mouth pull up in a smile. "Tired of making Kate jealous?"

Yes. "I'm just trying to keep a distance from Yen."

He nods. "That I can do."

For once, there is a task he is able to complete.

"I am pretty good at keeping people distant," he adds then walks off of the porch.

But I do not move. I watch him for a moment. Something in his tone made me believe he was not talking about Yen and myself, but referring to the space between him and the rest of the house. To keeping himself an outsider. And for a moment, I start to think that maybe his continuous failures are simply a way to distance himself from the others.

"You coming?" Kate asks quietly, bringing me back to the present.

I nod and walk off of the porch, still wondering if Luther is not better at being a vampire than he makes himself out to be. But I try not to think about that too long. I would much rather just enjoy my time with Kate than let Luther cloud up my thoughts.

Together, we walk down the cold streets to the bar. Kate's arm looped around mine, Yen telling Luther about her personal suffering during the Spanish flu pandemic of 1918. As if the humans did not endure worse. Comparably, her own drought of fresh blood is not significant when one considers that close to a quarter of the world's population was infected. Sure, we were all worried about an extinction of the humans, but they survived, and so did we.

As we approach the bar, I can smell the stench of alcohol pouring from the door, and hear the sound of one of the local bands beating the drums. Not quite as good as the record of the song they are imitating, but close enough to have drawn a crowd, I am sure.

Taking the handle, I notice a hand-painted sign stating, *All is welcome*. Doubting that includes me, I push open the wooden door and step inside first. The room is large and spacious, with only a few billiard tables along the back wall which is decorated with a large banner with the words, *Welcome 1978*, in gold letters. On an adequate platform, the band belts out the slightly off-key notes of a more recent rock song while several people dance in front of the stage. Obviously, the drinks in their hands must have interfered with their hearing, because the music is not that impressive. I suppose quality is not as important as making this a fun night for them.

Standing in the doorway, my eyes go directly to the bar where Bradley stares at me. Slightly dumbfounded that I would walk into his bar, his expression quickly turns to irritation.

Smiling at him, I loosely salute him with my index finger. A friendly enough gesture, but that is not how I intended it and he knows it. He pulls the towel off of his shoulder and throws it onto the counter petulantly.

Regardless of the fact that he does not want us here, he nods his head for me to go to him. Stepping to the side to let the others in, I shrug as if I am thinking about going to him, then shake my head.

Kate and the others walk in, and Bradley's face turns to anger. Grabbing the edge of the bar, he drops his head for a moment to calm himself, but it does not help much, because when he looks back up at me, his eyes are still hard.

Ignoring him, we walk toward one of the billiard tables. I take the pool sticks down from the rack on the wall and start to hand one to Kate.

Putting her hand up, she says, "Play Luther. The next game is between me and Yen." She raises an eyebrow as she glances over her shoulder at Yen.

As Bradley begins stomping toward us, I nod at Luther. "Looks like you're up."

I toss a pool stick to Luther. "Rack them." Then I walk past him to meet Bradley away from the table.

Coming closer, Bradley looks back as though he is expecting to see his pack behind him, but they are not here, and he is completely alone with four vampires. Despite his temper, I can tell that he is uncomfortable being so close to us.

Keeping his voice low, he nearly snarls, "What are you doing here?"

With the loud music and the not-so-sensitive hearing of the majority of the room, I do not have to try very hard to keep our conversation from reaching the humans. "I was invited."

"Not by me. Your kind is not welcome here," he says through gritted teeth.

I figured that much, but really I do not care about what one insignificant wolf has to say. "That's not what your sign says." I cross my arms loosely. "In fact, I have on a shirt and shoes. I think that means you have to serve me?" I say to rile him.

He steps toward me, fighting back his aggression.

"Easy, boy," I smirk. "Our truce does not say I can't defend myself." And I would, too. Given even the slightest of chances, I would take him down – with or without his pack behind him.

"There is nothing in here for you," he insists.

Causally, I look around the room at the humans, dancing and drinking. "Are you sure?" Meeting his eyes again, I continue, "Looks like you offer a wide variety of drinks. After all, I'm sure your nephew is here somewhere, and he is so very human."

Grabbing my shirt collar, he pushes me back against the wall, letting a growl slip from his lips.

Luther starts toward us, but I put my hand up to stop him. "It's fine, Luther." I am surprised, however, that he was the one to step forward first.

Staring into Bradley's eyes as a challenge, I tell him, "You can bark all you want. But you better ask Cyrus before you bite."

Though I use a great deal of strength to pry his fingers from my shirt, I do not show any signs of struggling with it.

While it is true that wolves who do not phase during the full moon are extremely eruptive, I continue, "Be careful. They might put a muzzle on you."

Stepping back, Bradley pinches the bridge of his nose between his fingers. I have done that several times. Enough times to know that it does not help. But when he looks up at me again, it seems to have worked for him.

With regained control, he states, "Stay away from my nephew."

I do not take my eyes away from him but can smell his nephew approaching us.

"Speak of the helpless," I say quietly to Bradley before I turn toward the blond man coming closer. "Luke," I say, smiling.

Sliding past Bradley, I tousle Luke's shaggy locks about playfully.

Laughing lightly, he shoves my hand away. "What's going on here?" Luke asks me.

Knowing that means he saw Bradley pin me against the wall, I turn toward Bradley. "Just a misunderstanding." Simply to annoy him, I straighten Bradley's collar. "It won't happen again. Will it, Bradley?"

His eyes harden but he manages a fake smile. "Tell you what, Nicolas, you can have as much alcohol as you want. On me."

I laugh to myself irritably. Of course he would offer me free drinks. I would be hugging the toilet with the first sip of anything that is not blood. And obviously, he knows that, too.

"In that case," Luke starts, wrapping his arm around my shoulders, "I'll take a scotch on the rocks on Nick's tab."

With a smirk, I reply, "I'll take you up on that. Have someone bring me rum with lots of ice."

Bradley seems slightly surprised by my request and so does Luke. As far as he knows, I don't drink alcohol at all. That is what I have maintained for weeks now, every time he has offered to bring me here, insisting that I would not leave without a companion as long as I listened to him. Like I would need his help with that.

Resuming its hard appearance, Bradley's face grows stern. "I'll get right on it."

And he will. But not for me. He will only be prompt because his favorite and only nephew asked for a scotch on the rocks. Without Luke, my order would never be filled.

Bradley walks away much the same way he approached; rigid and angry.

Leading Luke, I walk back to the pool table. Luther, still standing near the end of the table, has the balls racked and ready to start. Yen is perched on the edge of the table with her feet dangling a foot from the floor.

"Luke, this is Luther," I say, pointing. "And my friend, Yen."

Luke shakes Luther's hand then reaches for Yen's. "Yen? Is that like yin and yang?"

Irked by his comment, she does not reach for his hand. "No," she says harshly.

Perhaps I care for Luke more than I let myself believe, but I attempt to soften the tension in the air around us by explaining. "Yen basically means 'to desire'."

"Oh," he says quietly. Then looking at Yen again, he adds, "Then you are aptly named."

Not being able to help herself, she smiles genuinely and slides off of the table. With the grace and poise, I have only ever seen in Marcella, she walks over to us. "That was too little, too late," she says to Luke. "But cute just the same."

Then passing us, she goes to Luther and takes one of the pool sticks off of the table where he had laid them. "I'm taking your game, Nick," she informs me.

Leaning over the table, she breaks the triangle of pool balls, making them crack loudly.

Smiling to myself at how predictable her moves are, I pull Luke with me as I walk toward the chairs along the wall.

As I get closer to where I left Kate, I look up at her. On the edge of the chair with her legs crossed, wearing only a pair of tight blue jeans and a bright halter top that shows her stomach, she sits as though she was waiting for me. With the color of her top accentuating her skin tone, and her long hair hanging over her shoulder, she has never looked so tempting.

And for once, she renders me speechless for a moment. I stand, frozen in front of her, following the curves of her flawless form and attempting to not let her notice me doing so, but failing miserably.

When my eyes do fall on her face, she is smiling with pride, as though her sole intention on choosing her outfit was to have this moment play out just like this. Damn, she's good.

"I'm Kate," she says to Luke, reaching to shake his hand.

He takes her hand but does not shake it; instead, he holds it in his hand for longer than necessary. "Kate?" He presses her hand with his as I begin to wonder why he is still holding onto hers. "Wow, Nick didn't lie. You are beautiful."

Interest sweeps over her face and I realize what she heard in his words.

It is one thing to have someone tell you that you are beautiful to your face, but it is an entirely different feeling to know they say it behind your back, as well.

I shake my head. "He is taking that out of context," I tell her.

But of course, Luke is no help. "You've said several times, Nick."

And there it is. She knows I find her attractive and now I cannot take it back. Sighing, I run my hands through my hair.

Pulling herself up with Luke's hand, Kate loops her arm in his. "Walk with me, Luke. I want to know more of the things he says when I'm not around," she says in a sweet voice.

I have heard that tone in her voice before. It's just slightly unnatural; enough to sound as though it is laced in honey but not enough to be unnerving. She uses it to get her way, and it usually works.

Luke smiles at her. "Sure," he says, misreading her interest as flirting.

She lets him guide her away from the table, allowing him to believe that he has more control than he truly does. Relinquishing power to someone else is not something most vampires are comfortable with until it serves a purpose, and I smile to myself as I consider her motive. Her curiosity is driving her to go against her nature. Curiosity about me, that is.

I sit down in the chair Kate vacated. Still warm from her, the vinyl seat flattens beneath me as I lean back against the hard wooden back. Looking around the room, my eyes find Mary dancing with her friends. I watch her for a moment before she sees me and waves happily. I wave back as Marie walks over to me with my drink.

"For the gentleman," she says, holding the short glass toward me.

Taking it from her, I notice that there is no ice in my drink; this much I expected. It happens to be the reason I asked for ice in the first place, just to ensure that I would not get any. It takes away from the smell of the rum which is the only part of alcohol that I can still enjoy.

"Thank you," I tell her softly.

Putting her hand on her hip, she leans to the side. "I didn't know you were a drinker, Nick."

I smile. If she only knew. "I'm selective."

Nodding, she says, "Me, too. I'm a beer girl."

Then from across the room, Bradley calls, "Marie."

She turns in time to see him wave her toward him. I was wondering how long he would let her speak to me before interrupting. I suppose I just received my answer.

Looking back at me, she shrugs. "I guess he needs me." She nods toward the rum in my hand. "Let me know when you want another."

She walks backward for a few steps before she turns back toward the bar and hurries to Bradley.

"The humans know you too well," Yen says.

I glance at her as she leans over the pool table, lining up her shot. "You shouldn't be on a first-name basis with so many of them."

Striking the ball quickly, she stands up as two solid balls split and drop into different pockets.

"I'm not going to kill them," I tell her, trying to make it sound convincing.

A half-smile creeps on her face while she lines up another shot. "Liar."

She is probably right, of course, but I am trying not to hurt any humans on this vacation, as difficult as that may be.

I look at Luther, who is watching Yen make another ball into the pocket. His eyebrows are drawn together in a curious and almost disappointed expression.

"I hope you didn't bet money on this game," I tell him, making him meet my eyes. "She's a shark."

Smiling, he nods. I suppose he has already figured that out for himself.

Without raising the glass to my nose, I inhale the rich smell of rum, bringing back memories of my human life, memories of happiness and pain, of being weak and vulnerable, of never being enough for my father. For a moment, I wonder what he thought happened to me after I was turned.

I spend close to forty minutes listening to the humans dance and laugh around me; to Luther huff quietly each time Yen beats him, and Yen's smug chuckle after each win; Inhaling the smell of my past and letting it blend with my present; The heavy odor of rum and the savory scent of blood mixing in the air around me, lavishing in the sweet smell.

But my focus is broken when the music stops abruptly. Setting my glass aside, I look around the room as Bradley steps onto stage and takes the microphone.

Glancing back at the large clock on the wall, he hesitates for a brief moment then starts, "Ten. Nine..."

The crowd counts with him. A countdown to the new year. I smile slightly, thinking of how many times I have done this before. There is nothing new about New Year's Eve for me; nothing exciting about another year. Just more of the same awaiting me. But for these people, it holds so much potential. A new beginning. A new chapter.

Just then, I see Kate push through the crowd, rushing toward me as Bradley continues, "Seven. Six..."

Smiling widely, she hops onto my lap, crossing her legs and looping her arms around my neck. "You're mine, Nicolas Rider," she says playfully.

Confused at first, Bradley's countdown reminds me of what she intends.

Shifting uncomfortably, I take her wrist from behind me. "I don't think we –" I start.

Pulling her wrist from my grip, she places her finger on my lips to silence me.

Bradley's voice is nothing but background noise as he counts, "Four. Three …"

Leaning toward me until our noses nearly touch, she whispers, "If it truly meant nothing, you wouldn't be worried about a simple kiss."

I could stop her. I could pull her from my lap. Push her face away from mine. But I do not, and I am not sure why.

Instead, I close my eyes. My heartbeat quickens in anticipation. And though it is only seconds, the moment seems to be long and slow.

She places her hand along my jawline as I hear the crowd erupt. "Happy New Year!" they shout happily.

But I do not care about the balloons that are falling on the humans, or the cheers and squeals of the women. I only want one thing, and Kate does not disappoint. She presses her lips to mine, pulling my face toward her.

A heat rolls through me as I fight the urge to pull her closer. Keeping my lips soft, I move them with hers. Her fingers press into the back of my neck, making my spine tingle.

I slide my hand along her thigh slowly, stopping when she pulls her lips away.

A smile spreads across her face. "Good. Now I just need to kiss Luke."

And jumping from my lap, she starts into the crowd, leaving me wanting more. Wondering what just happened, I stare at the place where she disappeared into the crowd for a moment, until Yen kisses me on the cheek.

"Happy New Year, Nick," she says without noticing my distraction.

Glancing over at her, I fake a sincere-looking smile. "Happy New Year."

Smiling back at me, she trails her fingers along my cheek causally. And if my mind was not filled with the taste of Kate's lips, I may have wondered what Yen was thinking behind her gentle eyes, but all I can do is try to not make it obvious that my thoughts are about someone else.

She halfheartedly skips back to the billiard table and I sigh with relief. It is not often that I keep something from Yen. It is not something I enjoy, even though I am fairly good at it.

Standing up, I start toward the bar, simply to put some distance between the others and myself. It is not that I do not want to spend time with them. I just need a moment to myself. Although the bar is nearly empty, it probably is not the best place to try to be alone; not with an inquisitive Marie waiting for me to sit in front of her.

Choosing a stool toward the end of the counter, I slide onto the seat. I look at Marie and raise my hand up for another drink. After all, I'm not paying for them.

She smiles and grabs a glass. Her eyebrows come together ever so slightly as she focuses on pouring the rum, something she does without realizing it. Setting the bottle of half-empty rum aside, she places the glass on the counter, and, just like in the movies, she slides the drink down the bar with one quick push. But unlike the movies, when I stop the glass, it hits my hand hard enough to splash some of the alcohol onto my hand.

Apologetically, she shrugs and mouths the word 'sorry.' If it had been Bradley who had spilled the drink on me, I would have been angry. But I know Marie didn't mean anything by it so I smile at her with my lopsided grin and she goes back to wiping the counter.

I shake the excess rum from my hand onto the floor. Laying my forearms on the counter, I inhale the smell of the rum. A better quality than the other drink had been. Marie did not cheat me with the same cheap alcohol Bradley had.

Watching the vibrations of the music in the rum, my mind goes back to Kate. The way she smelled – the light hint of coconut that before was so familiar and unassuming, and now seems inviting. I never wanted to have feelings for Kate. I never want to bring her the pain the way the women I fall for inevitably feel. But yet, when she kissed me, I did not want her to stop. The soft skin of her hand on my face. Her long hair brushing against my arm. I close my eyes for a moment but it does not help. I cannot remove her from my mind.

Turning around, I scan the crowd until I find her, laughing and holding onto Luke's arm. A heat ripples through me, but I stop myself when I realize what I am feeling. Jealousy? I cannot be jealous. All I have done for the past thirty-four years is push her away. I have no right to be upset when she finally does move on. So why am I?

Kate whispers something to Luke that makes him smile – a ridiculous, childish smile. It nearly makes me gag. Then she pulls him to his feet and starts toward the door. They are leaving. Leaving together? Why? Luke is a human – and not even a handsome one. What could she possibly see in him?

Logically, I know that I should not think about Luke so negatively. He is my friend, but still, I cannot help it. As I watch them exit the bar, I refocus. Why am I jealous? I do not even want to be with her. I mean, I didn't. And I still don't... do I?

Before I can consider my feelings, a young, blond woman steps into my view.

"Hi," she says with a smile.

I look beside her at her red-haired friend who looks as though she is about to burst into laughter. Judging from the smoothness of their skin and the fresh scent of their blood, I assume the women to be close to twenty years old, though the friend seems younger. Bringing my eyes back to the blond, I say, "Hello."

I am not really interested in conversation and do not pretend that I am. I turn back toward the bar to watch the ripples in my undrinkable rum.

A little perturbed, the blond leans against the counter and clears her throat to regain my attention. I suppose she is not used to a man's disinterest.

A half-smile creeps onto my face and I glance over at her. To be honest, there is something about the uneven features of her face that is appealing. The way her small nose does not quite fit above her voluptuous lips and the way the bright blue of her eyes makes up for their lack of size.

"Can I help you?" I ask sarcastically.

"As a matter of fact you can," she says, batting her eyes. She leans toward me so slightly that I do not know if she is aware of it herself. "I'm taking a poll for my sociology class."

That's a lie. I can see it in her eyes. Besides, I care very little about a sociology class. "Really?" I ask, sounding sincere, as I watch Bradley glare at me from across the bar.

"Yep. I'm surveying men to see how many sex partners they have had," she says bluntly, making my eyes snap back to her.

Surely, she is not asking me how many women I have been with. "That's kind of personal, don't you think?"

She shrugs lightly. "Only if you're embarrassed by it." A slow smile spreads on her face; she knows she has me. "So how many should I put you down for?"

She is serious. Obviously, I am not going to tell her the truth. I do not want that kind of judgment on me. Especially since, according to her, I am only twenty-two. But I need a good, solid number, nothing too high, nothing too low. What would a human say?

"Ten." Give or take.

The petite redhead giggles slightly and I wonder what answer they were expecting from me. Perhaps they did not expect me to answer at all. Perhaps I shouldn't have.

"Thank you," the blond finally says, "I'll be sure to add that to my poll." She nudges her friend in the ribs and they start to walk away.

Still curious as to why she wanted to know about my sex life, I call after her, "Wait." She turns toward me and I smile. "I was lying. But if you let me buy you a drink, maybe I'll tell you the truth." No, actually I won't.

Trying to conceal a smile, she bites her lower lip and glances at her friend. When the redhead nods her approval, the blond looks back at me. "One shot of vodka."

A shot. Something quick enough that she will not have to sit beside me for long if she should decide to rejoin her friend. Smart girl. She is not sure about me yet.

As she sits down next to me, her friend leaves us alone, which is not normally a wise choice, but I do not intend on breaking the pact with the wolves just for one meal.

"I'm Nicolas," I tell her, extending my hand toward her.

She looks at me for a moment before she puts her hand in mine and shakes it. "Hannah."

I glance at Bradley who is wiping out a glass with enough vigor to crack it at any time. Knowing that he does not like me talking to Hannah is all the more reason to keep the conversation going, not that I would do that just to spite him. Well, maybe I would.

As he walks toward us, I ask her, "So are you really in college, or do you just like asking highly inappropriate questions to random men?"

She drops her eyes, trying not to smile. "No, I do actually go to UAA."

She means The University of Alaska in Anchorage. I wonder what she is majoring in but before I can ask, Bradley approaches us.

"The lady wants a shot of vodka. And you can put that on my tab," I smirk at him.

But he ignores me and keeps his eyes on Hannah. "You've had enough," he says roughly, "Jericho told me to limit you tonight."

Jericho. The werewolf I saw in the alley with his human mate. The werewolf I left alone in the snow unconscious.

Hannah taps her fingers on the counter irritably. "Jericho is my brother, not my boss. Get it right, Bradley."

Her brother. Just perfect. No wonder Bradley did not want me talking to her – a fragile human with a werewolf brother. Perfect.

"Tell you what, you go back to your table and sit with your friends and I'll bring you a drink," Bradley offers.

Though he did not say the words, she hears his dislike for me. Maybe she wants to make him angry, or perhaps she actually does like me somewhat, because she tells him, "No thanks. I'm comfortable here."

"Hannah –" he starts to protest as a fight breaks out in the back of the room and someone flips over a table, letting it crash onto the floor. Bradley jumps over the bar and hurries to get in the middle of it. Typical werewolf.

Disregarding the commotion in the background, my curiosity gets the best of me and I ask, "Why did you ask me how many women I've been with? It wasn't for any class."

She looks at me with light in her eyes. "A bet," she says. "Sometimes me and my friends try to guess different answers that people will tell us. Winner gets free drinks for the night."

I laugh to myself lightly. Sounds like a game Kate and I would play. "What did you guess for me?"

"Twelve. But Lily said eleven so she won."

I assume that Lily is the redhead she was with earlier. Not that it matters much.

"That's too bad," I say softly. "You don't strike me as someone who likes to lose."

With a mischievous smile, she leans close to me. "I didn't." Unexpectedly, she lays her hand on my upper thigh, making me inhale sharply. "I am taking you home, aren't I?" she whispers.

Part of me is unsure of what changed her mind about me so quickly, and the rest of me does not care. For whatever reason, she wants me and I will not argue with that. After all, thirst is not the only desire that needs filled.

I push her long locks away from her face and place my hand along her neck, feeling her pulse pound against her skin. And holding back my fangs, I say quietly, "Then we should go."

Her eyes move to my glass of rum, and just when I think she is going to insist that I finish my drink, she reaches for it. Throwing her head back, she downs the rum in one smooth gulp. As a drop of rum runs from the corner of her lips, she wipes it gently with her finger. "Let's go," she says, taking my hand and leading me toward the door.

As the fight in the back starts to die down, she grabs her coat and we leave.

Though her house is only a few blocks away, it is enough time for her to explain to me that she is only here to visit her brother for Christmas break, which means she only has ten days left of her vacation before classes resume. Overlooking the fact that her brother is a werewolf, and that I could kill her if I lose control, the more she speaks, the better this sounds. She is not looking for anything serious, which is good since I cannot offer anything long-term. Besides, the more she speaks, the more I enjoy the sound of her voice melting in my ears.

We walk up to the door of a sizable two-story home with several windows shining a dim light onto the snow around us. She slides the key in and unlocks the door. As she pushes it open, the smell of a werewolf hits me; it is faint enough that I know a wolf was here recently, but is gone now. Probably Jericho, but as long as he is nowhere in sight, it is not a problem for me.

There are other smells, too – human scents. But as I begin to determine whether or not they are currently home, Hannah grabs my shirt and pulls my face to hers. Crushing her mouth to mine, I hear her heartbeat quicken. Her flesh begins to flush with a rush of blood to the surface of her skin. My vampire wants her. But I want her more.

My breaths grow heavy and a warmth rolls through my body. She slides her hand to the base of my skull as I move my lips with hers.

Gently, she pulls me inside the house, which is enough of an invitation to suffice being asked. As I glide my tongue along her soft lips, her breaths become jagged and her fingernails press into my skin, which only makes me desire her so much more.

I kick the door shut as I slide my hands over her shoulders, pushing back her coat and letting it fall to the floor. Running my hand under her thin shirt, I move my hand to the small of her back and pull her to me, closing the space between us.

There is a possessiveness behind her kiss that nearly disguises the urgency of her hands pulling at my shirt that has my heart racing.

But the sound of light footsteps above us makes me grab her wrists and stop her from taking my shirt off. "Do you have a child?" I ask quietly, although she would not have been able to hear the pads of small feet upstairs.

She looks at me slightly confused for a moment until a young boy, maybe only five years old, appears at the top of the stairs.

Glancing over at him, she backs away from me. "Wyatt, what are you doing up?" she asks him as he sits on the top step.

In Scooby-Doo pajama pants and a faded sweatshirt, he crosses his arms over his knees. His dark hair hovers over his eyes and his face is uneasy. If he did not resemble Jericho so much, I might think he looked kind.

"My mom's in the kitchen. I think she is crying," he says timidly.

That does actually make me feel for him, but I am sure the werewolves would rather I stay out of whatever is happening here.

Hannah sighs quietly. "I'll take care of it." Then she says very softly, "Go back to bed."

Though he does not look happy about it, he stands up and walks away. I listen to his steps as he goes back to his room.

"That's my nephew," Hannah tells me, making me look over at her.

"He's cute," I say and honestly. He is, though the thought that he could one day be a wolf that will undoubtedly hate me, does make him a little less adorable.

Looking past me toward the kitchen, she exhales forcefully. "I'm sorry. Could you just give me a minute?"

A minute to check on his mother? Why not? The chances of regaining the same passion that was here a moment ago are slim anyway. "Sure."

Halfway smiling, she is not hiding her worry well. "Thanks," she mumbles.

As she walks to the kitchen, I lean my back against the wall and listen for the quiet noises of someone crying, but hear none;

only the sound of liquid being poured in a swallow glass, and a heavy bottle being placed on a wooden table.

Then Hannah's voice, muffled by the walls, "Are you okay?"

There is a pause, and then the sound of a now-empty glass hitting the table before a woman's voice replies, "I'm filing for divorce in the morning."

A chair scratches across the floor as it is scooted out from the table by, I assume, Hannah, "What happened?"

I imagine Hannah taking the woman's hand, rubbing her fingers across her knuckles. Concern written across her face. And I admit, part of me wants to know what distress looks like on her lovely face.

Pushing off of the wall, I walk quietly toward the kitchen, crossing through the living room.

Although I am not actually trying to eavesdrop, I hear the woman say, "Jericho is an ass." Of course he is, he's a wolf.

I tread lightly so they do not notice me as I pass the couch.

"I know," Hannah says softly, "I grew up with him, remember?" she tries to cheer her up, "What was it this time?"

"He was supposed to take Wyatt tonight, but backed out at the last minute so he could be with his friends... again," the woman says sharply.

I do not often take the side of a wolf, but perhaps she is being a tad bit too harsh on him. After all, it is a full moon and he is a werewolf.

Stepping around the corner, my eyes do not see the small space, worn cabinets, or the pale paint on the walls. They only fall on the woman sitting across from Hannah.

I have seen her before – in the alley with her mate; the woman who ran from me after I stopped Jericho from phasing in front of her – stopped him from hurting her. And I see it in her eyes that she remembers me, too.

Hannah turns around to face me and smiles gently. "Rebecca, this is..." she pauses, thinking, "I want you to meet..."

I suppose I should not expect her to remember my name.

"Nicolas," I tell Rebecca, the woman with dark, medium length hair, who happens to be staring at me intently.

The soft features of her face hold a tension with her surprise at seeing me. "It's you," she whispers.

Hannah looks at her slightly confused. "Do you know each other?"

"No," I say quickly, though it may have been too quickly. Then turning to Hannah, I start again, "I think I'm going to go."

Rebecca pushes the bottle of scotch to the side. "I'm sorry," she says to Hannah. "I didn't realize you had company."

"It's okay," I say to ease her worry, though the troubled look on her face still makes her seem as appealing as ever. "I have to work in the morning anyway. I should get some sleep." Not that I need it or will even try to rest.

Rebecca wipes the stale tears from her pink eyes and I wonder how someone could look stunning after crying for so long. I have seen well over a thousand people cry, usually while muttering about not being ready to die, but still I have only found a few that can keep their beauty while doing so. In fact, the most striking woman I have ever seen cry would have to be Kate. Something about knowing that I am the only one she feels comfortable enough to be so vulnerable in front of, makes her all the more beautiful.

But I should not think of Kate like that.

Hannah takes my hand. "You don't have to."

The warmth of her skin is almost enough for me to consider staying, just to feel her against me. Almost.

Leaning down, I kiss her on the cheek lightly, holding my lips to her longer than necessary. "Goodnight," I tell her quietly.

I start toward the door but stop just before I leave the kitchen. "Rebecca, I know this is none of my business, but…" I look over at her with soft eyes, "when you tell your husband that you want a divorce, wear his favorite perfume. It'll drive him crazy," I say with a slight smile.

For a moment, I see her smile back. "Goodnight, Nicolas," she tells me.

I walk out and through the living room until I reach the door. Feeling eyes on me, I turn around to find Wyatt sitting on the top step, listening keenly. He puts one finger up to his lips to silence me.

Perhaps I should not let him hear what his mother is saying about Jericho, but at the same time, it is not my place to say otherwise. So I nod once as a goodbye and slip out of the door quietly.

Keeping my eyes on the snow in front of me, I walk home, my hands tucked deep inside my pockets. My breaths hang in the air, reminding me of the frigid temperature around me.

Even if I couldn't sense that I was being followed, there would be no hiding the odor of him. The musky, wooden scent of a wolf accompanied by the human smell that had filled Hannah's home. Jericho.

I wait, letting him stalk me, until we are outside of the city limits. Then stopping, I raise my head slowly as a smirk spreads across my face. "It's very kind of you to walk me home, but you're not really my type, Jericho."

I turn around to face him as he steps out of the shadows, his face twisted in hatred toward me. His eyebrows are drawn together, his lips pressed thin and tight. His dark hair still disheveled from phasing so recently.

"You have a lovely home," I continue. "But I have to ask, did you mark your territory in every corner, or does the stench of your wolf just smell that bad?"

A low growl rumbles behind his lips. "You stay away from my wife and sister."

Surely, he does not expect me to listen to an order from a wolf.

Although I know he means both Rebecca and Hannah, I tease, "Your wife is your sister?" I shrug, "Figures, dogs are incestuous creatures."

Without hesitation, he leaps toward me. His clothes explode from his body as he phases in midair. Stepping to the side quickly, I move just in time as he lands where I had been standing. He turns his head toward me, snapping and gnashing his teeth together violently. But I answer his anger with a kick to the ribs that sends him back into the snow.

Jumping to his feet, he charges at me as fast as he can. I stand still, letting my eyes change to black and my fangs press into my lips. My fingernails grow, waiting to dig them into his flesh.

When he is seconds from me, I flip over him, placing my hands on his back and grabbing handfuls of the fur. As I land on my feet, I swing him over my head and drive him into the ground in front of me, just to hear him whine painfully.

He slashes his claws at my face, but I grab his paw and thrust my hand into his arm, feeling the bones shift apart. Dropping his arm on the ground, I put my foot over the injured area and apply enough pressure to let him know that I could crush the bones completely.

I can hear the padding of paws but do not take my eyes off of Jericho. Instead, I put my hand around his thick neck and squeeze until my nails are cutting into him.

I lean toward him and hiss, exposing my fangs as three werewolves emerge from the dark, two in their wolf form, and one, Cyrus, in his human form.

Cyrus puts his hands up to stop the others. "Enough."

"Down, boy," I whisper to Jericho, mockingly. Then loud enough for Cyrus to hear me, I say, "Everyone in that house was alive when I left. I have done nothing wrong."

I stand up, keeping my foot on Jericho's arm. "The pact we made with you is our way of showing your kind mercy. Not the other way around," I inform Cyrus, though I think of all of the wolves, he is the only one who already knows it. "If you want to tell me who I can be friends with, you better bring your whole pack. But until then …" I shove Jericho away with my foot, making him slide across the snow to Cyrus' feet, "keep that pup on a leash."

"Nicolas –" Cyrus starts with a harsh tone.

But I interrupt him. "We are finished here – unless you plan on apologizing for your mutt."

Jericho pulls himself onto his paws but keeps his front leg from touching the ground.

"Go home, Nicolas," Cyrus says bluntly. "You might not have one for much longer."

I half-smile at his weak threat. I am not afraid of such a small pack. My family could take them on easily. Truthfully, the only reason we made a truce with them is to keep the humans ignorant about us during our stay here, and with this city having so few numbers of humans, a deal with the wolves seemed the easiest.

"Let's go," Cyrus tells them.

The wolves follow him as he walks away from me. But from the way their yellow eyes narrow on me, I do believe that if he was not the alpha, they would not leave so willingly.

"*Well, do you want to be with Kate?*" A simple question, but how do I respond? Kate is wonderful for me. She is smart and powerful, beautiful and alluring, and fun and easy to talk to. There is nothing about her that would turn me away. Nothing.

I exhale forcefully. "I don't know, Tara," I say into the telephone honestly. At least I can afford to be truthful with the only werewolf who cares for me.

Playing with the phone cord, I continue, "She would only get hurt and I can't do that to her; she's my best friend."

I lean back in the chair and prop my feet up on Doctor Price's desk and, yes, he would be angry if he knew that I use his phone for personal calls to Rome, but that is all the more reason to do it.

There is a light laugh on the other end. "I thought I was your best friend?"

The humor in her voice makes me smile. "You know what I mean." I mean my best vampire friend. My oldest friend. The one who knows me better than anyone else, including, at times, even me.

"Nick, she may not get hurt. It's not set in stone, you know?" she says softly trying to comfort me.

If she was talking to anyone else, she may be right. But this is me she is speaking to, and with both of my more serious relationships ending in death, it seems that destiny does not agree that I should be loved. Besides, my heart still longs for Ann, leaving little room for anyone else.

I shrug, even though I realize she cannot see me. "Maybe, maybe not. Either way, I can't risk it."

There is a long sigh in my ear, followed by her quiet voice. "It's okay to be afraid."

I snap the chair up quickly, sitting up straight. Me? Afraid? "I'm not afraid of anything," I reply almost defensively.

"I think you are," she says and I can tell that she believes it. "I think you're afraid of finding someone who could replace Ann."

Nobody could do that.

"I think," she continues in my pause, "she symbolizes the last bit of your humanity that you hold on to. And without her, you don't know who you are."

I flip a pen from the desk over my fingers. Maybe she is right; she has a point. My reservoir of compassion for the humans is limited as it is, and without it, I would be no better than the nomads.

Coming down the hallway, I hear the heavy steps of someone walking toward Doctor Price's office. Leaning near the telephone, I say quietly, "I have to go."

"Don't forget, I'm coming to Alaska," Tara hurries out. "You're picking me up at the airport, right?"

WITHOUT SHADOWS | 93

I smile to myself. "Yes, of course," I whisper to her, "Now, I really have to go."

"Okay, then hang up," she whispers back, mocking my quietness with her own.

The footsteps stop a few feet from the door as I laugh lightly to myself. "Hey, wait," I say, "I can't wait to see you."

Letting the smile show in her voice, she answers, "Goodbye, Nick."

"Bye," I say quietly enough that I am not sure whether she could hear me or not.

Regretting the necessity of hanging up, I place the receiver back on the base and walk to the door. I press my ear to the door and listen. Even through the thick wood, I can hear Doctor Price talking to one of the nurses about the older, grouchy man in room twelve.

Opening the door slightly, I peek into the hall to confirm my assumptions. Sure enough, Doctor Price has his back to me. So sliding along the wall, I slip out of his office, closing the door behind me. I start down the hallway away from him and toward the stairs that lead to the inpatient level.

It is funny to think of all the times that I have snuck into his office. I call overseas to Tara, take all of the staples out of his stapler, hide the key to his filing cabinet, things to frustrate him. Just because.

Upstairs, the smell of stale lunch fills the hallway. Caramelized butternut squash surrounds me, but it is sweeter than I would cook it, making the air heavy and thick.

I walk to room twelve, Mr. Kenton's room. The grouchy old man hates everyone, even his family, who rarely come to visit him. His personality is off-putting which, I am sure, is the reason the staff here keep a distance when they can. But alas, I cannot stay away. It is an orderly's duty to bathe Mr. Kenton, and I happen to be that orderly today.

Pulling my mouth into a forced smile, I step into the room, and with a friendly tone, I say, "Hello, Mr. Kenton."

He darts his eyes to me. "Oh, it's you." Crossing his arms over his chest, he continues, "Well, don't just stand in the door. This body isn't going to wash itself," he says harshly.

Turning around, I let my smile drop as I close the door. It is patients like him that make me earn my redemption and make me wonder why I even try to work with the public.

I start toward the sink. "It looks nice outside," I say, trying to make small talk when I do not wish to.

"I wouldn't know," he huffs.

I glance over at the large window, but the curtains are drawn. "Well, let me open your drapes so you can see the stars and maybe even the northern lights," I tell him, walking toward the window.

"Leave it," he snaps, making me stop in my tracks. "Just leave it closed. There is nothing to see out there but darkness. Besides, the window lets in a draft and I am sick enough. Not that you people care."

That is certainly true. At least about me; I care very little whether he feels bad or not. He makes others dislike him in such a way that I am pretty sure his family is hoping he dies here, which says quite a bit about him in general.

"Sir –" I start, but he raises his hand to interrupt me.

"Just do your job, half-pint. And keep your trap shut."

His offensive tone sends an angry heat rushing to my cheeks, but somehow, I am able to bite my tongue and not say what I want to.

I go to the sink and turn on the hot water, letting it run for a minute to warm up. I reach for the bathing basin in the lower cabinet when Mr. Kenton comments abrasively, "Make sure it's hot this time. You always make the water too cold. It's like you're trying to make me catch my death."

Trust me; he would know if I was trying to kill him. "Just give it a minute to heat up," I tell him.

I hear the chopping sound of air, and move in time to see a box of tissues hit the cabinet near my head. I spin my head around to find Mr. Kenton glaring at me.

"I said, keep your mouth shut," he orders.

My blood boils beneath my skin and my jaw clenches tightly. There is nothing I would like more than to sink my fangs into his jugular. If I did not have the pact with the werewolves, he would be lying in a pool of his own blood right about now.

Through gritted teeth, I utter, "Mr. Kenton, do not throw things at me."

"Or what?" he asks, shooting his eyebrow up.

Or he will die by my hands, even if it causes a rift between the wolves and my family. But because I cannot say that to him, I simply reply, "I will have you put in restraints."

Mulling this over, he drums his fingers over his lips. I turn back to the sink and put my hand in the hot water to check the temperature.

When I grab the basin, I hear Mr. Kenton start again just as severely, "I want a woman to bathe me. Why does it always have to be a man?"

I let out a long sigh. "It's the policy, you know that." Which I have explained time and time again.

"Make that cute little candy stripper do it. You know, the little blond one," he adds with a hint of a smile.

Jennifer, I assume, he means. The sixteen-year-old volunteer. Absolutely not, even if it weren't against regulations, there is no possible way I would ask a child to bathe this retched excuse for a man.

Reaching over, I turn the cold knob on and feel the water cool on my hand. *Good enough*, I think to myself.

I place the basin under the faucet and begin to fill it as a slow smile spreads across my face.

***

Sitting alone at my usual table in the odoriferous cafeteria, I try to forget Mr. Kenton. Everything about him, from his obtuse attitude, to bathing his wrinkly, loose skin, makes me irritable.

I hold a quarter upright with the tip of my finger and flip it with my other hand so that it spins across the table like a top, trying to be distracted by something. Anything.

Glancing up from the tops of my eyes, I see Luke coming toward me with a tray of food. I slap my hand down on the quarter to stop it. Finally there is someone who can preoccupy my mind for a while.

Placing my foot on the edge of the chair that is across from me, I kick it slightly, just enough to slide it out from under the table.

He smiles at my offer and lays his tray on the table. He flops down in the chair. "Where's your food?" he asks.

I could say, "You are my meal" as he sits down across from me, but I don't. Instead, I shrug. "I already ate."

"You say that every day," he disregards, waving his hand in the air.

He scoops some of the mashed potatoes with his spoon and shovels it into his mouth, almost the way you would expect a child would. He opens wide to try to fit too much neatly inside his mouth, but fails.

"Did you have fun last night?" he asks with full cheeks.

I watch him slop his food around for a moment before I answer, "Yeah, it was all right." Except for the part where he left with Kate, although I still do not know why that bothers me so much.

A part of me has to know what happened after they left, but the rest of me is more concerned with not being obvious. I do not want to be Kate's boyfriend, but at the same time, I really think I might like it more than I would admit to myself. Either way, I certainly do not want Kate and Luke together.

"So Kate is really smokin'," he starts, and I am glad he was the one to bring her up. "But I think I blew it with her."

I hide the smile I feel inside. At least nothing happened between them that would make me want to kill him.

"Why?" I ask innocently.

Swallowing, he shrugs lightly. "I don't know. I must have had too much to drink or something, 'cause I ended up passing out."

"You did?" I remembered him at the bar, and he didn't seem like he had drank very much. He actually seemed really sober for a change.

"I guess. I remember leaning in to kiss her, and then the next thing I knew, I was waking up this morning on the couch. Alone."

I smile my lopsided grin. She enthralled him – made him go to sleep so she did not have to kiss him. That has to be what happened. It is the best explanation. At least, it is for me.

He misreads my smile and tosses a roll at me. "It's not funny."

Laying the roll on the table, I reply, "I'm not laughing." And I am not. I do not find this hilarious in any way. Just pleasing that she did not fall for his boyish charm.

From behind me, a warm hand touches my shoulder gently, "Nicolas?"

Turning around in my chair, I see Hannah wearing a soft pink sweater with her hair pulled back into a loose ponytail.

"Hannah," I say, slightly surprised to see her here.

"Do you work here?" she asks.

Her question makes me think that maybe this conversation is not the friendly, social meeting I am hoping it is, and that she will ask me something job-related instead.

But my worries are quickly relieved when she continues, "I'm sorry about last night. That wasn't how I planned my night to turn out." Her hand trails down my upper arm, making chills rush to my skin.

"It's all right," I insist. "Things like that happen."

A smile lights up her face. Placing her other hand on the table, she leans toward me slightly with mischief in her eyes, which is enough to make my heartbeat pick up its pace.

"Why don't you come over after work? We will have the house to ourselves this time," she says insinuatingly.

I can see Luke's jaw fall without looking at him and hear him drop his spoon onto the tray in shock. But I keep my eyes on hers as the animal inside awakens at the chance of being alone with a helpless human. The man in me smiles at the idea of being alone with a woman.

Concealing much of the hunger in my eyes, I tell her, "I'll be there."

I watch as she bites her lower lip gently, making me want to taste her lips on mine. She grabs my shirt collar and pulls my face closer to hers. "Damn right you will."

The authority in her voice is intoxicating, and if I were standing, it may have made my knees weak. But sitting in this chair, it only makes me want to pull her onto my lap and take her right here, right now. I do not mind all of the observers, or their judging eyes, and I get the feeling she would not object to it either. I want her. She wants me. What else is there? There is Kate. *Stop it*, I tell myself, *don't think about Kate like that.* Kate is not meant for me. She deserves someone better. Someone without so many sins.

Hannah lays her cheek against mine. "See you soon," she whispers seductively.

As my breathing stops, she lets her fingers slide off of my shirt and trail across my chest as she walks away. My eyes follow her to the door unwillingly and when I finally do turn around in my chair, Luke is staring at me in astonishment.

"How did you do that?" he stammers out. "I've been chasing after her since the eighth grade."

Truthfully, I do not know why Hannah is interested in me, so I shrug. "I'm honest, I guess." As honest as I can afford to be, anyway.

He picks his spoon up but hesitates to use it. "I'm honest, too," he tells me. "I say, 'Hey, you wanna bang?' but that never works."

Scratch what I said before about him having boyish charm. I laugh to myself. Surely, he is not serious. Between chuckles, I say, "I have to get back to work." Standing up, I continue, "I'll see you later."

"Yeah, sure," he answers as he shoves another bite of potatoes into his mouth.

Still smiling, I walk out of the cafeteria and back to the inpatient floor, where my new favorite patient is waiting for me.

Sitting on the bed, Jennifer is trying to take the blood pressure of one uncooperative little girl.

"Please, sit still. It'll only take a minute," Jennifer reasons.

But Punzi wants no part of it, and jerks her arm, trying to free it from Jennifer's grip.

"Hey, Punzi," I call into her room.

Her face perks up and she turns toward my voice. "Nicolas? Is that you?"

As I walk toward her, I continue, "Yes, and you really need to hold still for her."

Slumping her shoulders forward, she sighs. "I don't want to. It squeezes my arm and it hurts."

I sit down on the edge of the bed near Jennifer and take Punzi's hand. Seamlessly, I attach myself to the fibers in her being, enthralling her, so that what I say she will believe without question.

"It doesn't hurt," I tell her softly, and I can feel the pulse in her wrist begin to slow.

I nod to Jennifer and she slides the cuff on her tiny bicep. Even as she moves quickly to get the blood pressure, I keep my focus on Punzi. Looking at her blank eyes is harder than usual. I find myself wishing Jennifer would go faster so that I could release Punzi from this drone-like state.

Finally, Jennifer slips the cuff off of her arm and smiles at me. "Thanks," she whispers. Then, quietly, she walks out, leaving me alone with Punzi.

Without hesitating, I let go of her frail hand and watch as she blinks a few times instinctually, to clear her mind.

"Is she gone?" she asks me.

"Just us," I tell her.

"Good," she says. "Did you know that they tried to feed me broccoli?" she whines, "What kind of kid eats broccoli?"

Normally, pouting does not bring me pleasure but, for a reason unbeknownst to me, it makes me smile. Perhaps it is because I actually want to spend time with this child. I am not worried about putting her in harm's way or that her and her family will die by my hands. I simply get to enjoy being around a child who wants to be around me, which I really haven't had much experience with. At least, not since Roddy, Tara's son was little, but he has been grown for some time now.

"Not this kid, that's for sure," she huffs. "It ruined my whole day."

It is pleasing to me that she has decided to talk to me so freely. I was hoping that soon she would feel comfortable with me. Though, I was expecting it to take slightly longer than a day.

"Well, I'm sorry about that," I tell her. "So what can I do to make it better?"

"I don't know," she says almost as a whine. Sighing, she flops backward on the bed as though she is exhausted. "It's so boring here."

Smiling to myself, I push the loose strands of hair away from her face. "Surely, it's not that bad," I say softly.

She lets out a long exhale, blowing her bangs up in the air for a moment when an idea forms in my mind. It's not something I am supposed to do but, honestly, I cannot just sit here and watch her suffer. How am I expected to say no to such a sweet face?

"I'll be right back," I tell her, making her squeeze her eyebrows together in confusion.

I walk to the storage room at the end of the hall and take a wheelchair out. Nobody notices me as I hurry back to Punzi.

She hears me come in but does not know what the sound of the wheels are. "What is that?" she asks.

"Your chariot," I tell her, stopping the chair beside her bed. "We have to hurry, Princess Rapunzel. The witch's army is drawing near."

"Oh no. Quick get my royal cloak," she says with a wide smile.

Lifting her out of bed, I play along, "There's no time for that. We must make it to the magic forest before nightfall."

"Ready the horses. We leave at once," she tells me as I set her in the wheelchair.

I spin the chair around quickly. "We'll take the commoner's path over the Canyon of Winds."

Pushing her quickly, I turn the chair around the door sharply. She slides across the seat, laughing.

"Faster, my good man!" she cheers.

Running down the hallway, we pass the nurse's station with Punzi squealing. Several nurses look at us with wide eyes and a few of them even smile.

"We're almost to the canyon but, oh no, the bridge is out. What must we do?" I ask her.

Crossing her legs in the seat, she tells me, "Jump it."

"Are you sure?"

"We only live once," she says bravely, making me smile.

Picking up the chair, I add, "Here we go!" I spin the chair around in the air. "We're caught in a whirlwind!" I shout.

"We'll never make it!" she calls.

I bring the chair back down with a jolt and she laughs loudly.

Quickly, we start down the hallway again. But as I round the corner, Pricilla, the dayshift supervisor, stands with her arms crossed over her chest and a stern look on her face.

I stop abruptly just in front of her.

"Why did we stop?" Punzi asks.

I lean close to her. "It's the witch." Pricilla purses her mouth irritably. "I think I've been captured," I tell Punzi.

"Trish," Pricilla says to the nurse near us, "Take this patient back to her room."

"Yes, ma'am," Trish says quietly. She takes the wheelchair from my hands and starts down the hallway.

Before they make it far, Punzi calls back to me, "Be brave, my prince."

Barely holding back my laugh, I cover my smile with my hand.

"Do you think this is funny?" Pricilla asks harshly.

I want to say that it is, but instead, I tell her, "No, ma'am."

She steps closer to me. "I could have you fired." "For what? Running?" I say sarcastically.

Apparently she does not find me amusing, because her eyes narrow on me. "For disrupting."

"Then I apologize," I tell her. "I didn't realize that entertaining a patient could upset the delicate balance of care and boredom that we provide to children here."

"You better watch that mouth of yours," she replies sharply. "This is going on your record, and if I can, I'll have your job over it."

She stomps away quickly as I shake my head. Firing me would be a mistake.

***

Perhaps going to Hannah's is a mistake, but regardless, I find myself lingering in her yard. Knowing that she is a werewolf's sister should make me leery, but pacing along her driveway does not change my mind. I like Hannah, just not as much as I like Kate. However, Kate is not option, at least not for me, whereas Hannah is, and if vampires are anything, we are opportunistic.

Stepping onto the porch, I knock on the door lightly.

I do not wait long before I hear Hannah say, "Come in."

Watching the snow swirl around my feet as I step inside, I keep my head down until the door is closed. Then looking up, my heartbeat quickens. Standing at the top of the stairs is Hannah, wearing a bra and panties which are sheer enough that I can make out her dark nipples through the material.

I want her. There is nothing else to it. I didn't expect her to be as beautiful as she is. I didn't expect her skin to be so flawless or her body to be so impeccable. Curving in all the right places, she strongly resembles a vampire. The only difference being the way her scent calls to me. My lust for her intensifies, demanding that I have her.

Seeing the hunger in my eyes, a sly smile spreads across her face. "Come and get me," she whispers seductively.

She walks away, trailing her fingers along the banister as she walks down the hallway. I make it up the stairs faster than a human would, not caring whether she notices or not. Grabbing her waist, I turn her around toward me and back her against the door.

As she inhales sharply, excitement lights her eyes. "You're fast," she breathes out.

I pull her to me. "Not with everything," I tell her, then crush my lips to hers. A fire rushes through my body as her hand burns its way down my chest. With handfuls of my shirt, she pulls my top over my head, letting her breasts brush against me.

She kisses me with an urgency behind her lips as she caresses her tongue with mine. I can hear her heart pounding as her hand rolls over the ripples of my abdomen. With my hand on her cheek, I keep her face to mine. She grabs the top of my pants and works quickly to unfasten them while I glide my hand down her neck and along her chest. Rubbing her breast, I fight the urge to rip the bra from her as I press her into the door.

She drops my pants, kissing down my neck. Sliding her hand in my underwear, she massages me gently. My breaths become jagged and sharp and I rub my hand along the soft skin of her cheek. Pulling her face up, I press her lips to mine intensely. I can feel my fangs trying to extend but I hold them back as I bite her lower lip lightly.

Gliding my hand around to her back, I unhook her bra and slide the straps from her shoulders. As one hand strokes her breast, rubbing her nipple with my fingers softly, the other hand opens the door behind her. I feel her smile through the kiss as she pulls her hand from my underwear. Taking her bra in both hands, she wraps it around the back of my neck and leads me into the room.

She kicks the door closed as she tosses the bra to the floor. Sitting down on the edge of the bed, she leans back on her elbows and smiles playfully, biting her lip. Her eyes move from my underwear to my eyes and she says, "Take them off." Her eyebrow darts up as she continues, "I want to see what I'm working with."

Grabbing the band, I slide my underwear off and watch as her eyes widen slightly and she holds her breath for a moment.

Stepping toward her, I lean over, placing my face close to hers. "Does that work for you?"

Her eyes meet mine with desire burning in them. She smiles seductively. "Definitely."

Pressing my lips to hers, I slowly glide her panties off. I slide my hand along her legs, grabbing her thighs and moving her legs apart. She pushes herself back further onto the bed, leading me with her lips. Pulling me with her, she leans back onto the comforter.

I kiss along her jawline and down her neck, feeling her pulse thump against my lips. Her fingers tangle themselves in my hair as she lets out a pleasurable exhale.

Moving my hand to her butt, I hold her against me as I rock my hips into hers. With a light moan, she grabs my shoulders and pulls me closer. Her fingers press into my skin as she arches her body toward me. My heart races in response to the way her legs tighten around me.

I run my hand along her ribs and breast to her cheek and her skin warms with my touch. I kiss her lips fiercely, letting her feel the need behind them. Between our uneven breaths, her moans grow louder, sending a heat charging through me.

As she digs her fingers into my back, I slam my hips into hers. She rolls her head to the side, closing her eyes and parting her lips to let a rough breath escape. I trail my tongue along her ear, tasting her flesh and fighting to hold back my fangs. She rolls her hips with mine and I exhale sharply. My hot breath on her neck forms chills on her skin which only makes it harder to not bite into her delicate throat.

Breathing hard, I kiss down her chest. I roll my tongue along her neck, raking my teeth and biting her chin gently as my hand pulls her body against mine.

"Oh, you feel so good," she says in a pant.

A surge of greedy desire washes over me and my eyes change to solid black unwillingly. Keeping my face beside hers, I try to focus on turning my eyes back to the soft green they were a moment ago, but the smell of her blood close to my nose makes it difficult.

Nearly in control of myself, I hear her breathily say, "I want you to come inside me."

Knowing I have no chance of appearing human, I close my eyes and lean away from her. I grab her at the waist and pull her onto all fours quickly. Since she can no longer see my face, I open my black eyes and watch her arch her butt into the air as I rub my hand along her spine. Then holding onto her hips, I guide myself inside her again.

***

It is difficult to keep my eyes off of Hannah's naked body lying next to me, and she knows it. Rolling over toward me, she smiles, "So, Nicolas," she starts, "what's your last name?"

I half-smile at the question since it is something most humans learn before sex and not after. "Rider," I tell her.

"You're not from around here, right? I would remember you," she asks as a strand of hair falls in front of her face.

"No," I say as I push the loose locks behind her ear. "I'm here on vacation."

She lets out a disbelieving chuckle. "Nobody vacations here; especially in the winter."

"I do. I like the night," I tell her. "To be honest, I have a condition where I am basically allergic to the sun. I can't be out during the day at all. So, to me, this is paradise."

Intrigue sparks in the eyes. "That's called, um," she pauses a moment, thinking, then continues, "solar urticaria." "You've heard of it," I say, surprised.

She shrugs, smiling proudly. "I am at the top of my class. Pre-med."

I smile to myself. "You don't seem like a pre-med student."

Her eyebrows shoot up. "Med students can't have fun?"

My lopsided smile shows itself as I reply, "It's not that. I've just never seen a doctor who looked like you. You will probably give patients palpations just by walking in the room."

She laughs lightheartedly, shaking her head. The door downstairs shuts loudly, grabbing Hannah's attention.

"Becca's home," she tells me. "You should probably go."

"Sure," I say quietly as the sounds of Rebecca's footsteps travel up the stairs.

Looking around the room, I hear her add, "Your clothes are in the hallway."

Of course they are. "Right," I mutter to myself.

I slide out of bed and pull my underwear on. At least those are in the room.

"You can come over and we'll do this again sometime," she says softly.

She pulls the blankets around her and closes her eyes. Her body shifts for a moment until she is comfortable then settles with a sigh.

"I'll just let myself out then," I tell her.

Without opening her eyes, she sleepily replies, "Okay."

Feeling like this is a trick, I am slightly unsure of what my next move should be, but still I walk to the door and listen as Rebecca's footsteps go into the next bedroom.

I know this is my chance to slip out unnoticed by Rebecca, so I open the door and step into the hallway. Grabbing my pants and shoes, I slip them on quickly, but just as I pull my pants to my waist, Rebecca steps into the hallway.

"Oh," she says, surprised, "Nicolas. Sneaking out, are you? Imagine that," she adds sarcastically.

Slightly annoyed by her comment, I drop my eyes and smile to myself. Then looking back up at her, I tell her, "That's not exactly what's happening."

"Really?" She walks over to me and I smell her perfume clinging to her. She must have taken my advice and wore it to see Jericho today, which softens my irritation with her.

She stops in front of me, crossing her arms over her chest. "Tell me then. What part am I wrong about?"

Knowing that Rebecca is mostly right, I answer her, "Me." I grab my shirt from the banister and pull it over my head. "Goodnight, Rebecca. It was nice to see you again."

I walk around her and start down the stairs when I hear Wyatt call, "Mom."

Rebecca goes to his room as I leave the house and step into the winter wind. Standing on the porch, I feel Jericho's eyes burning into me, even though I do not see him. I smile widely, knowing he is watching, and zip my pants up. A low growl ripples through the air, making me laugh quietly.

"You're too easy, Jericho. You need to learn to watch that temper," I tell him, and before I can add anything to that, I hear a sharp scream – a scream full of pain and terror. A scream reserved for vampires. Afraid that it is because of my family biting into a frail human, I bolt toward the sound.

Not far ahead, I feel the other vampire's presence, but it is not one of mine. I slide to a stop in front of an alley and see someone I did not expect. Drinking the blood of a woman is the man who changed me all those years ago. My maker; the one who killed my Ann, and mercilessly chose not to kill me.

"It's you," I mumble to myself.

His head snaps up and the blood rolls down his chin as he smiles at me. "Hello, Nicolas."

He lets go of the woman and she drops in the snow. Wiping his face with his sleeve, he continues, "I wondered when we would meet again."

My shock is quickly replaced with anger and my eyes change to black. I lunge at him, knocking us both to the ground. We tumble over one another until he pins my shoulders down.

"You're weaker than me," he gloats.

Grabbing a piece of wood from a nearby stack, I slam it into his head, sending splinters and fragments into the air.

"Doesn't look that way," I tell him as he falls off of me.

I jump to my feet and stomp at his head but he leaps up just in time. Behind me, he grabs my hair and shoves my head into the building, bloodying my nose.

I reach behind me, taking his wrist, and pull him over my shoulder. He lands in the snow on his back. Putting his hands beside him, he starts to jump up but I drive my fist into his sternum, pushing him to the ground.

He claws at my arms as I tighten my hands around his throat and dig my fingernails into his neck. My blood streams down my forearms toward him, but I do not stop for the pain.

He curls his body and kicks me back a step. I swing my fist toward him as he gets to his feet. I hit him hard enough to push him against the wood stack. I punch again, but this time he blocks it with his forearm. He grabs my wrist and I elbow him in the nose, making him lose his grip on me.

Grabbing his collar, I slam my forehead into his face and hear his nose break. He stumbles back a step, shaking his head to clear his vision. Taking a piece of wood from the pile, he hurls it at me. It cuts through the air past me as I barely dodge it.

I flip over, landing in a crouch near him. I sweep my leg around, knocking his feet out from under him. A mist of snow heaves into the air as I leap onto him. I grab a handful of hair and jerk his head to the side. With my fangs exposed and ready, I lean in for the kill when he pushes my arms out away from him. He slams his hands into my chest, sending me flying backwards. I hit the adjacent building hard and feel a sharp, piercing pain. I cry out slightly as I hang suspended above the ground from, what I know is an ice hook in my back. Close to my heart, it punctured my lung, making it difficult to breathe calmly.

He stands up and walks over to me. Smiling, he pulls on my feet, pushing the hook in deeper. The pain twists my face but I refuse to scream.

"Tell Marcella I said hi," he says with a smirk, "and sorry that I forgot to send a Christmas card this year."

In the distance, we hear the werewolves howl as they quickly approach.

He looks in the direction of the howls and I take the opportunity to kick him in the face. He backs up, wiping the blood from his lip. He smiles as though the pain satisfies him somehow.

Grabbing the edge of the roof, I lift myself up off of the hook, screaming through the ripping pain as the cold, metal hook slides out of my back. The sound of heavy paws draws closer and he sprints out of the alley as I drop to the ground. The blood streaming from my back stains the snow a deep red when I stand up.

I run after him, but as I reach the opening of the alley, I slam into Cyrus in his werewolf form. Tripping over him, I land face first in the snow with a thud. I look up but do not see the vampire anywhere.

"Damn it, Cyrus!" I shout as I kick the dark grey wolf in the ribs.

The four wolves that are with him growl but do not step toward me as Cyrus phases into his human form again. He grabs my ankle and slams my body into the building.

"Do not touch me again, Nicolas," he snaps with the wild look of his wolf still in his eyes.

I stand up and face him. "I could have had him."

"Had who?"

Honestly, I do not know how to answer. I could say 'my maker' but then I would have to explain that. Since I don't know the vampire's name, I sigh. "Forget it. You wouldn't understand."

I start to push past Cyrus but he shoves me back. "Where do you think you're going? There is a human hurt in there," he says, nodding to the alley, "and I want to know what happened. Just so you know, I haven't enjoyed the taste of a vampire in a long time, so your story better be a good one."

I glance around at the wolves standing behind him, and for a moment, consider what the odds would be if I tried to take them all on. When I see Jericho, the caramel wolf, I tell Cyrus, "It was a vampire, but not one of mine. I tried to stop him." That's sort of what happened. "He ran and I could have caught him if you didn't show up. Jericho knows it's true. He was with me when we heard the screams."

Cyrus looks over his shoulder. "Jericho, is that true?"

Jericho glares at me briefly before he lowers his head in a nod.

Cyrus' mouth twists while he thinks to himself. Then looking at me, he continues, "If I find out this vampire is connected to you, well, let's just say I know where you live."

I half-smile at his weak threat. If he were to attack me at home, with my family there, and without the sun to protect him, his entire pack would die.

"Cyrus," I start, "if you want this vampire dead, stay out of my way."

The sound of the woman choking on her blood grabs Cyrus' attention, and he looks into the alley.

I can see him deciding what he should do to help her, so I tell him, "It's too late."

His eyes meet mine and I smile coldly. "But you do whatever you want. She's your problem now."

I do not wait for a response and walk away, but as I do, I hear Cyrus say, "Jericho, get her to the hospital." Like that will do any good.

Chapter 5

I *slam the door shut* as I storm into the living room. Sitting on the couch next to Yen, Marcella looks surprised by my   disheveled appearance as her eyes widen with concern.

"We need to talk," I say through gritted teeth.

She stands up. "What happened?"

Ignoring her question, I sharply insist, "Somewhere private." Although there is not much privacy in a house full of vampires who can hear everything.

Nodding, she walks toward her bedroom as Yen smiles like a child who just watched their sibling be punished.

I follow Marcella without another word, biting my tongue through the frustration.

When we reach her bedroom, I close the door, trying not to slam it. Marcella crosses her arms over her chest. "What?" she asks defensively.

Attempting to sound reasonable, I start, "My maker knows my name. He called me Nicolas, not Vincent. And he knew your name, too. How does he know your name, Marcella?"

Without batting an eyelash, she lies, "He must have followed us at some point."

I exhale irritably. "No. It sounded like he knows you personally. Besides, you don't seem surprised to hear I met him tonight."

Bringing my hands to my mouth, I calm myself before I add, "I want the truth, Marcella. How do you know him?"

There is a long sigh as she hesitates to answer, but finally she drops her arms. "I made him."

I was not expecting that answer, and my face must show it because she waits a moment for me to process it before she continues, "His name is Salem. We had a falling out, and he has been trying to get in my good graces ever since."

"What?" I say disbelievingly. "What do you mean 'made him'?"

"I was lonely, Nicolas," she explains. "He was a mistake, that's all."

"That's all?" I snap. "He ruined my life. He took everything from me. He's not a mistake, he's a curse."

Stepping closer to me, she starts, "Please don't be angry." She reaches her hand toward me but I step away from her. "How am I supposed to feel? You have lied to me for centuries. I thought you cared about me."

"I do," she says softly.

Unsure of whether to believe that, I let out a sigh and run my fingers through my hair. "You said you had a falling out. Why? What happened?"

She shakes her head. "He was reckless. He turned people without thinking about the consequences. He brought unwanted attention to us. So I left, but I still watched him.

Killing the ones he changed, until you." She steps closer to me. "I just couldn't kill you. You reminded me so much of Noah."

She had told me very little about Noah, but I do know that he was her favorite son, and that leaving him to become a vampire was the worst choice she has ever made.

She rubs her hand across my cheek gently and it is comforting. "You must understand why I kept this from you. Salem is my son, too, and I will protect him."

Reaching up, she places her other hand on my cheek, cradling my face. "Can you forgive me?"

I swallow the lump that has formed in my throat. "I understand, but that is all you can expect me to do right now."

Taking her wrists, I pull her hands from me and walk out, not sure I can handle any more information at the moment. Thankfully, she does not follow me, knowing that I need to be away from her.

As I start toward Kate's room, I see Luther standing by the door as he says, "Kate, please let me in."

The concern in his voice makes me worry. "What happened?"

He shrugs. "I don't know. We were watching a western and a tribe was attacked. She just started crying and locked herself in her room. She's been in there for over an hour."

He has been standing out here for an hour, listening to her cry and doing nothing to help her? "You are a vampire, Luther. You can bust this door down," I tell him irritably.

He looks at me sharply as though he does not understand my frustration. "I don't think she wants me in there."

"Really?" I say sarcastically then shove him back. "Out of my way."

I knock on the door firmly. "Kate, let me in."

There is little sound of movement from her room so I start again, "I will tear this door from the hinges. I have had a terrible night and I need my best friend."

The door opens slowly and I see Kate's tear-streaked face. "I need mine, too," she says weakly.

With those words, my frustration with Marcella and my encounter with Salem mean nothing. I only care about clearing the red from Kate's swollen eyes.

I step in and wrap my arms around her waist. I pull her into me, wetting my shirt with her tears. I swing the door closed in Luther's face. Then grabbing her legs, I carry her toward the bed. Holding onto my neck, she cries harder. I sit on the edge of the bed, sitting her on my lap.

Her hand slides down to my chest as she whispers, "I can still see them."

"Me, too," I tell her softly. It does not take much to remember the field painted red with the blood of her tribe...

I stumbled upon an attack of one of the local tribes. Their distress and pain had called to me. Crouching low in the bushes, I watched as the soldiers slaughtered the people. Some of the Cherokee were holding their children close, protecting them from the gunfire. Some were fighting back, but their arrows were no match to the guns.

The massacre did not last long, nor did they kill everyone. The soldiers started to go, leaving the women crying for their dead, but there was one woman who did not cry.

She hurried to a corpse and laid her hand on his soft flesh. Then looking up at the soldiers walking away, her eyes hardened. With blood on her fingers, she streaked the crimson across her cheeks. She grabbed a nearby bow and stood.

She took aim and shot the arrow into the back of a young soldier. Screaming, he dropped to the ground. The others turned to face her. They drew their weapons but she did not run. She did not hide. She only stared at them with hatred and contempt.

The bullet was fired but I jumped in front of it before it hit her. I rolled to my feet with black eyes. Fearful, the soldiers ran, but I was faster. I tore through them, exacting her revenge.

I went back for her and she was waiting. She was not afraid of me, not my brave Kate. I held my hand out for her, wanting her to come with me, and without much hesitation, she put her hand in mine...

"Nick," she starts, "why does it still hurt so much? It was so long ago. I should have healed by now."

I rub my hand along her back. "No, you shouldn't have. You cared about them, Kate. It's okay that memories bring pain. It's better than forgetting them."

Gliding my hand across her cheek, I wipe the cold tears from her skin. "Allowing yourself to feel sorrow is not a weakness. If you don't embrace the things that seem human, you are no better than the nomads. And trust me you are definitely better than a nomad."

She looks up at me and smiles gently. Her hand slides along the back of my neck. It would be easy for her to pull my face to hers and press her lips to mine in a long kiss. The longer I stare into her soft eyes, the more I find myself hoping she does. It becomes harder to breathe as the air between us grows thick with desire. But she does not seem to notice the way my hands hold her just a little too tightly or the longing behind my lips.

A tear rolls down her smooth skin, but before I can catch it, she wipes her hand across her cheek. "When do you have to pick Tara up at the airport?"

Nearly mesmerized by her, it takes me a moment to answer, "In an hour."

She lays her head on my shoulder, nestling her face into my neck, "Hold me until then."

"Of course," I say quietly.

The smell of her hair wraps around me and I close my eyes, enjoying the scent. Logically, I tell myself not to fall for her, our relationship is perfect the way it is, don't mess it up. But her warm body against me feels so nice, and my arms around her feel so right.

"Did you need to talk to me about something too?" she asks softly.

Actually, yes. I do want to tell her about Salem, but it doesn't seem to be the best time for her, so I say, "No, yours is more important. Mine can wait."

I press my lips to her forehead and rest my cheek against the top of her head. I hold her for most of the hour before she tells me she feels better. Then, after she hops in the shower, I head for the airport.

I do not have to wait long before Michael, the pilot, lands and I see Tara get out of the single-engine plane. She smiles when she sees me and rushes to my arms, dropping her bag by my feet.

"Nicolas, I have missed you," she says, hugging me tightly.

"I missed you, too," I tell her honestly. "How was your trip?"

She leans away from me, keeping her forearms resting on my shoulders. "Fine. And I suppose you expect me to thank you for the in-flight meal since I'm sure that wasn't routine."

I shrug, "Michael owes me." I pick up her bag. "Besides, it's not like *I* was going to feed you," I joke.

Laughing, she hits my arm playfully. "Come on," I tell her, "let's get out of here."

We start walking toward my truck when she loops her arm through mine. "Take me somewhere so I can stretch my legs." She raises her eyebrows, insinuatingly.

"Sure." I open the door of the '68 Chevy C10. "Hop in." Then, in a deep voice, I add, "If you dare." I let out a fake dark laugh.

She rolls her eyes, smiling. "One on one, you're not that scary." She bounces into the seat. "Besides, am I supposed to be afraid of you or your driving?"

Chuckling sarcastically, I tell her, "You're so funny." I set her bag behind the seat and close the door.

I slide into the driver's seat and pull out of the parking lot before I glance over at Tara and watch her run her fingers through her hair, which now only hangs to the bottom of her ears.

"Your hair looks nice short. It suits you."

She looks over at me with raised eyebrows. "Tell me what I really want to know," she says.

Smiling, I turn my eyes back to the road. "Kate and I are just friends."

"So you haven't kissed her since New Year's?"

"Nope. And I'm not going to," I say matter-of-factly.

She huffs. "Do you know what wolves hate? Cats. Especially scaredy cats."

I laugh at her sarcasm. "You know, a good dog waits until you say 'speak' before it opens its mouth," I joke.

Smiling, she inhales sharply. "You did not just say that!" She hits my arm. "Nicolas Rider, where are your manners?"

Simply because I cannot resist, I say, "Probably on someone's nightstand."

She bursts into laughter, leaning forward and covering her mouth as she does. "You are full of it tonight, Nick. And to think, I actually missed you."

"Of course you did. Who wouldn't?" I say, giving her my lopsided smile.

"Lucid people."

Chuckling lightly, I ask her, "How long are you staying?"

"Just a few days. I wish it was more pleasure and less business, though."

"Business?" I start. "What kind of business do you have in Alaska?"

She smiles softly at me. "Do you think we are far enough out to go for a run yet?"

Feeling her hesitation to answer, I pull over. "Sure."

I walk around the truck, and as I open her door, she pulls a drawstring sack out of her bag. "Will you carry this for me?"

I take the sack from her hands, knowing it has a change of clothes inside.

"Turn around," she tells me. "No peeking."

With my back to her, I can hear the rustling of her clothes as she changes out of them.

There is something she is not telling me. There is an unease about her that is not usually present around me, and I fear it is because of me. Fumbling with the strings on the sack, I ask her, "Is everything okay?"

She does not answer with words. Instead a solid black wolf bolts across the field from where Tara had been undressing. I smile to myself. That little cheat.

I slam the passenger door closed and race after her. Dark as night, her fur rolls with the wind she creates. Her yellow eyes gleam as she looks back at me and her heavy breath fogs the air.

She is faster than I remember, but I am quicker. Although I could push myself harder, I let her keep the lead. Something tells me she needs to win.

Just miles into our run, she skids to a halt, sliding across the snow.

"Why did you stop?" I ask when I reach her.

She stares at me with her big yellow eyes without blinking so I add, "I wasn't letting you win."

Exhaling forcefully, she shakes her head as though she doesn't believe me.

"Fine," I say as I toss the sack of clothes by her feet. "You're the only woman I know who doesn't think that a win is a win."

Turning around, I continue, "You have too many morals for your own good. One day they'll get in your way."

The snow shifts under her feet as her body changes, and I hear, "One day you'll get in my way. And then I'll take you down."

I laugh to myself. As if she could.

"Morals aren't a bad thing to have, Nick. You should know that better than anybody. For a vampire, you seem to have a lot of them."

Define 'a lot.' Personally, I believe I have lost most of the morals I had as a human and I wasn't particularly that great of a human.

Tara walks around to face me. "Because of you and your morals, I survived the forties."

"Because of me and my morals," I lean toward her, "a lot of humans didn't."

She smiles. "I know. Eric never lets me forget that."

Eric, her husband. Of course he would remind her of the reasons we shouldn't be friends. He hates everything about me, and I don't exactly like him, either. To be honest, the only member of her pack that does slightly like me is Finn. But maybe that's because I helped him survive as well.

"What does he think about your hair?" I ask her.

"He hates it."

Good. I hope she keeps it short then. "All the more reason for me to like it."

She laughs lightly to herself then looks over toward the dark sky. Sitting down in the snow, she keeps her eyes on the snow when she says, "You're my best friend, Nicolas. That's not always a perk for me. But I'm hoping it will be right now."

I sit down next to her as she looks over at me. "Roddy is refusing to marry," she continues.

Her son, Roddy, has been a werewolf for just under two decades. "He's still very young. Do you really want him to marry right away?" I ask.

"No. But he is also refusing to come home; refusing to join the pack. And that is a problem." She shakes the snow from her foot. "As long as I don't know exactly where he is, there is nothing for me to confess to Eric. And trust me, if Eric knew where Roddy was, it wouldn't be pretty."

She looks up at me with big eyes and I feel a favor coming on. "I need my friend, my best friend, to find Roddy and convince him to come home for me."

She bats her eyes quickly, making me smile.

"And you have no idea where he is?" I say.

"I didn't say that. Roddy sent me a letter, postmarked Denali."

"So he is in Alaska," I think out loud.

She shifts her feet but the sound of the snow does not distract me from the growing feeling inside. The feeling that we are not alone.

I sit up straighter and look out over the barren field of white and watch the snow dance in the wind.

"I hope he still is," Tara says, but her words are only background noise for me. "Will you help me, Nick?"

"Shh," I tell her as I look around carefully.

Something slices through the air behind me. Turning quickly, I shove Tara away as an arrow slashes my bicep. Before the first drop of blood hits the ground, my eyes change to black and I expose my fangs in a hiss at the vampire a hundred yards away from us.

Strands of stringy, black hair hang over her pale face as she lowers a bow. "Salem sends his regards," she calls just before she laughs wickedly.

Tara phases into a black wolf. She lunges forward but I grab her tail, making her nearly bite my hand. I pull Tara back as I sprint toward the woman. Running quickly, the vampire clears close to half of a mile before I jump onto her back.

We tumble over one another until I slam her shoulders into the ground abruptly. She snaps her fangs at me but I keep her pinned and away from my throat.

"Where's Salem?" I shout at her.

"You'll have to do better than that," she sneers as she grabs at the snow.

Forcefully, she crushes a rock into the side of my head, leaving a powder of stone on my shirt. I fall off of her and she leaps to her feet. She picks up the bow and swings it at me but I flip back and it misses me.

Following me, she steps closer, still swinging the bow. It hits my ribs hard enough to push me across the snow, but I still manage to grab it from her hands. Bringing my foot up, I kick her in the chest, knocking her to the ground.

She grabs an arrow from the quiver and hisses as she jumps up.

Raising the arrow, she rushes toward me. I block it with the bow and slam my elbow into her ribs. Dropping the arrow on the ground, she claws at my face, leaving four deep slashes along my cheek and neck. I drive my palm into her sternum, pushing her back a few steps.

Spinning the bow around me, I hit her head, splintering the bow. I grab her hair and pull her head back. "Where's Salem?"

She propels her head forward, smashing into my nose and ripping out her hair in my hand. With blood dripping over my lip, I strike her side, digging my fingers between her ribs. She screams out painfully but that does not stop me from making a fist around her bones and jerking her body to the ground.

Tossing the hair that remains in my hand, I wipe the blood from my nose with my sleeve.

Taking a larger fragment of bow from the ground, she leaps at me. Just then, I see black fur leap past me. Tara clamps her teeth into the vampire's neck and shoulder, pulling her to the ground.

Between the snarls, I hear the woman scream out as Tara drags her backward, smearing blood across the snow. Tara shakes her head, flinging the vampire from side to side.

Before I can stop her, the woman stabs the bow into Tara's shoulder. Not letting that slow her, Tara slides her teeth further up along the vampire's neck and bites down harder, pulling and growling ferociously.

Stepping over the woman, I pull the bow from Tara's shoulder and jab it into the vampire's chest, piercing her heart. She disintegrates into ash, leaving a dark stain on the crisp, white snow.

I watch Tara as she phases back into her human form. Still crouching down, she spits out some of the ash from her mouth and wipes her hand across her tongue.

"I hate that part," she says quietly.

What I want to say is 'I didn't want you to get hurt', but what I actually say is, "I didn't need your help."

She stands up, hearing the harshness in my tone that I was trying to hide. "Did you miss something?" she starts irritably. "I am a werewolf, Nicolas. Werewolves kill vampires. I may overlook what you are, but I have not forgotten my instincts," she snaps.

"I wanted her alive."

She steps closer to me with an angry look on her face. "Then why did you kill her?"

Because she hurt you. Because I was afraid she could kill you. "You wouldn't understand."

"I don't need you to protect me," she huffs.

Maybe she does understand. "I want to," I say before I can stop myself.

Taken aback, she loses all of the hardness in her face and stares at me. Her blood rolls down her bicep and it captivates me.

I rub my hand along her arm, collecting her blood, and she does not shy from my touch. The heat of the crimson on my fingers makes my heartbeat quicken and my mouth water at the thought of just tasting the blood once.

Fixing my eyes on the blood, I hear her say, "Don't even think about it."

I look up at her smile and let my eyes change back to green. "I wasn't," I lie.

Hating that I have to waste it, I wipe the blood on my pant leg. I would have much rather pressed it to my tongue and tasted its sweetness.

I slip off my coat and hand it to her. "Cover up."

Taking it, she wraps the coat over her shoulders and holds it across her chest, leaving her injured arm exposed.

I rip my shirt sleeve off and begin wrapping it around her stab wound.

"You don't have to do that. It will heal soon enough," she tells me softly.

Tightening the sleeve, I say, "This isn't for you." I glance up at her. "It's distracting me."

I lean away from her arm, hoping that will clear some of the luscious smell from my nose, but it doesn't.

She slips the coat on, pushing her injured arm into the sleeve, and I know the aroma of her blood will linger in it for days.

As she zips the coat, I take off my shirt and wrap it around her waist, buttoning it as high as I can to keep it from falling.

"Keep your shirt, Nick."

"Now, what would Eric think if I let you walk around here naked?"

"I'm sure he thinks you're capable of a lot worse things than that," she says with humor in her voice.

I smile to myself as I stand up again. "Probably," I agree.

"Why are you dressing me anyway? Aren't we going to run back to the truck?"

"Well ..." I run my fingers through my hair, "if I chase a bleeding wolf, I just might ..." I might let my instincts take over. Looking away from her, I finish quietly. "I don't really feel like it."

"Oh, I see," she replies, understanding what I didn't say. "Well, I think walking would be great."

Deep down, I think she knows I would never mean to hurt her, but she also knows not to push her luck.

She takes my hand and leads me toward the truck. "You know, I won't be in Barrow the entire time I'm in Alaska. I have some business in Fairbanks. I wasn't even supposed to come up here."

Sure that Eric ordered her not to see me, I look over at her. Sensing my thoughts, she smiles, "I'll deal with Eric later."

"When do you leave?"

"Tomorrow, while you're at work, and I'll be gone for two days so you have until then to find Roddy."

I show her my lopsided smile. "I didn't say I would do that."

"But you will."

I laugh to myself. Of course I will.

We walk the miles quickly, catching up on everything. When we reach the truck, Tara changes back into her own clothes, and hands me my coat. I was right; it does smell like her blood so I toss it behind the seat and try to forget the lure of it.

After I drop her off at the house she is staying at, I drive to my home and go inside.

Kate meets me in the living room. "Where's your shirt?"

I look down to confirm what I had started to forget: I don't have a shirt on. "It's a long story."

As I start toward the kitchen, Kate follows me. "Did that wolf hurt you?"

"No," I say defensively. "On the contrary, she was hurt protecting me."

"Oh," Kate utters as we reach my bedroom. "I guess that's okay."

I could tell her that it's not okay, but I see little point in arguing with her.

Grabbing a shirt from the laundry basket on my floor, I slip it on and drop my pants.

Quickly, Kate turns around, trying not to watch me. "Why aren't you with her now?"

"Tara had a meeting with Cyrus."

"About what?"

Pulling on my pants, I tell her, "It's just a courtesy wolf extend to each other when they're in someone else's territory. She just has to explain how long she will be here and why, that's about it."

"Why is she here?" Kate asks with irritation in her voice.

I walk around to face her. "You know, disdain isn't very pretty on you."

She grimaces at me, which only makes me smile.

"I realize you sort of have a love for wolves, but the rest of us normal people don't."

I laugh to myself. Since when are vampires considered 'normal people'?

"Honestly, if you had to choose, us or them, which would it be?"

I shrug. "If I choose vampires, do I have to take Luther, too?"

Laughing, she hits my arm playfully. "Nick."

"You know which one I would pick."

Her eyes drop slightly and she adjusts my collar. "I want to hear you say it."

I know what she wants me to tell her, and as her hand slides down my chest, trailing a heat along my skin, it becomes easy to say and I nearly whisper, "I'd choose you." Taking her hand and pulling her face up, I add, "I'll always choose you."

She does not respond with words; instead, her heart pounds in her chest, waiting for a kiss that I long to give. The air between us grows thick with desire as my hand aches to pull her to me and my lips hunger to taste hers.

I slide my hand to her cheek and rub my thumb across her soft skin. My eyes watch her lips as she parts them slightly, making it difficult to think clearly as I imagine the way her supple lips would feel. She presses my hand on her face, enjoying my touch and my breath catches.

I look into her eyes and see hunger in them. Knowing she must see it in mine as well, I pull my hand back. "I have to go."

Despite what I want to do, I know what is best for Kate. And it's best if we don't get involved right now.

I start toward the door when I hear, "Nick."

Turning to her, I painfully tell her, "I'm sorry." I think about saying something else, but nothing sounds appropriate. "I'm sorry."

Rushing out, I hear someone knock on the front door and James answer it.

"Is Kate here?" asks our neighbor's sixteen-year-old daughter, Molly.

"Hey, Molly," I say as I enter the living room.

Even though she looks confused at James, her face lights up when she sees me. "Hey, Nicolas." She waves a measuring cup at me. "I was just wondering if you had some sugar?"

"I'm sure we do."

She looks at James again. "I'm sorry, do I know you?"

Knowing that she has probably seen him on the news, I lie, "Actually, Molly, I used the last of the sugar this morning."

She does not glance at me even as I speak but keeps her eyes on James with a puzzled look on her face. "You look so ..." her voice trails off, "familiar."

Then a look of recognition sweeps over her and she inhales sharply, realizing who James is.

Nervously, she looks at me and forces a smile. "That's okay. Thanks anyway," she stammers out as she fumbles with the doorknob behind her back.

The door opens a crack and I place my hand near her head and slam it shut.

Jumping at the sound, she drops the measuring cup. "I won't tell anyone," she says with a shaky voice.

"I know you won't," I reply coldly.

Putting my hand over her mouth, I pull her outside. She screams and kicks against me, but she is too weak to do much of anything.

I open the door to her truck and slide in, pulling her into the driver's seat. I reach over her and close the door as she begins to cry.

"Drive," I tell her.

With trembling hands, she starts the truck and puts it into gear. "What are you going to do to me?"

Not what I want. Not what I could. Just what needs to be done. But instead of saying any of that, I simply turn on the radio and lean back in the seat.

Even with her uncontrolled sobbing, I still manage to hear the man on the radio say, "The search continues for a missing child in Anchorage named Penny Mason. The seven-year-old is believed to have run away from an orphanage in the early morning hours of December 29th and despite the extensive searches, no traces of her have been found."

"Are you going to kill me?" she whimpers.

I keep my eyes toward the window. "Yes," I say simply, then go back to listening to the news report.

"With the severe snowstorms that have battered Anchorage in recent days, authorities are beginning to wonder if they will find the girl alive."

"Can't you just let me go? I won't tell anyone, I promise," she says between sobs.

I look over at her and turn the radio down. It is obvious to me that I will not get to listen to it.

"Humans always tell someone. Then I would have to kill a lot of people that I don't want to. It's just better this way."

A tear rolls over her lip and drips onto her lap and it begins to make me feel bad for what I am about to do. But the situation remains the same so before I change my mind, I tell her, "Stop here."

She stops the truck in the middle of the road and looks at me with intense sadness in her eyes. "Nicolas, please don't," she pleads.

I take no pleasure in killing someone so young, especially when it isn't for food. But protecting our secret is an obligation we cannot afford to skip. Besides, death is a part of life.

"I'll make it quick," I say quietly.

Crying harder, she closes her eyes and lets the tears fall freely. Her body shakes with fear and I know that prolonging this will only make it more difficult... for both of us.

Without hesitation, I seize the moment. In one quick motion, I jerk her head and snap her neck before she even realizes that my hands have touched her.

I lay her limp body over the steering wheel and brush the hair away from her face. "I'm sorry," I whisper to her but it is of no consequence. She cannot hear me. She cannot feel my remorse. Not the way I can.

Knowing that I have little time to pity myself, I get out of the truck and walk to the back of it. I grab the tailgate and pull the truck so it is pointing off of the road. Then placing my foot on the bumper, I kick the truck forcefully, propelling it forward. Slamming into a large rock, the front of the truck crushes into the cab.

I stand in the silence, looking at the crumpled truck for a moment, and a part of me wishes Molly would crawl out of the rubble with no memory of what happened tonight. But she doesn't, and eventually I start home.

I watch my feet as I walk, kicking the snow. I try not to think of Molly, but trying only gets you so far. Memories of her face, her tears, her sorrow flood my mind. Knowing that tonight will not leave my thoughts soon, I think of something else. I focus on the news broadcast from the radio but that only distracts me a little.

Until suddenly, I snap my head up. "Penny Mason?" I say to myself.

I break into a sprint, leaving a powder of snow in the air behind me.

I should have seen this before, I think. Why didn't I connect the dots sooner? It is so obvious.

When I reach the house, I waste no time. I go straight to Luther's room. Without knocking, I barge inside, and thankfully, he isn't there.

Getting down on my knees, I slide his guitar case out from under his bed as Kate appears in the doorway.

"You can't take Luther's guitar," she protests.

Laying the case on the bed, I flip the clips and open the lid. "Watch me."

"He's going to kill you when he finds it missing."

I pick up the sleek Gibson and walk over to her. "I hope he tries."

Passing her, I start toward the living room.

"Where are you going?"

I turn to her and continue to walk backwards. "To the hospital."

"You don't work today," she says matter-of-factly, "and you wouldn't need a guitar if you did."

"I'm visiting someone."

She grimaces. "Who? That little girl?"

I stop and explain, "She's all alone, Kate."

Her face softens. "Nick, she's human."

"I know," I say quietly.

"You know what happens when we get too close to humans?"

They die. Every time. "I know."

But before I can say my hope that this time will be different, someone knocks on the door.

Swinging the door open, I see Molly's mother waiting nervously. "Hello, Ms. Duncan," I say with a smile.

"Hi, Nicolas. Have you seen Molly? She was supposed to be coming here..." Angst crosses her face as her words trail off.

"I did," I tell her. "She stopped by and asked for some sugar but we don't have any. I think she said she was going to the store in town."

Relief washes over her. "Oh. Thank you. She had me so worried," she says with a big smile.

I lean against the doorframe. "Kids will do that. I'm sure she's fine, though."

"Yeah, of course she is. You're right. She's probably on her way home already."

"She might get there before you," I say, making her laugh lightly.

"I should go. Thanks again," Ms. Duncan replies as she leaves.

Closing the door, I let my smile drop. Molly won't be coming home. And soon, Ms. Duncan will know that.

Kate lays her hand on my back. "Are you okay, Nick?"

"I'm fine."

But she hears the lie in my voice and wraps her arms around my waist. She slides her hands along my shoulders and she leans her head against my chest.

I put my arm around her, keeping her warm body close to mine. Laying my chin on her head, I inhale the coconut scent of her hair and it eases the guilt.

She will never understand how much I need her. "Will you take care of James for me?" I say quietly.

She looks up at me and rubs my cheek gently. "Of course."

Her touch feels good but I do not let that pull me from what I need to say. "Make sure you take him a hundred miles away first."

Her hand slides onto my chest. "Right, the pact with the wolves, I remember."

I start to open the door, but stop with my hand on the knob. "If you don't want to, I'll deal him when I get home."

She turns my face towards hers, heating my skin with hers. "Nick, I said I'll handle it."

I know what could make me feel better. It's the same thing that I badly want to do. I want to move my lips with hers, press her back into the wall, and start ripping at her clothes. Oh, the things I could do to her.

Cradling her face in my hands, I kiss her forehead. I close my eyes and let my lips linger on her skin.

"Thank you," I whisper to her just before I leave.

Once outside, I hurry to the hospital with the guitar in my hand. Upstairs, I find Punzi's room quickly. I watch from the doorway as Trish rewraps her hands. Seeing Punzi's frown and the way her eyebrows are drawn together makes me smile. Even when she is stubborn, she is adorable.

Trish wraps her so that her thumbs are still exposed, and even though Punzi can't see her, she smiles when she asks, "Is that better, Punzi?"

Sitting still, Punzi says nothing.

"Can I call you Punzi?" Trish asks gently.

The little girl just shakes her head no quickly, making me laugh quietly.

Trish starts picking up her supplies as I walk in and sit on the bed. "Hello, Punzi."

An instant smile spreads across her face. "Nick. What are you doing here?"

"I told you I would see you today." I look over as Trish walks away and see a needle lying on a small table. Knowing that Trish often leaves needles lying about, I motion for her.
"Wait."

Trish turns and I nod toward the table. She sucks in a sharp breath when she sees it.

"Thank you," she whispers as she picks it up.

As she leaves the room, I wonder if she realizes how close she is to being fired for that very reason.

"They gave me a shot," Punzi says, redirecting my attention, "in the butt," she whispers.

"Well, you're tough. You can handle it," I tell her.

"And look," she wiggles her fingers, "thumbs."

I smile at her. "Good. I brought you something you'll need your thumbs for, but first I have to tell you, they were talking about you on the radio today."

"They were?" she asks with a confused smile.

"I know who you are. You're Penny Mason."

Her smile fades as nervousness sets in, so I continue, "How did you get all the way up here from Anchorage?"

Her eyes dart around the room as she tells me, "On a plane. I thought it was heading south but I was wrong." She looks at me as though she can see me clearly. "You can't tell anyone. I don't want to go back."

"Penny, if you don't go back to the orphanage, how will you be adopted?" I ask softly.

Defensively, she says, "I won't get adopted, Nick. I'm blind. Nobody wants a broken child."

I slide closer to her. "You're not broken –" I start, but she interrupts.

"Yes, I am," she snaps. "If something doesn't work then it's broke. My eyes don't work. People want to adopt a perfect little *baby*. I'm not a baby anymore, and I don't fit into their dream family."

Tears begin to roll down her rosy cheeks. "Foster families don't even want me. They look at me and just see a problem. Something they have to deal with. I can't be thought of as a bother anymore, Nick. I just can't."

She covers her face with her hands as she cries harder.

Gently, I lower her hands down and wipe her eyes. "I won't tell anyone, Punzi." I pull her to me. "You have to know that I think you're perfect just the way you are. I wouldn't change a thing about you."

"Not even my eyes?" she says between sniffles.

"Not even your eyes. I think you're blind for a reason."

"Why?"

I slide her off of my lap to face me and brush her hair away from her face. "You don't realize it, but you are the most beautiful little girl I have ever seen – and I have seen a lot of children. I think if you could have seen how pretty you are, you would have been vain and ugly inside. But you're not. You were protected from that so that you could be beautiful inside and out. Not many people are like that."

I rub my finger along her chin. "You're not a problem. You're special. And if people can't see that, they're the ones who are blind."

A small smile lights up her face. "You really mean that?"

"Every word." I drop my hand and grab the guitar. "Now, do you want to know what I brought you?" She nods.

"Here's a hint," I strum the strings and she smiles bigger at the sound.

"A guitar?"

"Yes. That was a C cord. And this," I play another note, "is an F. Did you hear the difference?"

She shakes her head slowly.

I smile to myself. "You'll notice when I play them together. Have you ever played a guitar?"

"No," she says quietly.

"Then it's about time you did."

I slide in behind her on the bed and hold the guitar against her chest. Reaching around her, I take her hand. I lay her thumb on the guitar and hold the note for her. "Just glide your thumb across the strings."

She strums the guitar weakly but still manages a soft F cord.

Happily, she looks up at me. "I *felt* the sound through the guitar."

Laughing lightly, I move her hand away. "Let me try." I brush my thumb across the strings, playing a slow song. Quietly at first, I sing the words to her, but she isn't the only one who hears me. Nurses begin to stop and stare from the doorway. Some are surprised that I can sing well, some are pleased to see her happy. Either way, most of the nurses smile at us.

The audience does not bother me, though, as I smoothly proceed from one song to the next.

Punzi reaches up and wraps her arm around my neck, pulling my cheek to her lips. Her gentle touch only makes me smile more. I keep playing as the nurses begin to disperse and Punzi relaxes her head into my shoulder. With her warm little body leaning against me, I begin to find a new kind of comfort. A comfort from an unfamiliar place. From a child.

The ringing of a phone pulls me from my sleep. A woman's hair tickles my nose and I inhale the scent of coconut. With her body pressed into mine, I know that I am lying much too close to Kate, but still I smile.

I open my eyes as she rolls over to face me, keeping my arms around her. This isn't the first time I have woken up curled around her, but it is definitely the first time I have enjoyed it so much.

"Hey," I say quietly.

She smiles softly. "Hey."

The way she bites her lip bashfully makes my breath catch. The air grows thick and my hand curls around her hip as I attempt to resist the urge to pull her closer. With my eyes locked on hers, I listen as my heart pounds against my chest and I know she hears it, too. Soft and full, her lips draw me in, beckoning me to taste them.

"So …" I mutter, trying to think of something to say, "Did you sleep well?" Stupid question.

She laughs quietly to herself as she rolls onto her back.

"Yeah, Nick. I did."

I roll onto my back and stare at the ceiling. I can't say what I want to say. I can't tell her how beautiful she looks with her hair tossed about. I can't explain the way her skin glows after a feeding or the way my hand aches to hold hers.

"That's nice," I say quietly.

Sighing, she replies, "Nick, this doesn't have to be awkward."

To keep my hand from inching any closer to her, I lay it on my stomach. "Yes, it does."

She rolls onto her side again and props herself up on her elbow. "It's okay to have a crush on me."

I look over at her quickly. "I didn't say I liked you like that."

Raising her eyebrow, she smiles. "You didn't have to. I could tell by the way you were looking at me."

Smiling, I lean up on my elbow. "Well, I don't have a crush on you. I was looking at you strange because you smell funny."

Sitting up, she lays her hand on her chest. "I smell funny?" She runs her fingers along my ribs, making me twitch and cry out. "What do I smell like?

She leans over me, tickling my sides as I push at her hands. "What do I smell like, Nick?"

"Stop it," I shout cheerfully.

"Not until you tell me," she says as I squirm under her hands.

Between breaths, I blurt out the first thing that comes to my mind, "Bacon," I laugh. "You smell like bacon."

Her hands stop and I finally see her face. With a large smile and nearly laughing, she asks, "Bacon?"

I shrug. "Probably because you fed on a cop's son," I joke, referring to James.

Laughing, she falls back onto the bed beside me, draping her leg across my waist.

There is a light knock and the bedroom door opens. As Yen steps in, she says to me, "Nicolas, you have a phone call." Then looking at Kate, she adds, "It's Hannah."

Kate's laughter stops abruptly, making Yen smile.

"Thank you, Yen," I say sarcastically. "I'll be there in a minute."

Taking the hint, Yen leaves without another word. I look over at Kate, not knowing what to say.

"You better get that," she tells me.

It bothers me to know that being with Hannah hurts Kate, but it's better this way. Kate and I are not meant to be together. Although, honestly, I am starting to doubt that.

"Yeah," I whisper.

Looking back as I leave, I see Kate roll onto her side away from me and my heart sinks. I would much rather comfort her than answer the phone, but instead, I keeping walking.

When I get to the living room, Luther is standing near the telephone. "Since when do you give girls your number?"

"Shut up, Luther," I say dismissingly. Truthfully, I am not sure how Hannah ended up with my phone number, but I suppose that doesn't matter. She has it now.

"Hello," I say into the phone.

"Nick, it's Hannah. Do you have a minute? I need a favor."

Eavesdropping, Luther leans in toward the phone. I shove him back a step as I ask her, "What's wrong?"

"Jericho was arrested and Becca is at a PTA meeting. I need someone to watch Wyatt so I can run down to the station and sort this out."

Luther laughs loudly, having heard Hannah plainly. Slightly stunned, I clarify, "You want me to *babysit*?"

"Just for a minute. I swear I'll make it quick," she begs.

"I don't know if that's a good idea," I say. Of course, it's not a good idea. What part of letting a vampire watch a child is good? Not to mention that this particular child is the son of a werewolf.

"Please. There's no one else to ask."

I look over at Luther as he sways his arms back and forth as though he is rocking a baby. I push him hard and he topples over the chair and onto the floor.

"Okay," I sigh, "I'll be there as soon as I can."

Relieved, Hannah says, "Thank you so much, Nick. I didn't know what else to do."

"It's fine. Let me get ready and I'll see you in a bit."

"Okay. Bye," she tells me.

"Bye."

I hang up and look at Luther as he tries to pick himself up off the floor, despite his laughing.

"Wow, Nick. Just wow. You handled that really well. I see who wears the pants in your relationship."

I reach my hand out and help him up. "That's funny, 'cause knowing how to handle things is why Hannah keeps me around. And usually there are no pants involved."

He starts to say something, but I cut him off, "And yes, Luther, I realize you have no idea what I mean, so let me spell it out. Women like to have sex with a man and not just a person with a penis."

Without waiting for his pointless comment or sarcastic smile, I go to my bedroom, dress quickly, and leave before Kate can ask where I am going.

I make it to Hannah's house reasonably soon, allowing myself more time than necessary, since showing up too early only arises questions.

When she answers the door, I am glad I came. With her hair sloppily pulled back, she looks more frazzled than she had sounded on the phone.

"What did Jericho do?" I ask bluntly.

She half-smiles at me. "Drunk and disorderly."

Disorderly sure, but not drunk. By the time the police test him for alcohol, he will be sober. Werewolves burn up alcohol extremely quickly, which is one reason why they tend to drink so much of it.

"You should let him sweat a little."

This time she smiles for real. "Come in."

Stepping inside, I see Wyatt sitting in the corner of the sofa with his arms crossed.

"He doesn't know why I'm leaving," Hannah starts, "And I'd like to keep it that way."

"Sure," I turn to her and cradle her face in my hands. "Don't worry about us. Wyatt will be fine. Just go get your brother."

She rubs her fingers across the back of my hand. "I'll hurry."

Gently, I kiss the tip of her nose. "We'll be here."

Looking into the living room, she calls, "Bye, Wyatt. Be good." Then looking at me, she adds, "I owe you one." She is wrong. She doesn't owe me. Jericho does.

Grabbing her coat, she leaves and I walk over to the couch. I pick up the laundry basket full of folded clothes and move it from the sofa to the floor and sit down.

Looking at the television, I ask, "What are you watching?"

Wyatt doesn't answer me, so I try again, "Are you hungry?"

Getting nowhere, I glance around the room, drumming my fingers on my leg.

"My dad hates you," Wyatt says harshly. I look over at him quickly as he continues, "I mean, he really hates you."

"Good to know," I simply say, because there is nothing else appropriate.

He turns back to the television. Sighing, I lean back. This is going to be a long day.

***

I jump up from behind the couch and launch a balled-up pair of socks across the living room. Wyatt raises his hands to block the pretend explosion from my sock grenade.

"The Rebels are advancing from the west," I shout, pointing to the right.

With a white shirt tied around his tiny forehead, Wyatt rushes out from behind the couch, firing his toy gun toward the phantom soldiers.

I roll over the couch, hitting the coffee table and knocking it over.

Looking around the room, Wyatt shouts, "They're everywhere!"

I shove up the shirt I am using as a headband and fire my fake machine gun around the room.

Wyatt grabs my arm and pulls me down to his level. "Get out of here, Nick. Save yourself."

"No, I'm not leaving you."

He grabs another sock grenade. "That's an order, private!" He pretends to pull the pin with his teeth. "I can handle these bitches."

Scolding, I start, "Don't talk like that –"

But before I can finish, he hits my shoulder. "Stop breaking character."

Shaking my head, I focus on the game. "Yes, sir." I put my hand over the sock grenade. "Give 'em hell, Captain."

I jump over the couch and squat down with my gun ready. When I hear the sound of an explosion coming from Wyatt, I stand up and fire at all of the remaining Rebel soldiers.

Rushing around the couch, I bend down next to Wyatt amidst the sock grenades that riddle the floor. "Captain?"

Weakly, Wyatt responds, "I'm not going to make it."

"We'll see about that," I tell him as I pick him up and lay him over my shoulder.

I run around the couch, deliberately bouncing him more than necessary and, despite himself, he laughs.

"Stop breaking character, Wyatt," I tease.

He drops his gun as the door swings open and Rebecca steps inside. Even though it is difficult to sneak up on a vampire, there are times when I do not pay attention to my surroundings, and this was one of them. Her jaw drops as she looks around the room at the mess we've created.

Surprised to see her, I lightly toss Wyatt onto the couch.

Her eyes harden on me as she crosses her arms over her chest.

"Hey, mom. We're playing Civil War and I'm the Captain," Wyatt says as he rolls off of the couch.

Ignoring him, she says coldly, "Where's Hannah?"

Maybe it is because she is a mother, but the look she gives me makes me nervous. "She had to step out."

"Wyatt, go upstairs."

With her simple command, I get the feeling that I am about to be in trouble.

I set the coffee table upright. "Rebecca, don't worry about the mess. I'll clean it up," I say, although I know it's not the socks, she is angry about.

"Wyatt. Upstairs," she snaps.

"But mom," he whines, "there are monsters up there."

She takes a breath before she responds and her eyes are still sharp when she says, "How many times do I have to tell you? There are no such things as monsters."

He crosses his arms over his chest defiantly. "Yes, there are."

Pinching the bridge of her nose, I watch her as she focuses on her breathing, but it does not help much.

I bend down near Wyatt. Taking his shoulders, I turn him toward me. "Listen, Wyatt, I believe you. Monsters are real. But I know a secret about them. The bad ones, the really bad ones, can't come in your house without permission," Vampires for example. "And you haven't invited any monsters in lately, have you?"

He shakes his head.

"Then as long as you are in this house, you're perfectly safe," I tell him. "I need to talk to your mom for a minute, so go ahead and go upstairs. Can you do that for me?"

His face twitches. Even though he does not like the idea, he quietly agrees, "Okay, Nick."

As he walks away, I rub my hand over his hair. "Thanks, buddy."

He passes Rebecca, who stares at me in disbelief.

Sliding the laundry basket toward me, I pick up some of the socks and toss them inside. "So… I take it the PTA meeting was pretty rough."

She walks over and collapses onto the couch. "Parents are the worse part of my job." Rubbing her forehead, she mutters to herself, "This is typical Hannah. She's so irresponsible. I don't know why I thought I could trust her to watch Wyatt."

Going slower, I continue to put the sock grenades into the basket. "I'm sure she had a reason."

She looks up at me. "Yeah, a selfish reason."

Then leaning up uncomfortably, she pulls a ball of socks out from behind her back. Looking at it, she asks, "Civil war, huh? Is this supposed to be a grenade?"

"That is a Ketchum Hand Grenade."

Smiling, she picks up the toy machine gun lying on the couch. "And this?"

I give her my lopsided grin. "Okay, that is not historically accurate. Admittedly, it's not the most clever part of the game, but I was being resourceful."

She laughs lightly, setting the gun beside her again. Then her smile fades and she looks at me with sadness in her eyes. "I'm glad you were here when I came home and not Jericho."

I stop picking up the mess and sit down on the coffee table in front of her, not sure of what to say.

"He was a good father, and I know Wyatt misses him, but I don't want him here," she says, tracing her finger around a flower on the armrest.

I lean forward, resting my forearms on my knees. "So Jericho was just a bad husband then?"

Keeping her eyes on the flower, she shakes her head. "No. Just a liar. He kept something from me for years, and when I found out the truth, I decided that I didn't want my son to be around him anymore."

Jericho is not a very old werewolf. I can't imagine there is much from his past that would be very troubling. These days, werewolves are harmless to humans.

With a confused look on my face, I ask, "Why? Is he some kind of criminal?"

She half-smiles as she thinks for a moment then replies, "Well let's just say, he is a bit of an animal. Sometimes."

Surely she doesn't mean what I think she means. Did I hear her correctly? All he did was tell her about being a werewolf?

"Let me get this straight, you are keeping his son from him because of what he is?"

She looks at me curiously, wondering if I know about the wolves, too.

I huff lightly. "Rebecca, I might be crossing the line here, but if he is a good father, he deserves the chance to be one."

Her face grows blank as she blinks several times, thinking about what I said.

"You're right," she says quietly, "that is crossing the line."

I could tell her that she is wrong. I could say that Jericho would never hurt Wyatt. I could explain how Wyatt needs a man in his life, but instead, I tell her, "Then I apologize."

Glancing over my shoulder, I look at the remaining sock grenades when I hear, "I'll clean the rest. You can go."

I look back at Rebecca but she keeps her eyes down, so I say, "Next time, I promise I'll think of a less messy game to play." I pause for a moment but she doesn't look up, "And I'll try to mind my business, though I'm not very good at that." A soft smile spreads on her face.

"I'll see you later, Rebecca."

Standing up, I walk to the door and when my hand touches the doorknob, she says, "Nicolas, you can call me Becca. Everyone else does."

Meeting her eyes with kindness, I tell her, "You can call me Nick. Most people do, even when I ask them not to."

She smiles wide enough that I can see her teeth. "Goodbye, Nick."

"Bye."

Leaving the warmth of her house, I walk through the wind that whips the snow in my face and makes my breath fog the air.

I hurry to the bed and breakfast Tara is staying in but refuse to go inside, despite the fact that it is public enough for me to not need permission. Mostly because the older human who owns it has never invited me in, and I am kind enough to give her the pleasure of thinking that makes her safe. Besides, I doubt Cyrus would want me inside his sister's home.

Since Tara isn't exactly welcome in my house either, we find ourselves sitting on the snowy beach, watching the frigid waves crash onto the shore. We spend the next hour laughing at ourselves and dreading her departure, even though it is only for a few days. But finally, I take her to the airport.

So it is no wonder why I find myself thinking of Tara on the beach…

She was outlining an angel in the snow and looked up at me with a softness in her eyes. "You make one."

"I can't," I shrugged, "It's an angel. It'll burn me."

Sitting up, her eyes widened. "Really?"

"No," I laughed. "You're so gullible."

"Ugh," she groaned as she shoved my shoulder.

I laughed harder, which only made her push me more until she had me on the ground.

"I hate you," she teased as she shoveled snow in my face. "You think you're so smart."

As she dropped a handful of snow down the back of my shirt, I inhaled sharply from the coldness. I grabbed her hands, pushing them away enough for me to sit up again.

She giggled to herself as I tried to shake most of the snow out of my shirt. "I wish you were a wolf."

"Why, so I could be your alpha?" I joked.

"Pfft," she huffed. "You would never be alpha. Alphas aren't selfish."

I scoff sarcastically at her, making her smile.

"If you were in my pack, we would never have to be apart," she continued. Wrapping her hands around my arm, she leaned her head against my shoulder.

I rubbed my fingers across her hand and whispered, "I miss you, too." …

"Nicolas," Punzi grabs my attention, "were you listening?"

Sitting behind her, my hands work to braid her hair and I let out a small sigh. "I'm sorry, Punzi. I was distracted."

"By what?"

"Well," I start, and it brings a smile to my face, "I was thinking about one of my best friends."

"One? How many do you have?"

I chuckle lightly. "Just two."

I wrap her hair around itself when I hear her say, "I have a best friend."

"You do? What's she like?"

"*He,*" she corrects me. She pauses for a moment. Then speaking slowly and calculated, as though she is thinking, she adds, "He is very kind and funny. He knows how to braid. He works in a hospital."

Tying her braid, I ask, "Do I know him?"

"I think so."

I smile to myself as I move out from behind her.

"How do I look?" she asks, moving her head side to side dramatically.

Sitting down on the edge of the bed, I tell her, "Punzi, there are no words that can express your beauty."

Her cheeks flush as she smiles bashfully, but I have to look away for a moment to keep my mouth from watering, knowing that it is her blood that reddens her skin.

"Listen," I start, "I'm going to be out of town for a few days so I won't be able to see you. But I want you to practice the guitar, because when I come back, I'm going to teach you my favorite song."

"What is it?"

"You'll see." I glance back at the clock and sigh. "I have to go. I have some work to do before I finish my shift."

"Okay," she says quietly. "But I'll see you in a few days, right?"

I lean over and kiss her on the forehead. "I promise."

Regretting making a promise, since I am not very good at keeping them, I walk away.

Almost to the door, I hear her tiny voice, "Nicolas, I want you to adopt me."

My breath catches but my heart races. What do I do? What do I say?

"Nick, are you still there?" she asks, unsure if I have already left.

She listens for me but I stand still, considering how to tell her that I can't adopt anyone. I'm a vampire. She's human. It would never work.

As I think about all of the reasons why I can't adopt her, she collapses back against the bed and mutters to herself, "Don't be stupid. Why would he want you?"

Instantly, there is a pain in my chest that I am not used to. A pain caused by pity. The sort of pity I rarely feel for anyone, let alone a human. But somehow, staring at her tiny face with her gentle blue eyes, and the tear that rolls down her pale cheek, my heart breaks.

I don't want to be alone and she shouldn't be either, but I'm a vampire, not a parent. I want to say, yes, I'll take you home. I want her to feel loved and safe. But she would never be safe with me, not truly. So despite the way her sadness pulls me toward her, I walk out silently.

As I start down the hallway, I keep my head down so others will not see my pain. By the time I reach Mr. Kenton's door, I can think of little else but her tears. I hesitate there, trying to convince myself not to go back to her, and eventually, I push the door open and go inside.

"Ow!" Mr. Kenton shouts as Trish pulls a needle from his arm.

"I'm sorry, Mr. Kenton."

She lays the needle on the small table and covers the growing spot of blood on his skin with a Band-Aid.

The scent of his blood fills the room and wraps itself around me, sending a fire coursing my throat. My thirst burns enough to make me close my eyes for a moment in attempt to forget the way his blood was about to run down his arm; the way it would have pooled in his elbow; the way it would have tasted.

But when I hear him say, "Maybe you should kiss it and make it better," my eyes shoot open and a new heat rushes through me. Women should not be made to feel uncomfortable by any man, especially a pathetic excuse for a human like Mr. Kenton.

Uneasy and awkward, Trish just stares at him, not knowing what to say.

Ignoring the anger that man brings me, I force a smile and say, "Trish, you have a phone call."

A relieved smile spreads across her face and she exhales gratefully, "I'm coming."

I watch her walk toward me and lip the words, 'Thank you' as she passes. Then, once she is gone, I look over at Mr. Kenton and fake a smile, "How are you today, sir?"

"Shut your trap," he snaps. "Just make with the bathing already."

My smile fades but to keep from showing my disdain, I turn around so he can't see my face and close the door.

"I'll make sure the water is hot today, Mr. Kenton." Hot enough to burn his flesh off would be ideal, and the thought makes me almost smile. Almost.

I turn on the water to hot as he says, "It doesn't matter. Your hands are cold. They're always cold. Why don't you ask one of those pretty nurses to do this?"

I look over at him and start, "I can't do that, sir."

As I turn around, my eyes sweep across the small table and stop on the needle and syringe left by Trish. I try not to bring attention to it, knowing that Mr. Kenton is just cruel enough to have her fired for fun.

I feel the heat of the water running over my skin when I hear, "Well make it quick. The faster you get this over with, the less time I have to spend looking at you."

Fighting the urge to turn on the cold water, I focus on my breathing, that is, until a pillow slams into the back of my head. My eyes change to black but I am not worried about them. I am only thinking of reasons why I should not kill him.

"Please don't do that, Mr. Kenton," I say through gritted teeth.

"Why, does it hurt your girly feelings?" he asks harshly. "You don't like it? Get a different job."

Letting my eyes change to green, I shut off the water and carry the pan toward him. "I like my job," I say matter-of-factly.

"I don't know why," he starts as I set the pan on the table next to the needle. "You're not good at it. You're not good at anything."

My eyes fixate on the empty syringe as he continues, "Sometimes I look at you and wonder, how can someone be such a shit?"

The rage inside stirs and multiplies, making my hand nearly tremble as I reach for the needle. Through a flexed jaw, I tell him, "I would stop if I were you, Mr. Kenton."

"Well you're not me. You're not even half the man I am. You work a shit job, live with your mom, and have piss-ant friends…"

He continues, but I ignore most of his rambling insults as I focus on my breathing that has become rapid and heavy. My fist clenches around the syringe and I close my eyes tightly, trying not to imagine the ways I could hurt him.

He notices my anger but is oblivious to the consequences of it because he adds, "Go ahead and tell me I'm wrong. Say something smart so I can have your worthless ass fired."

Instantly calm again, my body relaxes and I look up at him impassively. Raising the syringe into his view, I pull the plunger back. "Do you know what happens when air enters your bloodstream?" I ask with a chill in my voice.

His eyebrows come together, not understanding where my question is going.

Moving unnaturally quick, I stab the needle into the side of his neck, and being a vampire, I never miss a vein.

With wide eyes, he raises his hands in a surrender, but it is too late for that.

I lean toward him and say coldly, "You die."

In one fluid motion, I push the plunger down, sending the 50 cc of air into his vessel. As I pull the needle out, he grabs at his neck in a panic but soon his hand slides down to his chest. Clutching at his heart, his hand draws into a fist, gathering his hospital gown into a bunch.

Inhaling quick, sharp breaths, he struggles for air. His body trembles in pain and his eyes fix on mine. Without looking away, I lay the needle on the table and let a cruel smile slowly spread across my face.

***

After the commotion of trying to save Mr. Kenton's pointless life, the hospital seemed quieter than usual. Nobody wanted to admit that they were glad he didn't survive, but everyone knew anyway.

I stayed busy until my shift came to an end. Then walking into the locker room, I notice something by my time card. A letter.

On the front is my name scrolled in Old English lettering. Curious but still leery, I open the envelope slowly and pull out a small scrap of thick paper.

Written by a fountain pen are the words: *Does it bother you to know that when you were blamed for Ann's death, your father didn't even defend your name? - Salem.*

Knowing the reaction he wants, I try not to feel the pain and anger his words cause. I crumple the paper into a ball inside my fist and toss it in the trash. He will have to do better than that if he wants me to come after him.

I punch my time card and walk out, inconspicuously watching for him. I may have decided not to hunt Salem for Marcella's sake, but that does not mean that if I see him, I will not attack.

I keep my head down as I drag my feet through the snow. With everything that has happened today buzzing around in my head, my thoughts keep coming back to Punzi and her sad little face as I walked away, the tears in her eyes, the desperation in her voice. Realizing that she would have to be desperate to ask me to be her father, I let myself feel her sadness for a moment, let the crushing pain fills my chest. I wrap my arms around myself, but that does not stop the misery from taking its hold on me.

The more I think of her loneliness, the more I wonder why I couldn't take her in. What is so wrong with having a vampire as a father? Sure, it's dangerous, but I could handle it. Sure, vampires don't hold the same value to a human life as parents should, but Punzi could understand why. Sure, vampires are not designed to be parents. Nature knows better than to allow it but… well… I have no argument for that.

By the time I make it home, my thoughts are completely absorbed my Punzi. I go into the kitchen and find Luther sitting at the table, scribbling in a journal.

"You can write?" I tease.

He looks up at me sharply.

"I was joking. Lighten up," I tell him. "Where is everybody?"

Closing the journal, Luther leans back in the chair. "Kate is at Ms. Duncan's. Her daughter, Molly, died – but you already knew that," he says like an insult. He crosses his arms over his chest as he continues, "Yen is hunting, either for a meal or a man. I didn't ask which. And Marcella is resting."

I smile to myself. "Do you want to wake her up for me?"

Luther chuckles lightly. "You have to admit that even I am not that stupid."

Pretty close, though, I think.

"Why don't you go in there? You're the favorite, remember?" he smirks as he tips the chair back onto two legs. "I'm just the screw-up. But I still didn't kill Lindsey, or Molly, or James. You did that, didn't you? Maybe that's because you have so much more control than me," he says sarcastically.

My smile fades. "I use most of my control trying not to kill you on a daily basis. If you have a problem with me, I suggest you spit it out. That is, if you're not too afraid."

He lets the chair fall forward onto all four legs again and stands up close to me. "Why would I be afraid of you? I've shit things bigger than you."

I hold back a laugh but my lopsided smile shows itself anyway. "Well, I always knew you were a giant asshole. I'm glad that has finally been confirmed."

Laughing to himself, he looks away as he tries to think of a comeback.

"You walked right into that one, Luther."

Nodding, he says, "I did. That's true. And you walked into this –" He screams, "Marcella!"

I punch his shoulder hard and cringe when Marcella calls out, "What?"

"Nick wants you!" he finishes with a grin.

Whispering so that only he can hear me, I tell him, "I hate you." But it only makes him smile wider.

"Come here, Nicolas," Marcella says sweetly, but I know her well enough to realize she is actually annoyed with me for waking her.

I go to her room and walk over to her bed almost timidly.

"What?" she asks, leaning back against the headboard.

Sitting near her feet, I start, "I could come back another time if you …"

Abruptly, she cuts me off. "What do you want?"

"A favor."

"Name it," she says sharply.

Nervousness takes over, and I swallow hard before I continue, "There's a child at the hospital." "The girl," she finishes.

"Yes. Penny, but I call her Punzi. She's an orphan."

Before I can say anything else, Marcella pulls the blankets back and stands up. "You have a nickname for her?" she asks incredulously. "You're getting too close, Nicolas."

"She needs a home, Marcella."

With a scolding tone, she replies, "We do not get involved in human matters."

"Make an exception. I know you have the connections. I'm just asking that you use them," I basically plead.

"No," she says harshly.

She starts to walk away and I go after her. I grab her arm to stop her and she turns to me with narrowed eyes. "Marcella, she's only seven years old. You have to help her."

"No, I don't, Nick. She's a human. That means she is none of my concern," she snaps.

My voice raises and I do not try to soften it. "She needs a family. There was a time when I needed a family and you took me in. I can't just walk away from her when she needs me."

Her faces goes blank. "What exactly are you saying?"

Calmly, I tell her, "If you do not find her a home, I will take her in myself."

She steps close to me. "Don't threaten me."

I take her hand gently. "Marcella, I refuse to abandon her like everyone else has."

Pulling her hand back quickly, she grimaces. "You're talking about kidnapping a human."

"Nobody is even looking for her. And she is blind, which is perfect. She will never see me as something frightening," I tell her.

"She may not see your fangs, but she'll inevitably feel them."

I know she believes what she is saying, and knowing she could be right only causes a pain to push against my chest.

"No. I would never hurt her," I say, but it sounds weaker than I intend, and I look away to hide the pain.

Marcella puts her hand on my cheek, comforting me. "Nicolas, you can't keep her," she says softly.

I meet her eyes with mine. "Then help her. Please, Marcella. I'm begging. I'll do anything, I swear."

She stares into my eyes for a long moment before she finally nods. "Okay," she says quietly, "I'll take care of it."

Slightly disappointed that I will not be raising Punzi, I let out a relieved sigh that at least she will not be alone anymore.

I kiss Marcella on the cheek and whisper, "Thank you." But I doubt she understands how much this means to me.

There are times when you realize you are dreaming but you choose not to wake. This is one of those times …

I stand near my childhood bed, looking at my meager belongings, half packed and ready for life on a ship. Listening to my father stirring the fire, I realize it is the last night I will sleep here, and it saddens me. I glance over beside my father's straw mattress and take the lone box from under his pillow.

Opening the box, I know what I will find. My mother's wedding band shines in the dim light. I slide it on my pinky and turn the ring around my finger. It is the only part of my mother I have ever held or seen, and sometimes it makes me wonder what sort of woman wore this ring.

I walk over to the edge of the loft and look at him below. "Father, may I take this with me?"

He does not need to look up to know what I am referring to. He keeps his eyes on the fire. "No," he says softly, "I need it more than you do."

But that's not true. I need it, too.

There is a knock on the door and he stands up. "That must be Sam."

As he starts for the door, I ask, "It's late, isn't it?"

My father just nods. "His daughters want to say goodbye to you."

I sigh lightly. "I have to be up before the sun rises, father."

It's not that I don't wish to see them. It's that I know goodbyes are hard, and I was hoping to avoid as many as possible.

"They'll be quick about it," he assures me.

He pulls open the door and Sam walks in with two of his daughters.

The oldest girl looks up at me and smiles, "Hello, Vincent."

"Hello, Ann."

"May I come up?"

Smiling, I shrug. "For a moment."

She starts up the ladder to the loft while Sam and my father sit at the table. I reach my hand out to help her up and when she grabs it, her soft skin warms mine.

She looks around at the mess on my bed. "You're really going?"

"Of course, I can't stay here forever."

Sitting on the edge of my bed, she looks at me gently. "I'll miss you."

I shove a shirt into my bag as I tell her, "No, you won't. I'll write to you as often as I can."

Her eyes light up. "You will?"

"Sure, as long as you promise not to grow up while I'm gone," I tease.

She smiles, but only briefly, before she fixes her eyes on the floor. "You're not allowed to forget me, Vincent."

"I won't," I bend down in front of her so I can see her face. "Not ever." …

My eyes open but the room I see is not my own. As pain begins to flood my heart, I sit up in Hannah's bed and place my feet on her cold floor. Leaning my face in my hands, I feel someone's fingers trail along my spine, and for a moment, I think it's Ann. But it's not.

"Are you all right?" Hannah asks sleepily.

"It was just a bad dream," I lie. It wasn't bad at all nor was it a dream. Just a memory, and a good one.

Lying naked under the blankets, she leans up on her elbows. "Was it about a girl?"

"Yeah."

Exhaling loudly, she tells me, "You know, Nick, what we have is open. If you want to be with someone, be with them. I don't care either way. I will be a little disappointed when this is over, but it's going to end soon anyway. Don't let me stop you."

I don't answer her. Perhaps that's because I don't want to explain that Ann is dead and there is no way to be with her. How do I say that I wouldn't let a human like Hannah stand between me and Ann if she were alive?

So it is just as well that Hannah continues, "You don't stop me."

Those words are enough to take my mind off of my dream. Smiling widely, I look over my shoulder at her.

"Really?" Shifting in the bed, I lean over her. "Well, *he* couldn't have been that good." I push her hair behind her ear. "'Cause you're in bed with me."

A large smile spreads across her face. "That's because our schedules coincide better, and when he was propositioning me pretty hard, I was busy."

I lean closer to her until I can rub her nose with mine. "You realize the only words I heard you say were: 'inside, position, and hard'? You keep talking like that and we may never leave this bed."

She laughs lightheartedly. "What if I make you jealous?"

A mischievous light flash in my eyes. "I don't think you can," I challenge.

"That man who hit on me, he was gorgeous," she starts.

"Mm hmm," I say with a quiet smile. Slowly, I kiss along her jawline, feeling her skin warm under my lips.

"He, um," she says distractedly, "was tall, dark, and handsome."

My hand slides along her ribs toward her hip and her heart races. A heat charges through me as her fingers dig into my shoulder, and I feel her jagged exhale on my skin.

She says, "He had huge muscles ..." but her words trail off as I position myself on top of her.

Tasting her flesh, I run my tongue along her soft neck toward her ear as I guide her leg to my ribs.

"He, um ..."

I let my teeth pull at her earlobe and her body nearly trembles beneath me. "I'd rather talk about you," I tell her, exposing the desire in my tone. "Or not talk at all."

"Me too," she says breathlessly.

As I lean up enough to kiss her, I can see the hunger in her eyes and it drives a necessity behind my lips when I crush them to hers. My hand glides to her butt and pulls her against me.

With the other hand, I drag the blankets over our heads so she won't be able to see my eyes.

***

As I sit up in the bed, Hannah's hand rubs across my back. The heat of her fingers warms my skin, making me look over at her and flash a most irresistible smile.

"Leaving?" she asks softly.

Nodding, I tell her, "Yeah, I have to go."

She rolls over, pulling the blankets to her waist and exposing the top of her butt. "That's too bad. I'm sure if you stick around, we'll end up having sex again."

I watch her lying on her stomach, naked and ripe for the taking. Her flesh is still flushed from being wrapped around me just a moment ago. My hand aches to slide my fingers along her spine, to feel the chills that form from my touch, to have the softness of her skin caress me, but still I answer, "I'm leaving town for a few days."

Walking over to my pants, I hear her say, "Where are you going?"

"Denali."

She perks up, leaning onto her elbows. "I have a cousin in Denali," her hand rubs across the pillow aimlessly but it draws me in just the same. "Donny. But I haven't seen him in forever."

Humans often say 'forever' as if they actually know how long that is. As if they have watched centuries pass, everything changing but you.

I slide my pants on and grab my shirt. "Do you want to come with me?" I ask without considering what Jericho might do if she says yes.

Her eyes light up. "To Denali? Yes."

I slip my shirt over my head. "Get your things together. We leave in a couple hours."

Smiling widely, she throws the blankets off and rushes to her closet.

Sitting on the edge of the bed, I put my shoes on. I glance over at her looking through her clothes. She stands on her tiptoes to reach a box on the top shelf and it makes me smile.

I walk over to her and grab the box. The dim moonlight does nothing to keep me from letting my eyes roll over her naked body as I hand her the box.

Staring at her nearly perfect body, I smile to myself, hiding my teeth that are begging to be let loose, to find their place in her throat, to feel her blood coursing into my mouth.

Placing her hand on my chest, she tells me seductively, "I'm going to make this the best trip you've ever had."

Her hand slides up to the back of my neck and pulls me in, kissing me passionately. Gliding my tongue over hers, I place my hand on the small of her back and close the distance between us. Leaning away, she pulls my lower lip with her teeth and it has my whole body tingling. My grip on her tightens as I fight to keep my eyes green.

"I thought you had to go," she says, smiling slyly.

She is right. I do have to go, but my feet do not move, so I lean in close and tell her, "This is to be continued."

Then, forcing myself, I walk out. Once I'm in the stairway, it is easier to breathe and I start to replay some of her words in my mind. *Tall, dark, and handsome*. That's how she described that man. *Tall, dark, and handsome*.

As I start to grab the doorknob, I look over and see Wyatt sitting on the sofa, the light from the television casting over him. "Hey, Wyatt. What are you doing up?"

He shrugs. "I couldn't sleep."

I glance up the stairs at the bedroom doors then back at him, wondering how long it will be before anyone else is awake. "Are you hungry?"

With a wide smile, he nods.

"Alright," I walk over to him and ruffle his hair playfully, "come on."

I go into the kitchen and he is right on my heels. He plops down in a chair and lays his arms on the table.

"Cereal is in the top cabinet," he says, pointing.

Laughing to myself, I tell him, "I don't do cereal."

He watches me curiously as I open the refrigerator and pull out the milk, eggs, and butter.

"Do you want me to make toast?"

"No," I slide the canisters of flour and sugar toward me, "I am making a crepe. Do you know what that is?" He shakes his head.

"It's like a dessert."

"For breakfast?"

I smile at him softly, "Would you rather have something else?"

"No, no. Dessert is fine."

Somehow I knew he would say that and it makes me show my lopsided smile. I open the cabinets above me and pull out the cornstarch, vanilla and almond extracts, and a can of peaches.

"That's a lot of stuff."

Taking out a large saucepan, I tell him, "That's because there are two parts to this. The crepe and the filling."

I mix the sugar and cornstarch in the pan when I hear him ask, "How do you know how much to put in?"

As I pour some water in slowly, I reply without taking my eyes off of the stove, "I have made this several times." For several different sheep.

I glance back at him as I stir in the butter and some of the peaches, "But this recipe isn't exactly like the one I learned in France."

"You went to France?"

"A long time ago. A woman there taught me how to make this. Of course hers were better than this will be but this is Alaska and I have to make do with the ingredients that are available."

The mixture begins to thicken and bubble so I turn the heat down.

"I've never seen a man a cook before," Wyatt adds.

Smiling to myself, I look back at him. "That's kind of sad, Wyatt," I tease.

Hearing the humor in my voice, he laughs to himself lightly.

I pull the mixture from the stove, add the extracts, and set it in the refrigerator for now. I take out a pan and set it on the heat.

Tall, dark, and handsome. That's how she described that other guy. Don't get me wrong, I'm not jealous. I'm not. But *tall, dark, and handsome,* really?

As the feeling that I know someone fitting that description begins to creep in, thankfully, Wyatt distracts me by asking, "Did you spend the night here, Nick?"

In a bowl, I mix the flour and some salt while I try to think of an answer.

"Yes. My boiler went down and it was too cold to stay at my house."

I mix in the eggs, knowing that the pan is hot enough to start.

As I pour the milk into the batter slowly, he asks, "Then where did you sleep?"

Without answering him, I stir in the butter and pour a thin layer of batter into the pan.

"I hope you're hungry because this won't take very long," I tell him instead.

He crosses his arms on the table and sighs loudly, noticing the way I avoided the answer.

"I told you I was hungry, didn't I?" he says sarcastically.

Smiling to myself, I lay the crepe on the plate and fold it over on itself into quarters. I pour some of the peach mixture over the crepe and grab a fork from a cup on the counter as Hannah walks in.

"Oh," she starts with a grimace on her face. "Nicolas, I think maybe having you sleep over gave you the wrong idea."

Picking up the plate, I start to stop her from saying anything else but she just continues anyway, "This," she gestures between us, "isn't going anywhere, and it's not the type of relationship where we make breakfast for each other." She cringes a little when she says it.

Since it occurs to me that she has no idea that Wyatt is sitting at the table or that this is actually for him, I tell her, "Hold that thought."

I walk over to Wyatt and lay the plate in front of him. "Voilà. As promised. Now normally, I would put whip cream on top, too, but I don't think your mom would like that very much."

He smiles at me so genuinely that it makes me smile back at him. I stand up as he digs into the crepe with his fork.

Hannah rolls her hands over themselves with an embarrassed look on her face.

I take her hand but she doesn't meet my eyes. "You know, if you wanted to give me an awkward lecture, I could offer to make you breakfast too, or we could pretend to be in a romantic comedy and make it together," I tease.

With her other hand, she covers half of her face as her cheeks blush. "No."

"This is amazing!" Wyatt tells us, making me smile.

"Thank you," I tell him. Rubbing my fingers along her cheek, I whisper to Hannah, "I will see you in a couple hours." I lean in and kiss her warm cheek.

"I'll walk you out," she tells me with her shy smile as she leads me to the door.

"This guy who hit on you, do you remember his name?"

Smiling, she asks, "Why, are you jealous?"

"Not a chance. Just curious."

She stops in front of the door, thinking and drumming her fingers over her mouth, "Lu … lu, lu…" Her eyes light up and she snaps her fingers together. "Luther."

My outward expression stays the same, soft and relaxed, but inside a fire races to my skin. I fight to keep my fangs from receding and my hands clench to keep from shaking in fury. "Do you know him?" she asks.

Nonchalantly, I shrug. "Nope."

That's partly true because I won't know him for much longer. Hiding my anger, I grab the doorknob. "I'll see you later."

I leave before she has the chance to say goodbye and start walking home, no longer smiling. Heat rolls off of my body and I imagine that if I were to touch the snow it would melt beneath me. My hands tremble at my side as I focus on keeping my eyes green for now. I stare at nothing as my mind floods with the things I'd like to do to Luther and the way his body would shatter into ash if I did any of them.

By the time I reach for the doorknob to my house, my breaths are calm, even, and calculated. As I enter, I see Luther lying on the couch watching the television. He laughs causally at whatever show is numbing his mind this time, and his smile makes my skin crawl.

"Hey, Nicolas," he says as I approach.

In a quick motion, I hit the television, sending it flying toward him, but Luther moves away and it slams into the wall near his head. He looks at me with wide eyes, unsure of what is happening.

"Stay away from Hannah," I say through gritted teeth.

A slow smirk spreads on his face. "You don't like your things touched? Then don't touch my fucking guitar." A guitar? That's what this is about?

Instantly, I grab his shirt collar, jerking him up and punching the smile off of his face. As he falls to the ground, I kick him into the wall, knocking some of the plaster onto the floor.

He is on his feet in seconds, charging at me, black eyes, fangs exposed, but he does not intimidate me. I flip into the air, wrapping my legs around his neck from behind, and as I fall onto my hands, I pull him over and slam him into the floor. I can smell the blood coming from his nose before I see it. I raise my fist to bash in his skull but he moves and I punch through the floor. He grabs a shard of glass from the broken television as I pull my arm out of the floor, slicing it on the busted wood.

He swings the glass at me but I slide back across the floor. The glass slashes my shirt the second time as I run out of room in the little space. Without hesitation, I bring my foot up and kick the glass shard, sending it through his palm until it punctures out of the back of his hand. Holding his wrist, he backs up but I do not stop to pity him. I grab the shard and pull it from his hand. I stab it into his abdomen with three quick jabs.

His fist hits my ribs, breaking at least two and I wrap my arm around his. I slam my hand against his forearm, snapping it and reminding him why he shouldn't strike back. Rolling my back into his stomach, I pull him over my chest and onto the floor. I drive my foot into his stomach hard enough to make him roll onto his side and spit out blood.

I pound my fist into his jaw, knocking a tooth onto the floor and grab his ankle. I swing his body around, and slam him into the wall, knocking over the table and lamp near the couch.

Standing up, he grabs the small table and raises it in the air at me. I block the table, and kick him back several feet. As he charges toward me, I flip another shard of glass into the air with my foot. Snatching the glass, I stab it into his side and guide it around, slicing along his ribs.

Gasping for air, he stumbles back, clutching at his cut. I drive my forearm into his chest and send him falling onto the floor in the doorway between rooms. Stepping over him, I go into the kitchen and take a large knife out of the drawer.

I walk over to him calmly and take his hand away from the slice on his side. With one quick, clean chop, I sever his hand and it turns to ash. Luther cries out painfully and starts to grab at me but I shove the tip of the knife under his chin, stopping him.

"Now you don't need your fucking guitar," I tell him coldly.

Of course, I realize his hand will grow back but a complete loss such as this will take nearly a month to regenerate, and that's enough to make me smile.

As his blood pools around my shoes, I walk over to the counter and toss a towel at him, "Put pressure on it. You're getting blood on my floor."

With narrow eyes mixed with a painful expression, he wraps the towel around his wrist and I walk toward my bedroom. Refusing to let Luther see me hurt, I stand straight and walk with purpose despite the way my ribs throb.

I step into my room and sigh at the sight of Yen.

Sitting on my bed, propping a magazine up with her knees, she smiles at me. "Did you kill him?"

I close the door and shake my head. "No."

"Pfft," she says as she closes the magazine. "You're getting soft, Nicolas."

Walking toward me, she lets the magazine drop from the bed. "The Nicolas I knew wouldn't stop." She rubs her hand along my chest and whispers in my ear, "He could go all night."

There is something in her voice that makes me wonder if she is still talking about fighting, and I smile to myself.

Pulling her hand off of me, I tell her, "I'd like to be alone, Yen."

She leans close to my face. "Did he hurt you? I could kiss it and make it better."

"You could leave, too, but I don't see that happening either."

She rolls her eyes. "Why do you want me gone? Is it because of Hannah or Kate?"

I walk away from her, toward my dresser. "I'm with Hannah."

"Barely. She doesn't even call you her boyfriend."

"It still counts to me."

She can hear in my voice that I am telling the truth. Thankfully, though, she does not ask why I am with Hannah in the first place because, to be honest, I'm not sure. A part of me is just glad to have the distraction from the new feelings surrounding Kate.

"You're no fun," Yen huffs.

I look back at her but only see the door close as she leaves. I pull open the top drawer of my dresser and shove my clothes to the side, exposing a Bible and I have to look away. My heart races as I pull my eyes back to the cross embossed on the book. My breathing increases into sharper, quicker breaths and if I could break into a cold sweat, I would. I try to ignore the crushing of my chest as I reach my shaking hand toward the cover.

I will never understand why something like a book could make us so uncomfortable. Humans deem it as a holy object, but why should that matter? Why should it burn us so? It isn't fair. Vampires have only two options; to lose our faith or to be denied it.

My skin touches the leather and it burns against me. Fighting back the cries, I open the book and flip over the pages. My hand trembles from the fire, but finally I come to a hollowed out section where a ring on a necklace is hidden.

Ignoring the blisters on my hand and the burning of the pages as my fingers brush over them, I grab the chain and pull my mother's ring from its protective place, the safest place in a house of vampires.

I slip the necklace on and hold the ring in my fist as I watch my hand heal. I take the ring in both of my hands and press it to my lips. Then I slide my mother's ring under my shirt and let the cold metal rest against my skin.

My door swings open and I look back quickly, expecting Luther to take his revenge, or at least attempt to. But standing in my doorway is Kate, and my breath stops.

"Nick, what happened? The house is destroyed and there is blood all over the kitchen," she says with more accusation than worry.

I know I should answer but the words do not come. It's all I have just to take a breath as I stare at her as she walks toward me. My mind races around how nice it would feel if she kissed me, the way I could lay her back on the bed, and … *Stop it, this is Kate*, I try to tell myself, but the thoughts keep coming. They circle around the softness of her skin against mine, the way her lips would taste, and her jagged breath on my neck.

My thoughts move so quickly that I start to lose track of reality and when she touches my hand, I jump back.

"Are you okay?" she asks.

But I'm not okay. I don't want to feel like this for Kate.

Shaking my head, I run my hand through my hair. "I'm fine," I lie as I try to slow my breathing.

"You don't seem fine."

She lays her hand on my chest and I close my eyes, trying to keep from kissing her.

"Nick, you're shaking."

I pull her hand away from me and walk toward the bed. Keeping my back to her, I say, "Something weird is happening to me." Weird, as in falling for Kate. "I'm not exactly sure why."

Of course, I am not exactly sure whether I want to feel this or not. I mean, I don't. But I do.

"I have to go away for a few days, and when I get back, I think it'll be better," I add.

At least that's what I am hoping for. A little time apart could clear up these cloudy feelings, right?

"Okay," she says quietly, "I'll see you when you get back then."

She walks out, still slightly confused, but like a good friend, doesn't push for more details than I am willing to offer.

Once she leaves, I let out a sigh. What was that?

I collapse back on the bed. I handled that so very poorly. How does she do it? How can she feel for me like this and still be so normal with me? She is better at this than I am, obviously, but I still need to pull it together.

It's *funny how people choose* to only believe what they see. How quickly their minds begin to tell them their memories are just dreams, imaginary figments that couldn't possibly be real.

It's strange to think that after a few centuries of hiding from the humans, they have forgotten us. Even werewolves are beginning to believe in our extinction. Just take Denali for example. The wolves here are blinded to us, believing in myths that we helped circulate.

As I walk down the sidewalk, I meet eyes with one such wolf as I pass him. His eyebrows come together in confusion. His wolf tells him something is wrong with me, but the human in him ignores it.

He continues walking, having only noticed the softness in my green eyes, and my meek demeanor. But what can I say; I am a great actor.

I hear the laugh before I enter the bar and I wonder if those humans inside would be so happy if they knew that we roamed their streets.

I walk toward the bar and see the reason I came here, and *she* sees me, too.

Smiling, she leans toward the human she sits casually on and whispers in his ear. She slides off of his lap and walks toward me with a drink in her hand, keeping her eyes fixed on mine.

As she passes me, she flashes her teeth in a smile but I know how much better she looks with her fangs extended.

I watch her as she approaches the jukebox. Her short, red hair exposes the tattoo of a deep, blue bird surrounded by flames – a phoenix, born from ashes, just like she says she was.

I suppose if I were rescued from two house fires, one as a human and one as a vampire, without so much as a burn or scrape, I might start to think of myself as a phoenix, too. But I doubt it.

She sets her glass down as I lean back against the wall.

"I didn't know you were a drinker, Phoenix," I tease.

Sarcasm lights her eyes. "When they start having meetings for what we drink, you can be my sponsor."

Turning the records, she continues, "What do you want, Nicolas?"

"To cash in a favor."

Her eyes run over my body. "Not interested. You're not my type."

I laugh to myself. That's not what I had in mind. "Sorry, sweetheart, but you're not my type, either."

She laughs blithely. "You don't expect me to believe that. I know you well enough to know your type. Let's see what's on the list, has vagina, check. Hmm, that's the only requirement. Guess I am your type."

Shaking my head, I tell her, "That's funny because the only reason you carry vodka around when you can't drink it is so the men at the bar will think it's the alcohol that makes you so easy." Whispering, I lean closer, "But we both know it's not."

Normally, I wouldn't be so frank with a woman when it borders on insulting, but Phoenix is different. I've known her for centuries, ever since I pulled her from that burning house. She understands that I don't mean anything harsh by it.

"Touché." She makes her selection on the jukebox and the music starts. With her voice concealed by the song, she asks, "What's the job?"

Finally, back on track. "Missing person."

"Human or vamp?"

"Wolf," I correct her.

Her eyebrows raise. "There's a lot of them here. You need anyone specific?"

"Very," I start, "his name is Roddy Brooks. You'll know him because he'll recognize what you are."

Her face grows serious. She glances around the room as she steps closer to me. "The wolves here believe vampires are extinct."

"Not this one."

"He's lucky I have found him then. I like being a myth. It makes my life easier."

I grab her arm, making her look at me. "I need him alive," I say with enough authority that it takes her a moment to begin breathing again.

"Why?"

Letting go of her arm, I answer, "That's my business."

Her eyes dart as she considers it. "Deal," she says matter-of-factly.

"Good. I'm staying at the –"

She cuts me off abruptly, "No, I don't need to know. I'll find you."

I smile at her playfully. "You think it'll be that easy?"

Crossing her arms, she lets a satisfied smile spread across her face. "You're almost as good of a tracker as I am, but you asked me to do it. Do you know what that tells me? You didn't come here alone. And the human you came here with doesn't know what you are, which is why you can't hunt down a werewolf. It's also why you checked into a hotel using your real name, because that's what she knows you as and anything else would be suspicious. So yes, it will be easy."

I have to admit, Phoenix is perceptive to a point of almost impressive.

"Maybe I'm busy. Maybe I don't want to get too close to Roddy and tip him off. Maybe I –"

She interrupts again, "That's a lot of maybes."

As the singer on the record belts out a high note, Phoenix leans closer. "I'll come by your hotel tomorrow with an address. If your wolf is in the city, I'll find him."

Without another word, she walks away, back to the man at the bar. Smiling to myself, I make my exit.

The streets are cold, but still crowded. The people here are used to the dark and do not shy from it the way others do. They do not realize the dangers in it, making them friendlier to strangers like me than they should be.

I keep my head down, not because I am timid amongst the wolves, but merely because I do not need to see to find my way back to Hannah. The streets are unfamiliar but her scent isn't, and it carries me to her cousin's apartment building.

The building isn't tall or grand but I suppose it fits a twenty-year-old who lives in a two-bedroom apartment with three other people.

I climb the stairs to the second floor and walk toward the small apartment as music pours into the hallway. Hannah had mentioned that there would be a party tonight for her cousin's birthday. She said she wasn't sure that I would fit in, and from what she told me of Donny, I'm not sure I will either, but nonetheless, I knock.

The door swings open and thick blanket of smoke rolls out. Leaning against the door, a lanky, blond man smiles at me wide enough that he nearly closes his eyes. "What's the buzz, dude?"

I stare at him blankly for a moment. "I'm sorry. What?" Instead of giving him time to answer, I change the subject. "I'm looking for Hannah."

His smile doesn't fade and his words are slow and even-paced as he tells me, "We're all looking for something, man."

"I guess," I say, slightly confused. "Is Hannah here? Or do I have the wrong apartment?" I ask, part of me hoping I do have the wrong apartment and I can just leave.

"Naw, your betty is right over there," he says, pointing. "Come in, I'll show you. I'm Chester, by the way."

"I'm Nicolas."

Reluctantly, I step into the fog of smoke and into the crowd of people, some swaying to the music, some leaning on their friends, laughing.

"Hannah said you work for the man," Chester says lazily as he leads me.

"I work for a hospital."

He nods as though there is something in my statement that he should be understanding of. "The man is always cutting me down, too."

"That's what is keeping you down? The man?" I ask sarcastically.

Chester looks at me confused and it almost makes me smile. Instead of listening to his rambling, I add, "I'm a writer, too."

His eyes light up. "Far out."

We stop near a small group of people huddled around a table and when Hannah sees me, she jumps up. "Nicolas!"

She grabs my hand and pulls me to the couch. Wedging me between the arm of the sofa and a burly-looking man, she plops down on my lap, wrapping her arms around my neck.

"Nick, this is Donny," she says, gesturing to the man beside me. Then pointing around the table, she continues, "That is Cody, Lizzie, Bruce, and you know Chester."

I notice Cody pass what looks like a hand-rolled cigarette to Lizzie, and even among the smoke and sweat in the room, I can smell it, and *that* is no cigarette.

Running his hand through his hair, Chester begins, "Hannah, you didn't tell me that your boy is a writer."

She looks at me, smiling with her glazed eyes. "I didn't know that." Her hand rubs over my shoulder. "What do you write?"

I shrug. "It's just for a magazine," I say, leaving out the novels I've written under several different pseudonyms.

The little white joint makes its way to Donny, and I glance over at him, and as he inhales, the tip lights up, burning the paper back.

"Oh yeah, is it for a medical magazine? Do you tell people how to correctly wipe a patient's ass?" Hannah says sarcastically.

Despite her bursting into laughter and the giggles from the group, I do not smile. I do not find it funny at all.

The smoke from Donny's exhale engulfs me and instantly I begin coughing, choking on the tainted air.

"No," I say between breaths. "It's a science fiction magazine." Mostly about werewolves and vampires, but I'll leave that part out.

"Do you mind if I go to the bathroom for a minute?" I ask, not waiting for the answer as I slide her from my lap and stand up.

"Sure, it's the first door on the left," Hannah says, pointing toward the hallway.

Making my way through the heavy smoke, I go to the bathroom and without knocking, I open the door. The haze is even thicker inside the bathroom, but still, I shut the door behind me.

Closing the lid, I sit on the toilet and wait for what seems like a long time. I don't want to be out there with that crowd. I kill humans like those and yet, I have to pretend to enjoy being around them. That's all I ever do though, pretend. I pretend to be human although I am clearly not. I pretend that people should like me when they shouldn't. What if I am actually just pretending to be a vampire? Wait, that doesn't make sense, of course I'm a vampire.

I go over to the sink. Maybe if I throw some water on my face that will clear my mind. But my thoughts keep circling. My whole life is a lie. Why am I just now seeing that?

Looking at myself in the mirror, I almost take a step back. Are those my eyes? They're so green. I lean close enough to the mirror to fog the glass with my breath. They're beautiful.

In the reflection, I see the shower curtain move and I turn around curiously. Someone is in there. Why didn't I know that? Why didn't I smell them?

I walk over and open the curtain. Lying in the bathtub is a woman in her bra and panties. She looks asleep but I nudge her anyway.

She rolls her head toward me as though it is difficult to do. It takes a moment, but finally her eyes meet mine.

"Hey," I say to her.

"Hey," she says sleepily. "Where am I?"

I kneel down next to the tub. "Donny's."

"Who's Donny?"

I think about it for a moment, but the only thing I remember is that he was sitting next to me. "I don't know."

She grabs my hand. "Hey, mister, do you like my shirt? I got it for Christmas."

I look again only to confirm what I already knew. "You're not wearing a shirt."

Glancing down at herself, she laughs. "You're right. I'm not."

She laughs harder, making me laugh, too. I sit down on the cold tile, floor wondering why that was so funny and why I cannot stop.

I do not have time to consider it long before someone opens the door. "Nicolas? Are you okay in here?" Hannah asks.

Still laughing lightly, I nod.

Smiling at me as though she knows something I do not, Hannah tells me, "Well, why don't you go back and sit with Donny and I'll be in there in a sec, okay?"

Hannah walks over to me and takes my hand. "Here, let me help you up."

Pulling me to my feet is more work than it should be. She doesn't seem to have any trouble, but to me, I feel heavy and as though I'm not helping much.

As Hannah pushes me toward the door, I call back, "Goodbye, naked lady."

And I hear, "Goodbye, random dude."

In the hallway, she kisses me quickly and it leaves my whole body tingling. Her lips felt so warm against mine. They were like pillows. Pillows on her mouth.

Hannah points toward the sofa. "You sit. I'll be right back."

"Okay," I agree, and as she walks away, I start toward the others.

As I approach the couch, Donny looks up at me. "There he is. We thought maybe you got lost."

I sit down next to him and say, "There is a naked lady in your bathtub."

He just smiles at me. "There are four men in this apartment, Nicolas. There is usually a naked lady somewhere in this place."

Even though I try not to, I laugh again. He didn't say anything too funny, so why is it?

Lizzie moves over close to me. "Do you feel okay, Nicolas?"

I nod. "I feel really good, actually." I do, too. I feel completely relaxed, like there isn't anything worth worrying about. It's as though there isn't a wolf in the world, no nomads, no pain, and no cares.

"You look like you feel good," Lizzie tells me.

"Thank you, Louzze." That's not her name. "Leessy, Liessy." Why can't I say it? "You have a funny name."

She starts laughing as Hannah walks in carrying a blue glass platter. As she lays it on the table, I see the long, thin lines of white powder.

Donny picks up a short straw and slides the platter toward me. "You're first, Nicolas. I insist."

I just look at him for a moment while I try to process how to tell him that vampires can't get high, and eventually say, "That would be a waste. I have a pretty high tolerance."

There is a low chuckle that rips through the group as Donny holds the straw toward me. "Your tolerance level is obvious to us. It's my birthday; don't be rude."

Taking the straw, I lean over the platter and see my blue reflection hiding behind the white lines. I plug one side of my nose with my finger and hold the straw to the first line. I inhale and it slides up my nostril like fire, burning more than I thought it would.

Sitting up straighter, I let the straw slip through my fingers and onto the floor. The group is laughing, but only thing I hear is my heart as it pounds faster and harder than it ever has before.

***

My eyes open and I sit up quickly near the end of the bed. I rub my hand over my cheek and feel the shag carpet imprint on my skin as I look around. I'm alone, but the hotel room still smells of Hannah. My throat burns like I haven't fed in months, making it hurt to swallow.

What happened last night? Vampires can't get high, but I definitely was. I remember singing the Rolling Stones song, *Paint it Black*, at the top of my lungs. I remember scaling the apartment building and standing on the edge of the roof in my underwear. Later, I was in the alley with my fangs in some man's neck. And at some point, I had sex with Hannah in the hotel elevator. My eyes were black. My fangs glided across her skin.

"Hannah?" I call nervously, despite the pain in my throat from speaking.

What if I killed her? What if she knows what I am? I can't let her live if she knows. Whether she is alive or not, this is bad.

There are footsteps that stop outside the door and I watch as the knob turns slowly.

I scramble to get to my feet as Hannah walks in with a bag of doughnuts.

"Hi, sleepyhead," she says with a smile.

Stepping close to her, I turn her chin so that I can see the scratches on her neck. I know they are from my fangs and the fire in my throat knows the potential meal that she is.

"What happened?" I ask.

She rubs her fingers over the scrapes. "I don't know. I was so messed up last night."

Walking past me, she tosses the doughnuts on the bed and flops down beside them. "I was even seeing things."

I sit down close to her, "What kind of things?"

Shrugging, she rolls her hands over themselves. "This is going to sound crazy but at one point, I thought your eyes were black."

She shakes her head dismissingly but I only swallow hard.

"I didn't buy the coke for last night so I don't know what it was cut with, but whatever it was, it was awesome," she laughs lightheartedly.

That's good, I guess. She doesn't believe what she saw was real, so maybe I won't have to kill her. At least, not today.

"Oh, I almost forgot," she starts excitedly, "Donny called this morning to check on us. Apparently, some guy was murdered last night like two blocks from Donny's place and we would have walked right past where they found the body." That sounds a lot like the man I tore my fangs into.

"We could've been killed," she continues.

No, she could have been.

"But that psycho knew better than to mess with me." She hops up on the bed. "I would have been like, hi yah!" She kicks her leg high. "And a little of this," she punches at the air. "And this!" She flops down, driving her elbow into the mattress. "And that's how I would have taken care of that," she boasts, making me smile.

Laughing quietly, I joke, "I admit, that was intimidating."

She rolls over onto her stomach and pulls the bag of doughnuts toward her. Taking one out, she stuffs it in her mouth and I am reminded of my own hunger.

I try to clear my throat, but that does nothing for the fire inside.

"Hannah, we need to talk."

Her chewing slows down as she looks up at me with only her eyes. Swallowing the doughnut in one large lump, she licks her lips. "It's time, isn't it?" Sitting up, she continues, "Time for the whole 'it's not you, it's me' speech."

I sigh lightly. "It really is me, though."

"People always say that."

But I'm not just saying it. I mean it. I could kill her. I almost did. Being so close to her isn't going to work for much longer.

I start to tell her some of the truth when she adds, "I *do* remember something very clearly from last night."

Her eyes lock onto mine but I can see a sadness in them. "When we were in the elevator," Right, having sex in the elevator, I remember that, "you called me Kate."

I close my eyes as guilt washes over me. I know that Hannah and I are not technically a couple, but that still must have bothered her. I drop my head and rub my hand across my forehead.

"I know I'm not the one you want, Nick. And I'm okay with that. And I'm okay with this ending," she says softly.

I feel the bed shift as she leans over and presses her lips to my cheek. As she stands up, I open my eyes but only to watch her from the corner of my eye.

She makes it to the door before I whisper, "I'm sorry, Hannah."

I didn't intend for her to hear me, but the way she pauses in the doorway makes me think she did. Without answering, she leaves, but I will see her again. We still have to fly back together, which will inevitably be uncomfortable for both of us.

I sit on the bed with my head in my hands for only a moment before there is a light knock. Go to the door, but I know who it is before I open it.

Smiling in the doorway, Phoenix says, "Are you losing your skills below the belt? Cause she didn't look too pleased."

I give her my lopsided smile. "I am less concerned with my skills and more concerned with yours." I push the door opens further. "Come in."

As she walks past me, I rub my neck, but that doesn't help the pain of speaking.

"Are you all right?" she asks.

Nodding, I answer, "I'm fine. Just really thirsty."

She pushes herself up onto the dresser and crosses her legs. "So what happened last night? You look terrible, and your handiwork is all over the news."

By 'handiwork' I assume she is talking about the man from the alley, the one that I carelessly tossed in a dumpster.

"I'm sorry about that," I tell her. But honestly, I am not sorry I killed him; only that it will make it harder for her to remain a secret now.

Leaning forward slightly, she raises her eyebrows. "And?"

"And the rest you wouldn't believe if I told you." I'm not even sure I believe it. Why did those drugs affect me? They're not supposed to. They don't affect vampires. Period.

I try to clear my throat, but that only makes me close my eyes painfully and grab at my neck.

Sitting on the bed, I run my fingers through my hair and ask, "Did you find Roddy?"

Exhaling in disbelief, she hops off of the dresser. "Don't insult me."

She walks over to me and pulls my chin up. Turning my face from side to side, she looks over me with her mouth twisted. Finally, she drops her hand. "You should've brought your sheep with you."

I suppose she means that my cold skin, the hunger hiding behind my eyes, and the way my pain keeps my eyebrows drawn together must make my thirst more evident than I intend.

"I can only help you hold over for a while. You'll have to hit up the safe house for any sustainable meal."

I know what she is suggesting, and it isn't something she normally offers, but the fire drives me to ignore my reservations as my mouth begins to water.

"Just promise you're not going to kill anyone else in my town," she adds.

She slides onto my lap, straddling me. With her face inches from mine, she pulls the collar of her shirt aside and leans her head, exposing her neck.

Placing one hand on the small of her back, I pull her body to mine. I cradle her face with my other hand as my eyes change to black.

Being as gentle as possible, my fangs enter her skin. Her blood rushes in my mouth, instantly cooling and soothing my pain. Her sharp inhale only makes my grip on her tighten. She doesn't struggle the way a human would; instead, her breaths become heavy. Her hand makes its way along my shoulder and her fingers tangle themselves in my hair. My heart races, matching hers as she arches her head back.

I slide my teeth out of her but I keep her close. She looks at me with her black eyes and smiles, exposing her fangs, and it makes my body crave her.

"I forgot how good that feels," she says, still breathing hard.

She grabs my face forcefully and runs her tongue from my chin to the corner of my lips, collecting her blood from my skin.

A very different fire charges through me, and my hands nearly tremble with desire.

"Now, back to business," she says abruptly and slides off of my lap.

Guess that's over.

As she walks over to the nightstand, I let my eyes become green again.

"When I give you the address, we're square, right?" she asks.

Half-smiling, I reply, "I saved your life. That's worth more than an address."

Her eyebrow raises mischievously. "I'm letting Roddy live. A life for a life. That's only fair."

My smile fades. That little schemer. It's tricks like this that make me remember why I like her so much. "Deal."

She reaches in her bra and pulls out a slip of paper. "That's an apartment he shares with a barely legal local."

I realize wolves and vampires don't really care about the age of a person but 'barely legal'? Come on, Roddy, use your head.

Glancing at the handwritten address, I hear her add, "And I don't think they're just friends."

Without looking up, I mumble, "That would explain why he's not getting married next month."

Phoenix laughs as if she knows an inside joke I am not aware of.

My eyes shoot up quickly. "What's so funny?"

"You'll see."

Smiling, she walks to the door. "This was fun, Nick. We should do this again, only next time, bring some cash 'cause you're all out of favors."

Then she laughs as she leaves.

I look down at the address. Seeing Roddy is important, but so is not killing any more humans while I'm here and my hunger isn't exactly satisfied. Sighing, I get up. First a free meal at the safe house, then find Roddy.

***

The apartment building is nice enough, recently updated, and cozy, which means Roddy hasn't been living in despair this whole time. At least that will make Tara happy to know.

I stop in front of the door with the 3C plaque on it. I already know that I have the right place since I've looked at the paper numerous times, but look down at the address anyway.

Taking a deep breath, I run my hands through my hair. What if he's not here? What if he is? What if I can't convince him to come home?

I lean toward the door. Listening closely, I can hear water running from a shower, muffling the sounds of voices. But the voice I do hear I recognize instantly.

"Babe," Roddy starts, "I love you, but you can't leave your socks on the floor."

The other voice mumbles something but I do not catch what was said.

"It is a big deal actually," Roddy snaps.

I do not hear any mumbling so I assume the other person scowls at him because Roddy changes his tone quickly. "I'm sorry," he says soft enough that I can only barely hear him. "It's just a pet peeve of mine, okay? Could you just try not to leave them everywhere?" His voice perks up as he adds, "I'm gonna take a shower. And if you could forgive me for being a jerk, I'd like you to join me – and hey, I might even share the water with you this time."

He laughs at his own joke but as his laughter grows quieter, I assume he leaves the room. Supposing that this is as good of a time as any to make my presence known, I knock.. But who answers the door leaves me speechless.

"Hi. Can I help you?" asks a young man. That's right, a man. Just a kid, really, maybe twenty, but I doubt it, with black hair and bright blue eyes.

Too stunned to do much else, I just stare blankly at him, repeating in my head 'Roddy was speaking to a man.' My mind races with a hundred questions but only one manages to escape my lips, "Does Roddy live here?"

The boy leans against the door with his eyebrows drawn. "Who are you?"

Finally able to process something other than surprise, I smile at him and reach my hand out. "I'm Nicolas, Roddy's cousin."

The boy changes in an instant. His eyes light up and a smile springs to his face. He pushes himself off of the door and grabs my hand, but instead of shaking it, he pulls me inside, too young and naïve to realize my lie.

"Roddy said he didn't have any family."

Roddy was keeping secrets. Surprise, surprise, "Well, we're not that close," I say smoothly as I look around aimlessly. "Is it just the two of you here?"

"Yep," the boy says as he closes the door, "there's only two bedrooms so we try to keep it just us."

Sure, that's the reason. Even if his eyes weren't darting when he said that, I wouldn't have believed it. Not with the present evidence. "What did you say your name was?"

"Oh, I'm sorry." He walks over and gestures for me to sit but I remain standing as he continues, "I'm Clint, Roddy's friend."

Friend? Friends that take showers together and pick up each other dirty laundry… well, I guess I have friends like that, too. But none of mine are men.

"Is um," I point toward the sound of the water, "Roddy in the shower?"

"Yeah, I'll tell him to hurry," Clint says.

He starts to walk away, but I grab his arm. "Wait, watch this."

I let go of Clint and raise my voice only slightly when I clearly say, "Roddy. Don't keep me waiting."

Before all of my words are out, the water stops. Clint looks over at me with a quirky grin and raised eyebrows as though he is impressed, but his smile fades when Roddy steps out of the bathroom with wide eyes.

Breathing quicker than usual, Roddy wears only his towel and lets the water run over his muscles. Nervousness, or fear, or maybe both, has taken the color from his cheeks as he swallows hard.

"Nicolas. What are you doing here?" He doesn't let me answer before he follows with another question, "Are you alone?"

"More alone than you are," I tell him with a smirk.

Knowing what I am insinuating, he lets his eyes dart to Clint then back to me quickly, wondering how much I know.

Roddy walks over to us, rubbing his hands over each other. "Could you excuse us for a minute?" he asks Clint.

From the look on Clint's face, I can only assume that he is second-guessing his choice to let me in, but he doesn't say his concerns out loud; instead, he simply nods and walks out.

As soon as the bedroom door shuts behind Clint, Roddy stammers out nervously, "Nick, I see you met my friend, Clint. He's my best friend. That's why we're roommates because we're friends. And that's what friends do. They room together 'cause we're friends."

With a disbelieving look on my face, I tell him, "Cut the shit, Roddy. I don't care who you're sleeping with. Finding out that your ship doesn't sail straight isn't the worse thing I could've walked in on."

"It's not?"

Of course not. I'm a vampire. My life isn't exactly sunshine and rainbows. It's not like I have a right to judge anyone.

"I thought you might think it was a sin," he finishes.

Sighing, I shrug lightly. "Do you know what I think is a sin?" I point toward the bedroom Clint had escaped to. "That is a baby. How old is that boy?"

"He's nineteen."

I raise my eyebrows as though what he said proves my point. I realize Roddy is physically only twenty-five, but he hasn't been nineteen for a very long time. "You're almost forty."

He shakes his head dismissingly. "Don't start with me, Nick. How many hundreds of years younger are the girls that you sleep with?"

It's a fair comparison. One that I don't really have a good answer for, so thankfully, instead of letting me respond with sarcasm, Roddy continues, "Besides, it's not like I went to the high school and pulled him out of study hall. I met him in a grocery store."

Nodding, I say, "Was his Boy Scout troop there for some reason?"

Even though he tries not to, Roddy laughs lightly.

I can tell by the way he shakes his head that I'm not that far off. Definitely not a Boy Scout, more like a bag boy. But I know Roddy. He probably went to the store every day and bought things he didn't need or wouldn't eat just to see Clint until he worked up the nerve to talk to him.

Growing serious, Roddy sits down on the coffee table with his eyes on the floor. "Nick, just let me have this, okay?"

The sadness in his tone makes me feel slightly guilty for being so hard on him. Sitting down on the couch next to him, I just listen.

"I realize that in another month I have to go home. And then I will have to pretend for the rest of my life," he adds quietly.

My eyebrows come together, "What do you mean pretend?"

He glances at me as if I should already understand. "Have you ever met a gay werewolf? They're either disposed of or disowned, usually both." He shakes his head lightly. "I can't watch my mom go through that." His eyes trail away in thought.

Grabbing his shoulder, I tell him firmly, "Roddy, you can't just be miserable your whole life."

Without looking at me, his words rush out, "What else am I supposed to do, Nick?"

"Don't go home," I tell him softly.

He looks over at me and I can tell it has crossed his mind, too. "It's not that easy, and you know it."

I do know. I know all about the bonds in a pack. How that once you are a member, the only way to really be free is if the alpha severs the ties that connect you to them. How until you are released, your bond with the pack will draw you back, make you feel as though something is missing until you return. It's not fair that only an alpha can decide whether you can leave or not, but that's the way the pack works.

And I know Roddy's dad. Eric won't let Roddy go. "I'll talk to your mom. She's alpha, too. She can break your bond to the pack."

He shakes his head. "No... I mean..." His words topple on one another. "Well... Yes, she can. But she won't. I'm her only son. She's not going to just let me go. Especially when you tell her where I am, 'cause that's why you're here, right? She sent you to find me."

"But I didn't find you, Roddy. When I got here, you were gone. Already skipped town to I don't know where."

Almost stunned, his eyes grow wider and his mouth opens slightly as I finish, "I can convince her to break your ties with the pack. She loves you. She'll do anything to make you happy." I stand up and start to leave, but then turning to him, I add, "Going home is just rushing into regret."

Holding the towel to keep it from slipping as he stands, he walks over to me. "You would really lie to my mother for *me*?"

No. I am not lying to her for Roddy. If he returns, he could be killed and she couldn't live through that. Keeping Tara from her son temporarily could save her from losing him permanently. I know I will feel guilty for this, and she won't understand my logic, but I don't see any other way around it.

"I'll protect her any way I can," I tell him.

And with those words, Roddy wraps his arms around my shoulders in a hug. "Thank you," he whispers.

When he leans away, I can see the relief and renewed sense of hope in his eyes.

Even though lying seems like a mistake, seeing him happy makes me smile, and I joke, "Roddy, next time you hug me, please be wearing pants."

I *should've spent my time* flying home, thinking of what I will say to Tara about her son, or feeling awkward at the strangely cordial conversation that Hannah engaged me in, but I didn't.

Instead, my heart was racing, my skin was tingling. I was growing more anxious by the minute, knowing I was that much closer to Kate. Will I still want her as much I did? Did this little bit of time apart help at all? Then I would smile because I was about to find out those answers. I was about to see her.

The plane lands on the lightly snow-dusted strip, and soon after, Hannah and I grab our things and start walking toward the parking lot.

"Do you want me to walk home?" I ask, unsure of whether she will want me to or not. And to be honest, I don't know that I want to.

Pulling her bag further onto her shoulder, she shakes her head. "No. I talked to Becca and she said Jericho was freaking out about me leaving." I would be, too, if my human sister left town with a vampire. "So now I have to go show him that I'm okay. He's so weird."

I smile to myself. "Okay, well, I'll see you around then."

"Yeah," she half-smiles, but something tells me I probably won't see her again. After all, she is going back to college soon and we don't exactly associate with the same crowds.

I walk through the snow, rubbing my hands together. I close my eyes, letting the wind wrap itself around me, but still I only see Kate's face.

It's distracting enough that I do not realize someone is close to me until I feel a hand on my arm. Startled, I jerk away, opening my eyes quickly.

Luke laughs at me. "Take it easy, man. I didn't mean to scare you."

As if I would ever be afraid of one human. I shake my head to try to clear my thoughts, but that doesn't help.

"What were you thinking about?" he asks, walking with me.

"Nothing."

"Doesn't seem like nothing."

I glance over at him and inhale as I start to explain my feelings for Kate, but then exhale slowly. "Forget it."

He shrugs his shoulders. "How was your trip? And how was your alone time with Hannah?" he asks, raising his eyebrows up and down insinuatingly.

I smile to myself. "It was interesting."

He hits my arm playfully. "Details."

Laughing lightly, I tell him, "A gentleman doesn't give details to someone with a big mouth."

"Pfft."

I look back down at the snow, still thinking of Kate. "It's over between me and Hannah, anyway."

"What?" he exclaims, "You had a perfect thing going with Hannah. No strings."

It's not perfect when you nearly kill the other person. Despite knowing what I intend to say, something else comes out, "Maybe I want strings."

My words surprise me enough that I do not hear Luke's response. His voice sounds distant and I cut him off quickly, "Look, I haven't slept since I left." Which is a lie, but a small one. "Right now, I just want to be home."

"Alright," he says almost as if I had scolded him.

I do feel bad for being abrupt, but I'm having my own crisis right now and do not have time to listen to why I should feel the way he thinks a normal twenty-two-year-old might feel.

"I'll see you later, okay?"

He nods. "Later."

I watch him as he walks away, but my mind is still on Kate. What if I still want her? I can't feel that way for Kate. I just can't. But would it really be that bad if I did? Of course it would be. She is my best friend and all I do is cause pain.

By the time I make it to my house, my heart is racing. I swallow hard as I hurry through the living room and kitchen, ignoring the glare from Luther, and go straight to Kate's bedroom.

The moment of truth. Here goes nothing. I push the door open and my eyes find her instantly. Standing next to the bed, she is folding her shirts and, in my opinion, has never been so beautiful. Her reddish-brown skin plays off of her white blouse and I watch as her hair slides off of her shoulder and drops in front of her face. My hand aches to move her hair so I can see her face again, but she reaches up and pushes it behind her ear.

Looking over at me, she smiles widely and it stops my breath. "Nick!" she rushes to me, wrapping her arms around my neck. "You're back."

I hold her against me, lavishing in the scent of coconut from her hair as it brushes my cheek. Feeling the warmth of her body through my shirt only makes my arms tighten around her. Surely, she notices the way I lean my head on hers and the way my body conforms around hers, but she does nothing to stop me.

"I was hoping I would see you before I left," she says, and my eyes open quickly, which is the only reason I notice the bag on the bed next to her shirts. She is packing.

I pull away from her just slightly, enough to see her face. "Are you going somewhere?" I ask quietly.

Slipping her arms from my shoulders, she walks back toward the bed. "Yeah. Ms. Duncan asked me to housesit for a little while. She's going to be staying at her father's in Maine."

Ms. Duncan, Molly's mother. I knew it would be hard on her to lose Molly, and believe me, I didn't want to kill her, but we all have obligations and mine revolve around being a vampire.

"It's the least we could do for her," Kate adds. I admit, that makes sense but does she really have to? "I kind of feel like we owe her."

My eyes drop to the floor and I do not even try to hide the sadness I feel. "I'm going to miss you."

I hear the smile in her voice as she says, "I'll just be next door."

Shrugging my shoulders, I glance around the room, trying not to make eye contact. "But you won't be in your bed, and I like sleeping next to you. I'm going to miss that," I say, just above a whisper.

There is a silent pause, and after a moment, I look up at her. She stares at me with a look that is mixed between anger and hurt.

Unsure of what I did, I ask, "What?"

Her voice has more pain in it than I expect when she tells me, "We both know that you want me. But if you're pretending that you don't, then pretend you don't. You can't say things like that. It's not fair."

Not fair? Since when is the truth about being fair? I've always been able to tell her anything. That shouldn't change. I don't want that to change.

I shake my head irritably. "So now I can't be honest with you?"

She shoves the last of her clothes in her bag angrily. "You're not honest with yourself."

"What do you want me to say, Kate?" I snap. "That I care about you? Of course I do. But apparently, I'm the only one here who realizes that we're both too selfish for this to actually work."

Her jaw clenches for a moment before she responds, "That's not the problem," she nearly yells at me. "The problem is you. You're just hiding behind Ann because you're too afraid to feel for anyone else!"

My hands nearly tremble when she mentions Ann. How dare she bring her into this! I have to bite my tongue to keep from saying anything at all because everything I want to say is highly disrespectful.

"Come on, Nick. Open your eyes," she continues irritably. Then, taking a deep breath, she adds in Cherokee, "Gv-ge-yu."

Of all of the languages she could use, she always chooses Cherokee because I have no idea what she is saying. It's a little infuriating, to say the least.

"What does that even mean?"

Hastily, she grabs her bag. "It means you're an idiot." She pulls the bag onto her shoulder. "You know where I'll be if you need me."

As she walks past me, she hits my shoulder with hers, knocking me back a step.

Feeling more than guilty for snapping at her, I pinch the bridge of my nose. Then opening my eyes, I go after her. "Kate!"

I hurry into the kitchen but stop there when I hear the front door slam shut. I am too late. Now she's mad and there's nothing I can do about it.

Exhaling forcefully, I look over slowly to see Luther sitting on the counter.

Unable to read his expression, I ignore him and glance down at the floor, thinking.

"Gv-ge-yu means 'I love you' in Cherokee," he says simply.

Quickly, I look at him. "How do you know that?"

He slips off of the counter next to me. "Because I was waiting for her to say that to me." He lays his hand on my shoulder. "But she never did."

My eyes drop, but I do not see anything in particular as Luther walks away.

She's right. I am an idiot.

"Kate!" I rush through the kitchen and living room, tearing open the door. "Kate, wait!"

Ignoring me, she keeps walking. I make it across the snow-covered yard quickly. Grabbing her by the arm, I turn her toward me, and without hesitating, I crush my lips to hers.

I place my hand on the small of her back as a fire rips through me, surging its way from my lips to my toes and back. Her bag drops to her feet and she wraps her arms around me. Her hand slides into my hair where her fingers tighten and pull, which only makes me press her closer.

My tongue glides over hers as my hand cradles her face. Hearing her heart racing only makes mine pound that much harder. With one hand, her fingers dig into my shoulder as her body curves into mine.

Pulling away slightly, I keep my face only inches from hers. Looking into her eyes, I let my thumb graze over her cheek. "I don't want to hide from you," I whisper to her.

I lean in to kiss her again, but just before my lips touch hers, I catch a whiff of a wolf. Not just any wolf. Jericho.

Looking over, I see him standing several yards from us.

"Get out of here, Kate," I tell her calmly.

She grabs my arm but she doesn't have to say anything. I know what she is thinking, so I look over at her. "I'll be fine. Trust me." I kiss the tip of her nose. "Go."

Looking sharply at Jericho, she grabs her bag and starts toward Ms. Duncan's again. Part of me wonders if she is really worried about me or just angry that Jericho interrupted us.

Either way, I turn toward Jericho and wait for his glares to become something verbal.

Sure enough, he unclenches his jaw to say, "You almost killed my sister."

"Almost" would be the key word there. But still I only smirk at him.

"If you even look at her again with those greedy little eyes, I'll break you," he adds.

He starts to walk away, since I assume he has orders to not attack unless provoked, but I don't really appreciate being threatened, even by an unthreatening person such as him.

"I wasn't aware that I had to listen to you. Wait, that's because I don't."

My words stop him in his tracks and he looks back at me from over his shoulder, so I continue, "Thing is, if I want to have sex with her, I will. And there's nothing you can do about it."

Then, just because it will give me the result I am wanting, I add, "Hell, I just wish she was a better lay."

That does it. His clothes explode from his body as he transforms into his caramel wolf. As he charges at me, I expose my fangs in a hiss.

His body collides with mine and I fall back to the ground with my hand on his neck, keeping his snapping jaws away as drool dips onto my face. My fingers squeeze into the soft tissues of his throat and his growls become raspy. He struggles out of my grip and snaps at me as I jump to my feet.

I kick him in the side, making him slide across the frozen ground. My eyes narrow as I wipe the saliva from my cheek. This ends tonight. I let my fingernails grow out as he rushes toward me.

Flipping over him, I grab handfuls of the fur on his back. As I land on my feet, I pull him over my head and drive his body into the ground. He scrambles to his feet, swinging his paw at me. His claws dig into my thigh, ripping through my muscles, and surely I will feel the pain later, but for now, I only feel anger.

I punch an upper-cut, into his jaw, throwing him into the air. As he drops to the ground, I kick his ribs and he flies into my truck, leaving his impression in the side.

The cuts on my leg begin to heal as he comes toward me again. I move to the side so that he runs past me, and as he does, I drag my fingernails along his side, slashing eight gouges from shoulder to hip.

He whines painfully but I do not wait for him to heal or retaliate. I grab his tail and bring his flailing body over my head, slamming him into the ground. Then again to the other side of me, listening for the breaking of his bones and smiling a little more each time.

With him lying on the cold snow, I kneel down by him and drive my fist into his eye, causing the blood to burst inside and fill his eye. I do not let up; I drive my fist into his face relentlessly, taking out all of my hatred for him.

Bleeding and broken, he phases into his human form, which I know for wolves is a surrender, but I'm no wolf and I don't play by those rules.

Laying my hand on his sternum, I press down, compressing his chest until he can barely breathe. His eyes widen with every painful inhale.

Wheezing sharply, he manages a weak reply, "Please."

A cruel smile spreads on my face. "That's good. It's better when you beg."

Pulling his head to the side by his hair, I quickly sink my teeth into his neck. His blood fills my mouth. Sweet and thick, it pours down my throat slowly, cooling its way to my stomach.

He pushes against me but his strength is no match for mine, and soon his hands go limp and fall to his chest.

Standing up, I stare at his dead, naked body in the snow but feel no pity or remorse. Grabbing his hair, I drag him to the truck and toss him into the bed.

I drive normally since driving too fast would raise suspicions, and eventually make to the lake. Still dragging his limp body behind me, I walk to the middle of the lake and stop. Bending down, I dust the snow away to reveal the thick ice beneath it.

Looking at the lake, I punch as hard as I can and drive my fist through the ice, splintering it into the air and breaking my fingers. I shove Jericho's body through the hole quickly, then watch as the ice reforms, sealing him inside.

I walk back to the truck and drive home. Leaving the dented truck in the driveway, I start toward Tara's with my hand still throbbing.

By the time I make it to the house she is staying at, my hand is nearly completely healed and the pain is minimal.

I look up at her window. It makes me smile to watch her for a moment as she dances in front of a mirror, unaware that anyone can see her. Carefree, she twirls around the room, and it makes me wonder what she is listening to. My smile grows lopsided and I almost forget about Jericho and every other wolf but her. Almost.

Despite Cyrus and two others approaching, I keep my eyes on Tara. Her face lights up when she notices me in the street and she makes a number one with her finger to tell me she is on her way down.

As she disappears somewhere in the room, I let my smile fade and I glance over at Cyrus.

"What?" I ask coldly.

He motions for the other two men to stop several yards from me but he continues until he is close, "Where's Jericho?"

I shrug lightly. "What's the matter? Did he break his leash?"

A low growl rumbles from the other men's chests but they stay very still as Cyrus ignores my comment and continues, "He was on his way to your house."

"I'm not at my house." Cyrus starts to open his mouth, but before his words can escape, I add, "But if I see him, I'll be sure to let you know… after I protect myself."

One of the men steps closer, but Cyrus puts his hand up to stop him. Then leaning close, he whispers, "I think you killed him. Probably in self-defense." Like I would ever be afraid of Jericho. "Dead or alive, I want to see him."

Impassively, I reply, "Then I suggest you fish him out of his hiding place, because I don't care about what you want. I warned you once; I'm not a dog person, so keep your mutts away from me."

As I start to walk away, Cyrus grabs my shoulder and it takes all of my restraint not to flip him to the ground.

"What happened to your pants?" Cyrus asks, looking at the slashes left by Jericho.

"Neighbor's aggressive dog," I smirk at him. "I guess they don't like me either."

The door opens and Tara walks onto the porch, but Cyrus and I keep our eyes locked on each other.

I shove his hand off of me. "Don't worry, I took care of it."

Tara walks over to us and stands between us. "Is there something wrong here?" she snaps at Cyrus.

His eyes move to her. "You should pick better friends. You don't know what he's capable of."

Glaring, she tells him, "You should pick better enemies because *you* don't know what he's capable of." Cyrus' jaw flexes but he says nothing.

"Now, excuse us. I'm hungry and Nick is buying." She grabs my shirt at the chest and nearly drags me away. She keeps her head up as we pass the other two men, who have narrowed their eyes on Tara. It's not every day a woman stands up to their alpha, and most do not know how to respond to it.

She doesn't look back at them, but I know she is listening for them to follow, which they don't. Eventually, she lets her defense drop enough to relax.

"Thank you, Tara. I –"

She cuts me off abruptly, "I don't want to hear about that mess back there. I want to know if you found my son."

Yes, Tara, I definitely did. I found out a lot about your son. But it doesn't matter how much I want to, I can't say that. Sighing, I drop my shoulders and shake my head. "He was already gone when I got there."

She looks away but I can hear the sadness in her voice. "Are you sure?"

The guilt crushes me, making it difficult to say, "Yeah."

I hate lying to her. It feels unnatural. It feels wrong.

I grab the door to the diner as she asks, "You could track him though, right?"

The restaurant is mostly empty and I am glad for that as I lead her toward a table in the back. "I don't think he wants to be found."

"Well, he can get over that," she says as I pull out her chair.

I sit down across from her, and softly say, "I think you should let him go."

She looks up at me sharply, trying to hide the hurt inside. "No. Without his ties to the pack, I won't be able to feel if... something happens. I need to know he is still alive somewhere. I can't give that up."

She snatches the menu and flips it open in front of her face in an attempt to stop the conversation, but I made a promise to Roddy, and for once, I'm going to keep it.

With my finger, I tip the menu down just a bit and continue, "That bond will pull him back, but if he feels like he was forced, he's going to resent it. He'll resent you."

Her chin quivers as the waitress walks over to us. Tara turns her face away from the lady, who slides a pen from behind her ear.

Taking the menus, I smile at the waitress. "We'll take two specials." I hand her the menus.

I look at Tara and my heart breaks. How can I do this to her? I am supposed to be her friend. But it's not my fault. This is because of the pack and their archaic rules.

"What to drink?" the waitress asks.

"Whatever is easiest," I say, not taking my eyes off of Tara.

From the corner of my eye, I can see the waitress look over at Tara. As Tara tries not to cry, the waitress's smile fades.

"Sure," she says before she walks away.

Once she is gone, I reach over and take Tara's hand. Gently, I rub my thumb over her skin. "You know I'm right."

A tear rolls down her cheek as she nods, "I know," she says weakly.

Taking a deep breath, she wipes her face with her hands. "Talk about something else."

I know the only reason she is asking is because she wants a delay from the pain of losing Roddy, and I know just the thing to distract her. "I kissed Kate."

Her head whips around toward me. "I thought you were with Hannah."

"Not anymore."

Sniffling, she leans forward. "Tell me more."

"There's not much to tell. I just kissed her right before I came here."

She sets one foot on her chair, wrapping her arm around her knee. "You said you weren't getting involved with her. So what happened? What changed?"

I lean back in my chair. "She basically called me a coward. I had to prove her wrong."

Tara bursts into laughter. "That is just like you."

It's nice to hear her laugh. It helps to take my mind off of the guilt left behind from my lie. My lopsided smile shows itself as the waitress approaches with our food.

She sets the plates down in front of us when Tara asks, "Are you going to go slow?" She raises her eyebrows as though she already knows my answer, making me nearly blush in front of the waitress.

I wait until the waitress leaves to reply, "And what? Get to know her first?"

Tara picks up a French fry from her plate and twirls it in front of her, inspecting it. "Thought so," Then just when I think she is going to drop it, she shoves the fry in her mouth.

I shove my plate away and lean forward, whispering, "Something happened in Denali."

Intrigued, she chews slower as though that would help her hear me.

"I went to this party –"

She cuts me off with sarcasm, "You? At a party?"

Admittedly, it's not my usual scene but still, I frown at her. "Yes," Then shifting uncomfortably in my seat, I start again, "I was at a party and there was a lot of…" Almost embarrassed that I would associate with those people, I hesitate to tell her, "there were a lot of…" I glance around the room as though I might find my words in the dim lighting or drab décor.

But I suppose Tara grows tired of waiting because she kicks me in the shin, making me blurt it out, "Drugs. There were drugs everywhere."

Swallowing her fry, she looks at me, confused. "So? I'm sure that's not the first time you've been around them."

As she picks up another fry, I tell her, "That's true but they've never had an effect on me before."

Dropping her fry, she grabs my wrist. "What do you mean 'effect'? Are you saying that you were *high*?"

"I think so," I shake my head. Who am I kidding? "I mean, yes, I definitely was."

Tara leans back in her chair, thinking. "That's not possible, Nick."

"I realize that."

"Then how do you explain it?"

"I can't."

She drums her fingers over her mouth for a moment before she huffs loudly. "There has to be a reason."

I shrug. "I can't figure it out. I'm not any different than any other vampire."

She tips the chair back onto two feet. "But apparently, you are."

Her eyes drift off to the side as she whispers to herself, "But why?"

Admittedly, I'd like to know the answer to that, too. I've thought about it every time my mind wasn't on Kate, and I can't find any reason. Nothing has ever happened to me that is so different from other vampires. No strange experiences, no unusual victims, just your basic vampire life.

Suddenly, her chair slams onto all four feet and Tara stares at me with a stunned look on her face. "Do you remember Ulrich?"

Of course I do. He was only the Nazi that tortured me for days until I finally was freed. The same Nazi that I left to suffer a pleasingly painful death.

"Yeah," I tell her, not really understanding where this is going.

"He gave you an injection, Nick," she says almost excitedly, as though I should be following her train of thought.

"Yeah, meningitis."

She leans forward across the table, shaking her head. "No, after that. When you were sick. He said it would make you better."

My eyes trail away. I remember that.

"What if he didn't mean the meningitis? What if he meant he could make you a better vampire?" she finishes.

That's crazy. But then again, he was crazy.

"That doesn't make sense. How would letting drugs affect me make me a better vampire?"

With a cocky smirk, she picks up another fry and twirls it in her fingers. "Because they were only interested in making better soldiers. And what better way than to make someone who can trade their inhibitions and regrets for insouciance and numbness."

Okay, that makes more sense. Drugs would make a vampire more dangerous and keep them from feeling the pain their actions bring.

"You might be on to something," I tell her.

She throws the fry at me and it hits my chest. "Admit it, I'm right."

Holding back a smile, I joke, "I will not admit that."

Grabbing a handful of fries, she throws them at me with a wide smile.

As I brush them off of my shirt, one drops from my hair onto my lap. "Hey, I have to live here, you know. You're making me look like a troublemaker."

She laughs lightly. "I'm sure your impeccable reputation as an ass will not be tarnished by a few fries."

Her sarcasm makes me chuckle to myself. "Fries? No. But when I tear into a mouthy wolf, that might change some opinions."

She rolls her eyes at me. "I hear you talking over there but you forgot something. My bark and my bite are bigger than yours."

Before I can stop my sarcastic remark, it slips out, "So is your butt."

Her jaw drops but she isn't angry. She sucks in hard. "Nicolas Rider!" she says, scolding me. Reaching across the table, she pulls my plate toward herself. "Just for that, I'm taking this. And," she says, adding emphasis, "you're buying me dessert."

I lean back in the chair and watch as she starts eating her food. I suppose it makes sense that Ulrich could have given me something that would alter my DNA. He was a scientist – and a smart one at that. But what could do this? What did he know that I don't?

As she takes a drink to wash down some of the fries, I mumble, "I think you're right."

She sets the glass down and holds her hand up to ear. "I'm sorry. What? I didn't hear you."

I smile to myself. Of course she heard me. "I said, you're right."

"Good. Now we can get started."

"Started? On what?"

A gentle smile lights her face. "Figuring out what was in that syringe."

"And how do we do that?"

She shrugs. "I can't think of everything."

We sit in the diner for close to two hours going over scenarios and possibilities, but none of them sound plausible. I eventually suggest that my friends in Europe could put a little pressure on a few people to get some information. But after ordering and devouring three desserts, Tara decides to involve some of her German allies instead.

She's probably right. After all, dead people can't help anyone. And my friends would leave a lot of dead people in their path.

Getting nowhere with the brainstorming, I leave Tara at her bed and breakfast and head to the hospital to see my newest favorite person, Punzi.

As I start up the stairs, I cannot help but to be excited. I haven't seen her little round cheeks in days, but it feels like longer. A soft grin creeps onto my face as I think of the happy smile she gets when she hears my voice.

I promised I would teach her a song and I am not leaving tonight until she knows it by heart. I walk down the hallway toward her room, going over the cords in my head and imagining her face when she gets it right.

But when I step in her doorway, there is someone else in her bed – an older woman with gray-streaked hair who smells of old perfume.

I grab a nurse's arm as she passes me. "Trish, where is Punzi?"

"Who?"

Of course she doesn't know her by that name. "The little girl that was in here," I say, pointing to the room.

Trish's face relaxes away from her confused look. "She's gone. A social worker came for her yesterday. She said something about an adoption."

My eyes drop to the floor but I do not see the tiles. She's gone. I know I asked for her to have a family, but deep down, I was still hoping to be a part of it.

"I'm sorry. I know you liked her," Trish says quietly.

Yeah, I do. As Trish walks away, I wrap my arms around myself and feel more alone than I ever have before.

I start down the hallway slower than usual, running her words over in my head. Punzi is with a new family now. Thanks to me. So why do I feel so bad? I know why. It's because I miss her. She was the only human I have let myself care about since Ann, and now she's gone, too.

The winter air bites at my nose but I ignore the way it tries to chap my cheeks, and head home.

Dragging my feet through the snow, I pass the bar when I hear Marcella's voice.

"I don't want him to know," she says forcefully.

I do not see her but I know where the sounds had come from. Pressing my back against a building, I lean my ear as close to the alley as I can.

"Why? Are you afraid he'll leave?" Salem taunts. "Don't you think that boy needs to know who he is living with?"

"I'm his mother. That's all he needs to know."

My eyebrows come together as I strain to hear them whispering. Obviously, she is either talking about Luther or me. But something inside makes me thinks this is about me. I thought she had told me everything about Salem, but maybe I was wrong. Maybe there is more.

"Mother?" he scoffs. "A real mother wouldn't have left her son to become a monster for her own vanity's sake."

Her son, Noah. I know very little about him or why she chose to become a vampire, but it sounds like Salem knows more.

Before I can think of it much, I hear the sound of a sharp slap and Marcella's voice. "Go to hell! You know nothing of the pain my choices have given me! You didn't watch your son grow old and die while you remained frozen. This life is a curse," her voice trembles as though she is holding back tears.

"A curse you so willingly shared," Salem says unaffectedly.

"I was lonely. I was desperate. I wanted my son back, and I'm sorry, but you just weren't good enough," she snaps coldly, much more like the Marcella I know.

I do not hear her leave but after a moment of silence, Salem says, "She's gone, Nicolas. You can come out now."

I step out from along the building and stare at him in the alley.

He smirks. "Are you going to try to kill me again?" he asks as though he is hoping I will say yes.

"Not as long as you're talking." I cross my arms over my chest. "What's she hiding from me?"

Laughing to himself, he whispers, "Good boy."

He walks toward me but stops when I lower my arms, ready for a fight.

His smile fades as he starts, "She searched a hundred and fifty years to find you. Nobody looked like Noah the way you do. Not even me."

My eyes drop. I look like Noah. Why didn't she tell me that?

"The first time she saw you, you were twelve and since we don't turn children, she waited. We watched you every night. She even cried when you left on that ship, but you came back, just like I said you would."

My stomach churns with nervousness. I don't want to know where this is leading.

"You don't honestly think you were an accident, do you?" he asks tauntingly.

He steps toward me, but with a million thoughts running through my mind, I just stare at the snow as my quick breaths fog the air around me.

"She begged me for you," he continues. "But had I known she would take you and disappear, I would have never done it."

He steps just in front of me, close enough to kill, but I can't even move.

He leans down so I can see his face. "You didn't just replace Noah; you replaced me," he says coldly.

My heart pounds hard. "You're lying," I say but it sounds weaker than I intend for it to.

"Am I?"

He is. He has to be. Marcella wouldn't keep that from me. It's too big. Of course if it's true and I had known, I wouldn't have stayed with her. And she does have a way of manipulating people. I am not naïve enough to believe she doesn't have secrets. We all do.

He could be lying, but knowing her, I doubt he is.

I look up at him with narrow eyes. "You were in that alley. You turned me. That I know is true."

Without warning, I grab him by the neck and slam him into the building. "Conversation's over."

My fingers dig into his skin, making his blood stream over his collar. He punches my ribs, breaking one but I do not lose my grip.

With my fangs exposed, I go for his throat. But just as my teeth press his skin, I hear him struggle to say, "She knew about Ann."

Slowly, I lean away until I see his face. "What did you say?" I ask coldly although I heard him clearly.

A smirk spreads on his face. "Let me go."

I take my hand away but keep my eyes black, ready to attack if I don't like the next sentence that comes out of his mouth.

He rubs his neck, smearing the blood. "Marcella wanted her out of the way. She only wanted you."

My hand flexes into a fist, but I hold myself back. I need to hear this. I need to know who Marcella really is.

"You have spent the last few centuries hating the wrong person," he adds. "But don't feel bad; she tricked me, too."

Half of me doesn't believe what I am hearing, but the other half knows it's true. My blood boils beneath my skin and I look at him coldly. I unclench my jaw to say, "You should run." He smiles at me. "Apparently, so should she."

He is right. I can't go home now. Not while I am so angry with Marcella. I have never hurt her, but this time would be different. This time, I wouldn't stop. This time, she would be ash.

Salem walks away, leaving me in the alley with my shaking hands. I have to calm down before I approach her. I have to find a way to think of something else for a while so when I do come back to this, I am in a better place to be understanding, because, right now, I am not understanding.

I know what to do. It's simple. It's what I always do.

It is difficult but I am able to focus enough to make my eyes turn green again as I start down the street. I walk quickly, trying not to talk to anyone, trying to hurry without being noticed.

Finally, I make it where I want to be. Leaving my shoeprints in the snow, I pass the little mailbox that reads: THE DUNCANS and the remaining Christmas decorations that should have been taken down already.

Stepping onto the porch, I pound on the door. There are quick steps and then Kate opens the door, surprised to see me.

I let my eyes change to black and tell her with a roughness in my voice, "Let me in."

She grabs my collar and pulls me to her, crushing her lips to mine. The hunger behind her kiss proves to me that she knows what I want, and she wants it, too. I kick the door closed harder than necessary and the key holder falls, scattering keys across the floor.

Pressing her against a hutch, I shove my coat off as she pulls at my shirt.

Her fingers trail along my chest, burning my skin. My tongue slides over hers while we tear at our clothes. I pull away slightly and slip her shirt off. She grabs my hair and sinks her teeth into my neck, sending a rush of heat surging through me. My hands glide to her butt as I close my eyes with the pleasure of the pulling at my veins her fangs brings me.

My grip on her tightens and I lift her unto the ledge of the hutch. She pulls her teeth out and kisses me again, this time letting her fangs graze my lips and making me want her that much more.

Her chest presses into mine with every quick inhale, and her fingernails claw into my back as she pulls me closer.

Jerking her panties to the side, I press my hips into hers. She inhales sharply, arching her head back. As I kiss along her throat, I guide her leg up to my ribs. I bite her just above her breast and her legs tighten around me. Her fingers wrap themselves in my hair as my hips slam into hers.

I pull my teeth out and she licks the blood from my lips, pulling at my hair enough to make my whole body tingle. My heart pounds hard, keeping pace with hers.

The hutch rocks back enough to knock some of the decorative plates down, breaking them into pieces around us. But I ignore that and run my hands up her back, curving her body with mine. Her lips taste like blood, keeping me wanting more as her tongue swirls the flavor around my mouth.

Her moans escape our lips and she leans back enough that I can feel her jagged breath on my skin. My fingers press into her shoulders as her body trembles in my grasp. Placing my hand on her face gently, I rub my thumb over her lips, parting them slightly. She leans forward enough to put my thumb in her mouth and bites into the tip gently, letting her mouth fill with blood and my breath catches.

I grab her butt with my other hand and thrust my hips against her forcefully. She inhales, pulling her teeth out of my thumb and letting the blood pour out of her mouth, streaming down her chin and chest.

Collecting my blood, I glide my tongue along her neck to her chin. I press my lips to hers again as a heat rushes through me, warming my skin as I think: Of all of the people I could choose to be here with, I'd choose her. Every time.

Chapter 10

I *admit, it is in bad taste* to kill someone's daughter then have sex in their house, but I did it anyway. And it is difficult to regret it as I lie on the couch with Kate leaning against me, covered by a thin throw.

"I don't know, Nick. I'm sure Marcella has her reasons for turning all of us."

As I rub my fingers over Kate's bare shoulder, I smile. "Not Luther. He is more like losing a bet."

She laughs lightly. "I'm glad she turned you."

Pulling my arm around her, she asks, "You don't really want to be human, do you?"

Brushing her hair away from her neck, I lean my mouth close to her ear and whisper, "Not right now."

Kissing along her neck to her shoulder, I feel her skin under my lips as chills form and she sighs lightly. Leaning forward, I slip out from behind her and pull on my pants.

"Where are you going?" she asks.

"I have to talk to Marcella."

Kate shifts on the couch, finding a comfortable position on her side. "Maybe you shouldn't."

I look over at her, but she is serious. "Maybe you should just pretend that you don't know."

"Why would I do that?" I ask, pulling on my shirt.

Slowly, she lays her head on her forearm. "Marcella loves you. You're just going to argue and push her away, and what good will that do? You're her favorite. She would rather be dead than lose you."

That sounds reasonable, I suppose. Although it's not something I would normally agree to. But something about the way Kate's eyes drift away makes me believe she is more worried that I will leave her.

Kneeling down beside the couch, I rub her arm, giving her a soft smile. "Well, you're my favorite. And I'll do whatever I have to so I can stay with you."

Her eyes meet mine and she smiles back at me.

I lean over and kiss her gently. "I promise I'm not going anywhere."

Then standing up, I let my fingers trail over her skin as I walk toward the door. I look back simply because I want to see her one more time before I go. Her smile takes my breath away and I blush, biting back my lopsided grin.

"I'll be right back," I tell her.

"I'm sure you will."

I shake my head but can't say much because she knows me too well. Stepping outside, I hurry across the field back to our property, thinking of what to say to Marcella. I don't want to be harsh with her. I should try to be understanding and just hear her out, but she destroyed my life. She's the reason I am what I am.

As I walk into the house, I meet Yen at the door. Carrying a small bag, she nearly walks right into me.

"Are you going somewhere?" I ask.

She smiles softly at me. "You're with Kate now, which means I failed."

Failed at keeping Kate and me apart. Not that Yen would keep me from what I want anyway.

"When this ends, and it will, you know how to find me," she adds.

She starts past me but stops when I ask, "You knew Marcella before me, right?"

Her eyes hide a reservation in them as though she knows what I am about to ask.

"Do you know anything about when I was turned?" I ask quietly.

Laying her hand on my cheek, she gently says, "Don't look at the past, Nick. You can only change the future."

She presses her lips to my cheek, "Goodbye, Nicolas."

Then she walks out, leaving me wondering if I should approach Marcella at all. Maybe Kate is right. Maybe I should just let it be for now.

I need to know, though. I can't pretend I don't.

I walk to Marcella's room slowly, thinking of her likely cold replies to my questions. Knocking on her bedroom door, I do not wait for her response and step inside.

Sitting on her bed, she smiles at me and closes the journal she had been writing in. But when I do not smile back, seriousness washes over her face. Laying the journal on the nightstand, she asks, "Is everything all right?"

"Why did you turn me?"

"I didn't. Salem did," she says, shifting to the edge of the bed.

Taking a deep breath, I try to stay calm despite her lies. "Please, Marcella. I'm not a child who needs to be comforted." I wait a moment for her to consider the truth before I ask again, "Why did *you* turn me?"

Her chin quivers and the tears begin to roll down her face. "I was so lonely," she whimpers out.

Having never seen her cry before, I wasn't quite expecting it, and I really don't know what to do. My instinct is to make her feel better. After all, she is my mother. But my mind is telling me that it is another trick.

"I just wanted my son back," she continues. Covering her face with her hands, she leans forward. "I'm so sorry." Sniffling hard, she says, "I wanted to tell you so many times, but I was afraid I'd lose you, too."

That makes sense, because I am not sure if I would have stayed.

"I realize you're not Noah, but you're still my son and I love you more than anyone else." She pauses a moment, unable to control her tears before she starts again, "Before you, I was a mess. I was heartbroken and miserable. But you... you made my life whole again."

As she drops her head, I walk over to her and kneel down in front of her. I should be angry. Angry about losing Ann – but Marcella is my family now. I should be ready to walk out the door, but she needs me.

She looks up at me with mascara streaming down her cheeks and my heart breaks.

Taking her hand, I start gently, "You took a lot from me." More than a lot, everything I ever wanted. "But you gave me something I never had before," I rub the mascara with my thumb, "a mother."

She tries to smile but her chin continues to tremble so I tell her, "I'm not going anywhere."

I want to ask about Ann, but inside I know I'm not ready to hear the truth, so instead, I lean toward her and kiss her forehead. Then I hear someone pounding on the front door.

Standing up, I look toward the sound and tell her, "Stay here."

I hurry to the front door just as the person pounds again. As I swing the door open, Finn starts in, "Where's Tara?"

I put my hand on his chest to stop him, and push him back outside. Stepping onto the porch, I tell him, "What are you doing here?"

He exhales irritably. "I'm looking for Tara. I know she's here."

My eyebrows come together with his tone. "No, she's not."

"Maybe not in your house, but she's in this town somewhere."

I step closer to him. "Then why don't you sniff her out like a good doggie instead of barking at me, because that won't get you anywhere."

He takes a deep breath, letting his exhale fog the air between us. "Don't push me, Nicolas. I like you. I do. Sort of. I might even feel bad if I killed you, but Eric sent me to bring her home. So that's what I'm going to do."

As if he could kill me. "She already has a plane ticket for tomorrow, so you can play fetch some other time."

"Where is she?"

"I don't know."

His tongue slides over his teeth as he tries to stay calm. "Don't know, or won't say?"

"Both."

"Look, Nick –"

I cut him off abruptly, "You look. Her flight leaves in fifteen hours. Eric has her all the time. Let her have these fifteen hours with me."

As he sighs, I can see that he is bending and finally he says, "Fine. But don't try anything. My orders are to bring her back at any cost."

Meaning he would try to kill me, which is laughable.

"How did you know she was here?"

Finn smiles at me. "Eric had me fly to Alaska to keep an eye on her and when he felt her break ties with Roddy, he told me to bring her home."

So she did let Roddy go.

"I could only think of one person who could talk her into that. Just can't figure out why you would."

And he's not going to find out, either. Exhaling forcefully, I sit on the snowy porch step. "How are your girls, Finn?" I ask, even though I have only met his twins a few times.

"They're good." He sits down next to me, draping his arms over his knees. "Micah wants to be a lone wolf," he says, shaking his head. "I talked her into staying through the winter, just to see if she changes her mind, but I doubt she does."

Knowing that female werewolves are rarer than males, I doubt if Eric would let her leave.

"And Sami is dating Trent," Finn says with disgust.

"Trent? He's what? Eighth in command?" Someone without much authority over the other wolves. And Finn thought he was low on the totem pole at fifth.

"Guess she's not like her mom," I mutter. I almost feel bad for bringing up his ex-wife, but he laughs anyway.

He hits my arm playfully. "Easy, Nick. Lydia is still the mother of my children."

"And your superior now," I say.

He rolls his eyes. "You don't have to remind me of that. Saul," – Lydia's new husband – "is next in line to be alpha. She's not stupid. She's not going to marry down."

As he slides his foot across the snow, I almost feel pity for him. It must be hard to have to take orders from your ex.

"She did marry down," I tell him. "Saul may have more power, but you're a better man than him." I lean back, resting on my hands. "Hell, you're a better man than Eric."

Finn smiles to himself as I say under my breath, "I just wish Tara would see that." Anyone would be better than Eric.

He shrugs. "She loves being an alpha. A real man would never ask her to give that up."

There is something in his tone that makes it clear to me what he really meant, was that he wouldn't ask her to. Smiling widely, I look over at him. "You like her," I accuse.

Quickly, he shakes his head. "No, I don't. Of course, I can't. I mean, I don't. I swear," he says, but his words tumble out on top of each other and sound defensive.

I laugh to myself. "You do. Admit it."

Slightly embarrassed, his face flushes pink as he fights a smile. "I do not. If I did, Eric would challenge me to a fight to get rid of the competition. And since I am not ready to take on Eric, I am *not* in love with Tara."

Who said anything about love? Hearing everything hidden in his words, I just smile at him. "Good to know."

The sound of a truck roars closer and I look up in time to see Bradley's Ford skid to a halt by my driveway. The two men in the bed stand up and my eyes change to black. The tension reverberates between us and my muscles twitch toward them. Finn grabs my arm, and even though he could not stop me, I stay where I am.

The two men pull something from the bottom of the bed and toss it on the ground. Large and heavy, it makes a thud as it hits the snow. I know what it is and smell it, despite the distance, and when it starts to move, Finn knows, too.

Under his breath, Finn says in disbelief, "Tara."

Bradley presses the gas petal down and the tires spin on the ice just as Finn rushes forward. Even though I would like to see Finn kill those werewolves, I know he wouldn't win. Not alone.

I hurry in front of Finn, pushing him back a step. "Stop. You can't help her if you're dead."

Finn watches the truck speed off with a deep hatred in his eyes, his chest rising and falling with his quick, sharp breaths. Then he turns his eyes on me coldly. "Get out of my way."

I step aside and he rushes to Tara, but I still manage to get there first.

I kneel down next to her and brush her blood-soaked hair away from her face. Lying on her side, she moans painfully. She holds her ribs, only taking shallow breaths, which tells me there is probably at least one fractured. The bruising on her face is already beginning to yellow as it fades. Seeing her so broken causes a heat to rise in me as I think of what I will do to those pathetic wolves.

I place my hand on her swollen cheek. "Tara, are you okay?"

With her eyes tightly closed, she murmurs, "Go away, Nick."

Finn slides his hand under her back and whispers, "Come here," as he leans her up.

Her eyes open when she hears his voice.

Reopening the cut on her lip with her words, she asks him, "What are you doing here?"

He looks her over carefully with worry drawing his eyebrows together. "Protecting you."

I watch as he cradles her in arms, seeing that there is more than just concern for his alpha there.

She laughs weakly. "Well, you're not doing a very good job."

Even as she lies in the snow, she is sarcastic and it makes him laugh lightly.

Tara pushes off of him and tries to stand. Finn and I both reach out to help her, but as an alpha, her pride keeps her from accepting it. She gets to her feet and stumbles back a step.

As I grab her elbow to stabilize her, she shoves my hand off. "I'm fine," she snaps.

But she is not fine and she cannot possibly think she is. So, just as irritably, I correct her, "No. You're not."

There is nothing about this that is fine. She is just pretending to be tough because Finn is here and she has to be in 'alpha mode', which is ridiculous.

I step closer to her so that my face is near hers. "You're coming inside. I'm cleaning you up, and you're explaining what happened."

"No –"

I cut her off abruptly, "Now," I order sternly enough to make me think that maybe if I were a wolf, I would have been an alpha, too.

Her eyes narrow but she cannot hide the way her throat moves as she swallows back her nervousness, making me feel bad for sounding so threatening. She has never been afraid of me and I don't want that to start now.

Relaxing my shoulders, I add quietly, "Please."

Even though I know the idea of being in a vampire's house doesn't suit her instincts, or even her creepiest desires, I can tell the option of sitting down someplace warm is appealing.

She exhales forcefully. "Fine."

Finn starts toward her. "I'll help you in."

But just as his hand almost braces her shoulder, I push him back a step. "You weren't invited," I say sharply. Although, I normally have no problem with Finn, the circumstances make me a little more territorial than usual. Besides, it isn't exactly safe for a wolf inside my house.

"Sorry to break it to you, but vampires know how to care for injuries better than just licking wounds."

A low growl rumbles in his chest but he still manages to ask, "You don't expect me to let her go in there with those leeches alone, do you?"

Before I can answer, Tara steps between us. "I expect it." She lays her hand on Finn's chest gently. "Don't come in. No matter what you hear."

"But –"

"That's an order," she says calmly. Then she looks over her shoulder at me and motions with her head toward the house.

I walk with her toward the house feeling Finn's eyes burning into me, but it doesn't distract me from the anger toward Cyrus' pack washing over me. How could those dogs do this to her? Obviously, there has to be a reason. Albeit, it won't be good enough to condone their actions but still, there must be one.

She doesn't let me help her as we make our way into the house, probably still trying to make her pain seem minimal for Finn. As I close the door behind us, she lets out a painful exhale as though she had been holding her breath to keep her ribs from aching.

Without waiting for me to suggest it, she walks over and sits down on the couch carefully, moaning slightly. As she leans back, I walk into the kitchen and wet a towel.

When I come back in, she has her eyes closed but does not look peaceful. I sit next to her and she leans up. She forces a weak smile but I do not smile back. Staring at her bruised face only makes my breaths quicken as rage stirs inside.

Hiding my anger, I dab the towel on her cheek, wiping the dried blood from her skin.

"I thought you would have a nicer house. One that didn't smell like blood and bleach."

I almost smile to myself, remembering why I had to bleach the floors after Luther bled all over the kitchen.

But I don't smile, instead I ask, "Are you going to tell me what this was about, or am I just going to kill a bunch of wolves for the heck of it?"

Taking my hand gently, she lowers it away from her busted lip. "I told you once. Being your friend isn't always a perk."

I have to swallow hard, choking back all of the harsh remarks I want to say, because I know it would only make her mad.

This is because of me. And probably Jericho, but mostly me. If they have a problem with me, which obviously they do, they should have come to me directly. I would have been more than happy to solve that issue without words.

It takes me a moment, but eventually, I sigh quietly and begin wiping the blood from her forehead. "Did you at least fight back?" I ask quietly.

"They didn't do anything wrong. You're a vampire. I'm a werewolf, Nick. I can heal quickly and they know that. I can handle this."

Surely, I didn't just hear her say that. Surely, she doesn't believe what she is saying.

I meet her eyes kindly, despite the heat fuming in me. "This, us," I motion from her to me, "may not be acceptable for most, but that doesn't make it wrong." And I will be sure to educate those mongrels on that.

Just then, Luther walks in and scoffs at Tara. She smirks at him. "What happened to your hand?"

"What happened to your face?" he snaps.

Even before her smile fades, I am in his face. "Say something else smart and I'll take your tongue next," I say severely.

He glances at me coldly. "She can't be in here."

"It's my name on the deed. And I said she could be here. If you don't like it, you can leave," I tell him matter-of-factly.

Tara clears her throat irritably. "Excuse me. Since when did two vampires ignore a bleeding woman just to squabble over nothing?"

She's right, of course. I should be more concerned with her than Luther, but right now, I just need to direct my anger at someone.

I sit down next to her again and start to bring the towel to her face but she snatches it out of my hand. "I can do it myself. I'm not dying, you know."

Stiffly, she stands up as though she had been sitting for hours. "Which way is the bathroom?"

Realizing that she doesn't need or want my help, my anger begins to recede into sorrow. Sorrow not just for her and the pain she is in, but for me and how much my revenge will disappoint her.

I lean back into the couch. "Just through the kitchen."

She nods. "I'll be right back."

I run my hands through my hair, letting a frustrated sigh out as she leaves.

To my surprise, Luther does not say anything disrespectful to rile me. He only asks, "What happened to her?"

"Cyrus' damn dogs."

"Really?"

I shrug. "They're animals."

In disbelief, he asks, "They do that to their own kind?"

Looking up, I remind him of the time, years ago, when I had to keep his hands off of Kate. "*You* do that to your own kind."

"Not to that extent," he defends. "She looks awful. How are you supposed to have good makeup sex when you're looking at that? The bruising, the swelling; she looks disgusting."

Leave it to Luther to come up with that logic. Despite how horrible I feel, I laugh lightly at his ridiculous reasoning.

As I rub my fingers over my forehead, I hear him ask, "What are you going to do about it? Whatever it is, I'm in."

I look up at him, expecting to see the lie in his eyes, but in its place, there is only truth. Even though she is not his friend and he cares very little for wolves, for some reason, I am not surprised that he is willing to step up for her. Maybe he just likes to fight. Or maybe he is not as bad as I pretend he is. Standing up, I put my hand on his shoulder. "Follow me." We walk outside to find Finn waiting on the porch.

"Where is she?" Finn asks. "You didn't just leave her in there alone, did you?"

Raising my hands between us to silence him, I reassure him. "She's fine."

He looks at Luther then at the house nervously, so I continue, "I need you to do something, Finn."

Staring at the door, he listens closely for any signs of a struggle, although his orders were clear and there is nothing he could do about it.

"Something for Tara," I correct myself, and that gets his attention.

His eyes meet mine and he nods as though he already knows what I am going to ask.

"Go back to your hotel. Stay away from Tara. She's going to try to give us both an order we don't want to follow."

An order to not retaliate against those wolves. An order which I do not intend to listen to.

"I'm the only one of us who doesn't have to obey it, and can lie when I agree to it. If she doesn't see you, she won't give you that order."

He doesn't think about it long, proving to me that he was already considering it before I asked him.

Nodding, he simply says, "Her flight leaves in fifteen hours. Make sure she's on it." Then he steps off of the porch and starts across the yard.

Of course, I should not have expected Luther's tiny brain would be able to follow our conversation, so I am not sure why I am disappointed when he asks, "So… what are we doing?"

I look over at him smugly. "I'm going to show you what vampires do for their friends."

***

"Promise me," Tara says, standing on the airport runway with no evidence of her attack remaining. Her hair is neat, the blood and bruising are gone, and the cuts are healed, but it takes more than a few hours to heal the heart. She may say that she is not angry with those wolves, and maybe she is not, but I am. My heart has not healed from the guilt of knowing it was their hatred of me that pushed them toward her. And it is my hatred that will push them back.

I roll my eyes. "Haven't I told you enough already?" As in, I stopped counting at eight times.

Grabbing my chin, she jerks my face close to hers. "I need to hear it one more time."

"I won't hunt down the wolves." At least not the ones in her pack, "Even though they would deserve it and it would give me great pleasure, I promise." …to kill every last one of them.

Staring at me intensely, she twists her mouth, trying to decipher whether I am lying or not. But if there is one thing I am good at, it's lying. Finally, she lets go of my face and takes a step back. "I almost believed you that time," she says playfully, but I can tell that she did, in fact, accept my lie.

"Well, believe this," I take her hand gently, "I am going to miss you."

"You know, you could always come to see me," she teases.

Just what I want to do, spend time around Eric. The last time I had to share her with him, it took everything I had not to chew into his neck.

"Sure," I say sarcastically, "and while I'm there, we could take a tour of every cathedral in Rome."

Laughing lightheartedly, she picks her bag up out of the snow and pulls it onto her shoulder.

"Call me when you land," I tell her.

She smiles softly at me. "Do you see this smile? It's for you. Keep it with you until we meet again."

I lean in and kiss her on the cheek, even though I know Finn is watching from a distance and is probably fuming over it. "I'll keep it in my heart. Always."

Wrapping her arms around my neck, she holds me for a moment, longing to stay just a little more. A part of me, a large part, considers asking her to ignore her pack's needs for my own personal wants. But Finn is right, anyone who really cares about her wouldn't ask that, so I stay quiet.

Her fingers trail across my hand as she backs away slowly with tears hanging in her eyes. Barely audible, she whispers, "Bye."

Then she turns and starts toward the plane, wiping the tear she didn't want me to see from her cheek.

I watch a man help her into the plane and close the door behind her. She forces a sad smile and waves at me.

Raising my hand, I give her a weak wave. "Goodbye," I whisper.

She kisses her fingertips and presses them to the window as the engine fires up. Grabbing her kiss in a handful of air, I show her my lopsided smile and watch her until the plane is in the sky.

As I begin to miss her, I feel Finn's hand on my shoulder. "You ready?"

Just like that, I am back to reality and the task at hand. "Are you?"

"Do you remember what she looked like the last time I saw her?" he asks.

How could I forget? Broken and bruised, my best friend in pain, yeah, I remember. Looking over at him, I nod.

"Then you know my answer." He walks away, carrying his bag of clothing he will need after he phases, once he shreds the current ones. He adds, "Let's go get Luther."

I catch up to him quickly but stay quiet, thinking of what to say to him. He must be dying inside. The woman he loves, but can't have, was hurting and there was nothing he could do. She doesn't want him to do anything about it. Conflicted with what she wants and what he feels is right, he knows Tara will not be pleased with his actions. Mine, sure, she expects me not to listen. But Finn? That will be like a slap in the face.

"What's the plan?" he asks quietly.

But I don't have a real plan. I know they will be at Bradley's bar. They always are. I know we will kill everyone, human and wolf alike, but Finn hasn't thought of the humans. Or maybe he has.

I glance over at him and shrug. "No mercy. No witnesses."

Without meeting my eyes, he nods slowly.

"I realize what I'm asking you to do," I start, "and I can do it without you. Don't feel pressured into this. You will always remember what we're about to do." The blood, the screams, the pain. "Just say it and you can walk away. I won't think less of you."

He looks over at me with pain in his eyes. "She's my alpha, Nick. I'm supposed to protect her."

"That doesn't mean getting revenge," I tell him softly.

His eyes drop to the snow at his feet again.

But he cannot hide what this is really about. "I know you love her more than Eric does. He wouldn't do this. He wouldn't kill humans for her. But are you sure you can?"

There is a pause and I almost start speaking again when he says, "Do you ever stop talking?"

I smile to myself but remain quiet the rest of the way into town where we meet up with Kate and Luther. Kate keeps her bow close while Luther hands me the 12-gauge shotgun I had asked for. Somehow they can sense the pain Finn is in and only say a few minor things until we reach the back door of the bar.

I put my finger up to silence everyone but it is really more of a reminder, since nobody is talking anyway. Finn lays his bag of clothing in the snow by the door as Kate pulls an arrow from her quiver. Pointing to Luther, I gesture for him to take his position at the front door to be sure nobody makes it out.

He rushes away, disappearing around the corner. I only wait a moment longer before I push the door open and creep into the storage room quietly. Finn and Kate flank me, but when I stop at the door leading to the bar, Finn walks past me to the breaker box.

I lift the shotgun up, aiming it at the door as Kate pulls back the bow string, both of us ready to fire. Looking at me, Finn flips the breaker and everything goes dark. There is a slight scream that quickly turns into a laugh as the humans inside make the fatal assumption that the power is merely out.

Finn pulls off his shirt, waiting to phase until our cover is blown, since the werewolves inside would be able to sense him in his wolf form.

As Bradley's heavy steps draw closer, I let my eyes change to black and my fangs press into my lip. Revenge makes the sweetest blood. Now is not the time for mercy and remorse, and I do not intend to have any.

The door opens and I wait the half of a second for Bradley's eyes to meet mine and see his death coming before I pull the trigger.

The sound echoes through the bar as his face explodes from the blast. The shot lights up the darkness as bits of bone and flesh fill the air and the humans cry out in fear, unsure of what is happening.

They scramble for the door that they cannot see through the darkness. The chairs clatter onto the floor, they trample over one another, too afraid to think clearly.

But the wolves do not panic. Phasing quickly, they rush at us as I pull back the forestock, loading another shell into the barrel.

Arrows fly past me as I pull the trigger again and take down a light tan wolf while the other four charge at us. Finn sheds his human self into a dark auburn wolf and pushes past me, eager for a kill. As Kate and I hurry into the bar, Finn lunges at a grey wolf, sinking his teeth into his throat and dragging him to the ground.

Grabbing the barrel near the sight, I swing the gun around as a brown wolf jumps at me. The stock cracks against his jaw, sending him colliding into the wall. An arrow passes my head and pierces the wolf through the eye. He phases back to his human form before his dead body even hits the floor.

I look behind me in time to see Kate pull another arrow from her quiver and send it deep into a human's abdomen as they run toward the door.

A dark grey wolf leaps at me and I bound over him, rolling over his back. As I land on my feet, he turns and snaps at my leg. Bringing my arm around, I slam my fist into his shoulder, pushing him back slightly. I step toward him and drive my foot in his ribs, feeling them pop against my shoe. He whines painfully as he backs away from me, probably trying to heal some before we proceed, but I don't mind, there are others to massacre.

I grab a human by the hair as he tries to make his escape. Wrapping my arm around his throat, I squeeze until he struggles for air. I dig my fingers into the soft flesh under his chin and pull up, removing his jaw before he can scream.

I dispose of him on the floor. Stepping over his trembling body, I slice my fingernails through another human's abdomen, spilling intestines onto the floor. He drops to his knees in his pooling blood and falls forward, smacking his face on the hardwood.

Amidst the panic, the humans pile themselves at the door, clawing and jerking at one another to try to get closer to their exit. Sinking my fingers into their skin, I grab them by the back and throw them aside, scattering them around the room.

I hurry to one of the women I had tossed, causing her to hit her head on the bar. Blood trickles down her forehead, her pupils are wide, trying to make me out in the dark. I take a bottle from the counter and shatter it against the wood. Shoving it into her chest, I keep my face close to hers, inhaling her fear and panicked sweat.

Leaving her to choke on her last bit of air, I walk over to another human and crush his head under my shoe, twisting my foot through the bloody pile of skull and flesh.

A smaller wolf jumps at me and I duck in time for it to fly over me. It skids to a stop on the hardwood and turns toward me just as my foot connects to his jaw. The wolf flips back from the force and lands on its back. It scrambles to get to its feet as I wrap my arms around it from behind. Squeezing its ribs, I feel the bones snapping under the pressure. The wolf whines and jerks wildly but my grip only tightens as its cries to become weak.

Dropping it to the floor, I grab the barstool. With its mouth open in a painful cry, I shove the leg of the stool in its mouth and out the back of its neck, severing the spinal cord and it phases back into the human it once was.

Hearing an angry snarl, I start to turn around to find the dark grey wolf charging at me. It jumps at me but it is closer than I thought and I am not ready. With an open mouth, its teeth are only merely inches from my face, close enough for me to smell the alcohol on his breath when something jerks it to the side.

It lands on its side beside the bar with two arrows deep in its neck. Kate rushes to it. Swinging her bow around, she slams it into the wolf's skull, collapsing it around the bow.

The wolf phases back into its human form as Kate pulls her arrows from it. Without hesitation, she readies her bow and fires her bloody arrows into some unassuming humans near the door.

I smile. She has never looked so tempting. But I don't have time to think like that now.

As I start toward the pool tables where some humans have taken to hiding, a human runs past me. I grab her by the hair, pull her back, and snap her neck quickly.

Stepping over her body, I walk toward the man holding a pool cue as if that would save him. I jerk the cue from his hands and shove it through his throat, lifting him into the air and tossing him aside.

I reach under the pool table and drag a man out from his hiding place. He screams and fights but to no avail. I sink my fangs into the soft tissue of his neck. Piercing his artery, I feel his warm blood course down my burning throat. Smooth and cooling, it eases my hunger as his body goes limp against me.

As a woman runs past me, I drop the man and snatch her by the arm. I slam her body onto the pool table, letting her head hang over the edge.

Kate's timing is impeccable. She is there before I realize that I want her to be. Kate swings her bow down on the woman's chin, snapping her head back violently so that it appears to be only hanging by skin.

A man with a cigarette dangling from his lips rushes toward Kate. Although, I don't believe he can see her or would be an actual threat, I bound over the pool table.

Landing near him, I grab him in a headlock. Quickly, I pull the cigarette from him and jab it in his eye, burning his pupil. Screaming, he squirms in my arm. Placing my hand on the back of his head, I drive his face into my knee, smashing his bones and stopping his heart.

I look around at the bodies strewn around the floor. Finn hovers over the last werewolf's human body in the corner. Blood pools on the hardwood, making puddles in the uneven floor. The room is quiet but there is still one heartbeat I hear.

Suddenly, the lights come on and Luke steps out of the storage room with a shotgun. He looks around for a moment but when he sees me, confusion sweeps over him.

"Nick?" he asks.

Knowing what is about to happen, I close my eyes just as the dark auburn wolf jumps at Luke. From the sound of brief, muffled screams, I imagine Finn has his teeth deep in Luke's throat. The gun goes off, making me open my eyes again.

I watch as Finn removes his teeth from Luke's dead body and phases into his human form. Bloody and naked, he stares at Luke in disbelief. Blood runs down his arm, I assume from where the bullet entered his bicep.

I hurry over and kneel down close to him. "Are you okay?"

He answers without taking his eyes from Luke. "He's not the only human I killed tonight," he whispers.

Placing my hand on his back, I try to console him. "You did the right thing."

"You don't understand," he says quietly. Looking over at me, he continues, "I liked it."

I had not considered that the animal in him would enjoy the hunt so much even when the prey is human.

I should not have let him come with me. He will not only carry the remorse of this massacre with him but also the guilt from the pleasure he took in it. And that guilt is so much more consuming. And lasts so much longer.

"I'm sorry," I tell him honestly.

His eyes drift away but I can tell he believes me. He wipes the blood from his mouth with the back of his hand. "I have to go. I'm getting dressed. I'm going home. And I'm going to forget this ever happened."

But it won't be that easy, and we both know it. Guilt has a way of sticking around for centuries, always reappearing at the worst times and reminding us that we are not any better than our prey.

Standing up, he walks into the storage room to dress. I start toward Kate with my eyes on the bloody footprints smeared on the hardwood. Hearing her sigh, I look up to see her standing with her bow over her shoulder, blood tainting her clothes, splattered in her hair, contrasting against her skin, and her eyes as black as night.

Smiling hungrily, I tell her, "You look so beautiful in red."

I step close to her and lay my hand along her jawline. Letting my fingers cradle her skull, I rub my thumb across her cheek, smearing crimson over her skin.

Between the smell of blood caressing my nose, and the sight of it staining my surroundings, my lips yearn to touch hers like never before, but still I pace myself, leaning in slowly until my lips brush hers gently. Her mouth parts slightly and her jagged breath grazes my skin. Pushing my lips to hers, I swirl the blood from my mouth with hers.

Without willing it, my hand reaches to the small of her back, pulling her into me and keeping her close so our noses nearly touch when I lean away.

"What about Cyrus?" she whispers, breaking my moment.

Sighing, I step back. "Can you and Luther handle this? I'd like to take care of Cyrus myself."

She smiles mischievously, letting her eyes change back to brown. "There's enough alcohol in here to start a pretty nasty fire, so yes, I can handle it." She closes the distance between us, laying her hand on my chest, "All by myself," she adds.

I kiss her softly and tell her, "Try to make sure Luther is trapped in here when it burns."

As she laughs lightly, I start out the door and walk outside and into a puff of smoke. I glance to my right and see Luther leaning against the building holding a cigarette to his mouth. True, vampires are not smokers but what is less suspicious than someone smoking outside of a bar?

He inhales and the tip burns bright red. Blowing out another cloud of thick smoke, he flips the cigarette into the street. "I don't hear any growling, so I take it we won."

I smile to myself. As if he ever thought we wouldn't.

"Better hurry and get that alpha," he adds.

Laughing slightly, I ask him, "Why? Are there witnesses that will tell him?"

His smile twists and he pushes himself off of the building with his foot. Leaning close to my face, he says, "Not on my watch."

Even though he is only inches from my face, I am not threatened. There is nothing he can do that would permanently injure me, and little that he could do to temporarily hurt me.

So with intense eyes, I tell him, "If I thought any different, you wouldn't be standing here with that absurd smirk on your face."

His smile fades and his jaw flexes, but before he can retort, I goad, "So why don't you just go in there like a good little boy, and clean up *my* mess for a change."

As I step past him, I hit his shoulder with mine. But I didn't need to touch him to feel the heat rolling from his body, so despite myself, I turn to him, "Oh, and Luther," he looks back at me with anger written across his face, "thanks."

I do not hide the honesty in my statement. I am thankful for him tonight. Although it may be the only time in the past one hundred years that I have been.

His eyebrows relax and his shoulders lower with his breath. "What did you say?" he asks.

Smiling, I chuckle to myself, "You're not getting me to repeat that."

Nodding, he shrugs. "I thought I'd try."

He pushes the door open and goes inside with a small smile lighting his face.

As I start toward Cyrus' house, the snow begins to fall; not heavily, just enough to dance in the air around me. I try to stay off of the main streets since I am sure my blood soaked-clothes would draw unwanted attention.

Eventually, I make it just outside of the town limits where a haze of smoke from a wood stove surrounds Cyrus' small home.

I walk onto the porch and knock lightly. No point in wasting time now.

When the door opens, I have to look down because the person who answers is only half my size. Her chubby cheeks are full of food, making her resemble a chipmunk. Her innocent eyes stare at me confused, either by my appearance or the late hour.

I bend down in front of the five-year-old. "You must Anita. I've heard a lot about you," I lie.

"Who are you?"

"I'm Nick. I'm looking for your father."

Without moving to fetch him, she asks, "What is all that red on you?"

I glance down at the blood on my shirt then back at her. "Would you believe I was in a food fight?"

Holding back, I chuckle quietly at my own joke. Food fight.

"Is it ketchup or barbeque sauce or something?"

I smile widely, exposing my teeth, but she doesn't know to be afraid, so she isn't. "It's something."

She steps onto the porch and her hand comes up between us. With her fingers so close to my skin, my heart races. The scent of her blood teases me, provoking me to give in, whispering that she could be my sweet revenge.

Fire surges through my throat as she reaches for the blood, curiosity pushing her to trace her fingers through it.

As the warmth of her flesh trails along my cheek, I close my eyes and focus on not being a vampire for a moment. Yes, killing her would hurt Cyrus, but it would be wrong, and I would hurt, too.

Somewhere in the house, I can hear footsteps coming closer. I open my eyes and stare past her into the empty living room.

Grabbing her wrist, I pull her hand away from my face, and with my sleeve, I wipe the blood from her fingertips.

"What are you doing that for?"

Because there is no part of me that wants to see blood on a child again, even when they still have a heartbeat.

"It will stain your clothes, and my shirt is already ruined," I tell her as Cyrus steps in the living room.

His face drops when he sees his daughter so close to me. My eyes lock on his and he rushes toward us. Without looking away, my grip on her wrist tightens.

"Ow," she says quietly. "You're hurting me."

He stops in his tracks near the door. I smile coldly at him for a moment then turn my eyes to Anita. "I'm sorry," I say as I loosen my hand without letting her go.

Standing up, I keep my hold on her wrist. "I'm going for a walk, Cyrus. Will you join me?"

My eyes drop to Anita and I run my hand over her hair. "Or do you want me to take someone else?" I add.

His breaths grow quick and uneven with nervousness, but not for himself. He is nervous because I am a good liar and he doesn't realize that I would not purposely hurt her.

He walks out onto the porch. "She needs to go inside. It's past her bedtime."

He says that, but what I hear is compliance. I release my grip and nudge her toward the door. "It was very nice to meet you," I tell her softly.

She nods back at me as Cyrus grabs her shoulders. "Anita, you go inside and lock the doors. Don't come out and don't let anyone in. Not anyone – for any reason."

He leans close and kisses her cheek to hide the tears in his eyes. "I love you."

"I love you, too, daddy," she says, hugging him tightly.

He takes a deep breath, pulling back his tears, and leans away from her. "Goodnight, sweetheart."

She starts inside as she tells him, "Goodnight."

He waits the moment it takes her to shut the door and we hear the lock scrape the metal before he looks at me. His eyes sweep over me quickly then out into the night where I am sure he can see the smoke from the burning bar in town.

Finally, he looks directly into my eyes. "Let's get this over with," he tells me.

Leaving the porch, he leads me toward the vacant field with his head down.

I say nothing. There is nothing to say. He knows why we are here. He knows what has happened. I am sure he felt his pack die before I even left the bar.

The snow crunches beneath our shoes, filling the silence, and as I begin to wonder why he doesn't fight me, fight for his life, he speaks.

"Thank you for not doing this in front of Anita. She doesn't know what I am and …" he trails off for a moment, "and the last thing I want her to see is me as a monster."

I could tell him that he's not the monster here. I could say, werewolves are less violent, less hungry for pain, more patient than vampires, but those would be lies.

"I know you don't owe me anything, but I'm going to ask for something anyway," he continues. "Spare her."

He lets out a shaky breath before he finishes, "Please."

As if I would slay her just get even with her dead father. She's a child, innocent and young, not for killing.

He shouldn't beg. I enjoy it too much. My eyes change to black and my fangs descend. His death and blood are so close, my body craves it, making my wait painful.

"This is far enough," I tell him callously.

He drops to his knees in front of me. Quietly, he tells me, "I understand this. I didn't know what they were planning, but they were my pack, my responsibility. Your friend was hurt and I should have done something about it, but I didn't. And for that reason, I am accountable for what happened."

Of course this is his fault. He is right. His pack. His responsibility.

"Could you please just show me a small bit of mercy and make this quick?" he asks as he leans his head to the side, making his throat even more accessible.

Mercy? No. There is no mercy. Not for wolves like him and his pack.

Standing behind him, I think of the ways to sink my teeth into him. I consider which vessels to puncture, whether to drag out his death or make him bleed out slowly. But something else crosses my mind. Something that, to the outside may seem forgiving, but to an alpha who lost his pack, it's a curse.

Leaving him in the snow, waiting for his release, I walk away. An alpha without a pack, without purpose, without power, will suffer far more alive than a few hours of death could ever give him. A living death, one of misery and mediocrity, will serve better as revenge than anything my fangs could deliver.

Letting my eyes change to green again, I head toward my house. I take the long way, avoiding the commotion in town surrounding the burning bar, which from the sound of it, has caused quite a stir.

I walk past the hospital, through its barren parking lot, slink from shadow to shadow behind the buildings and in the alleys.

I do not feel guilty, rather justified, instead. I am being very gracious by allowing the families of those wolves to remain among the living. My friend was hurt because of those dogs, and they deserved what was done to them. Sure, the humans who were killed in the mix may not have warranted death, but no adult is innocent. Humans die every day, tonight is no different.

As I pass the grocery store, something catches my eye. Stopping in front of the newspaper rack, my eyes run over the bold, black heading: MISSING CHILD FOUND DEAD.

Quickly, I pat my pockets, desperately searching for a coin and finding one in my pants. I pull the little metal coin out and slip it into the machine. Ripping the door open, I snatch the newspaper out.

I scan through the words, stopping at the most important phrases: ORPHAN GIRL, BODY FOUND IN FIELD, ANIMAL ATTACK. My breathing becomes chaotic as I read the words I expect to find: PENNY MASON.

Letting go of the newspaper rack, I hear the door slam shut but it is only background noise to the pounding of my heart. Penny Mason. That is, I mean was, my Punzi's name.

I've read thousands of newspapers about our meals. Always an animal attack, which is fitting, but this was no accident.

A heat rolls through me and I crush the paper in my hand. I exhale forcefully, ignoring the cloud of fog that appears in front of me. My anger blurs my vision, and for once, I do not care about my surroundings. My only concern is for holding onto what little humanity I have and not massacring the entire city.

Seeing nothing but blood, I close my eyes, but that does nothing for my trembling hands. Unable to focus on anything but the fire inside, my eyes open, black and intimidating, ready to enjoy pain.

I know who did this and I know where they live. Rushing through the snow, I push my legs as fast as they will carry me, not worrying about who might see me.

Finally, I reach the house. Without slowing my pace, I burst through the door. Luther sits up quickly on the sofa, but I march past him and go into the kitchen. I toss the newspaper on the table and it slides to a stop in front of Marcella.

"I dare you to lie," I say coldly with my heavy English accent.

She glances at the paper only briefly then pushes it away. "She was human."

"She was a child."

Standing up, Marcella says, "Which nobody misses."

Her words pull more fury from me than I expect. Grabbing the edge of the table, I toss it up into the wall where it breaks and splinters on the floor. "I miss her!"

Marcella's face twists with disgust. "She would have ruined everything."

I step close to her, putting my face near hers. "Like you don't?"

Her hand swings at my face but I grab her arm, twisting it back and moving behind her. I pull up on her arm so she knows how easily I could rip it off.

With my other hand, I hold her chin so she cannot move. Luther stops in the doorway, watching me as I whisper to Marcella, "I should kill you for this. You call me your son, but you so willingly hurt me over and over again. Don't you think I've had enough? Don't you think I'd be better off without you?"

"Nick," Luther starts quietly as he raises his hands between us. "Calm down. Let's talk about this," he says, but then he sees the scattered newspaper on the floor.

He kneels down and picks up the front page. He doesn't stare at it long before he knows all that he needs to.

Looking up at me with pity, he drops the paper. "Oh, Nick, I, um… I am so sorry."

He glances at Marcella briefly before he backs out of the room, understanding that if I choose to kill her, he won't be able to stop me, and is not sure he would even try.

I did not hear Kate enter from the hallway but I can sense her there just the same.

"You take everything from me," I tell Marcella coldly, "It's time I take something from you."

My fangs extend and push against Marcella's flesh. I can feel her pulse just under my teeth, tempting and calling to me the way vengeance often does.

Just as my fangs puncture her skin, I hear Kate's voice. "You couldn't keep her. She was human."

I turn my eyes to Kate as she continues, "It was her or us, Nick. You have to understand. I couldn't lose you."

Instantly, my anger is swept away by hurt. My grip on Marcella loosens. "What?" I barely whisper.

I am mistaken; surely I misunderstood. I must have. Kate could never kill Punzi. She would never hurt me like that.

"Nicolas –" she says as she steps closer.

I back away from her as my eyes fill with tears. "Tell me it wasn't you. Kate, please. You wouldn't…" I let my words trail as my voice fades.

There is a small pause as she watches a tear roll down my cheek. When she speaks, it is soft and tender. "It's for the best."

I shake my head at her lie. It's not for the best. Punzi was great. She made me happy. She made me feel human again.

My lip quivers as I tell her, "You knew… You knew what she meant to me. And you took her anyway. Why would you do that?"

No answer would suffice at this point, but I still want one.

"You would have left with her. Left to raise her, without me. She was in our way." Kate comes toward me with her hand out to touch my cheek. "I love you."

Backing away, I tell her, "No, you don't. You don't know how."

I look around the room at the smashed table, Marcella holding her arms around herself, the newspaper strewn across the floor, and Kate with her confused and pained expression. They killed Punzi to keep me, but all they have done is given me a reason to leave.

"This family is broken," I tell them, holding back the sadness in my voice. "And I want no part of it."

I step back into the doorway to the living room as I finish. "Don't look for me."

Turning my back to them, I let my tears fall, not just for losing Punzi, but also my family. So much to lose that cannot be replaced.

Kate screams out my name but I ignore her and walk outside where Luther is waiting on the porch.

"Are you really leaving?" he asks with a hint of despair.

I nod and he steps close to me, resting his hand on my shoulder. "I'll look after them."

But I already knew he would. I guess I've always known he could, but only if he had to.

He pulls me into a hug that I was not ready for, but do not shy from. I suppose he can read people well enough to know how badly I am hurting, and despite our bickering, I may actually miss him. Sort of. Well, probably not.

He leans away from me. Playfully, he slaps my cheek lightly. "You take care of yourself."

Then without another word, he goes back inside the house and leaves me to my escape.

I do not wait for Kate to come out and try to stop me, or Marcella, or even for me to talk myself out of this. I sprint through the snow, making a cloud of white powder in the air behind me. I wipe my frozen tears from my face, but more just take their place.

It takes less time than usual to clear the distance to Denali, and when I reach the city limits, I go straight to the only place I can think of.

I knock on the door quietly. When Phoenix opens the door, she raises her eyebrows. "You look like shit."

"Let me in," I say, but it is more of a question than a statement since I've never been inside her home before.

She holds the door mostly closed. "No."

I start to respond, but trying not to cry again, I only manage to suck in air. After my shaky exhale, I weakly say, "Please."

There is something about a man in tears that makes women everywhere melt. They will do anything to help him. Anything.

She pushes the door open the rest of the way and gestures for me to come inside, which is as good as words.

I walk inside, but do not see much, other than the orange carpeting.

"You should've gone to a safe house," she tells me.

"They'll look for me there," I say without explaining who will be searching. "I need your help."

She stares at me for a long moment, considering her options, then sighs. "I may know a human who could get you some papers."

She walks over to the telephone and picks up the receiver. "You have to go someplace nobody would ever look. Do you know a place like that?"

Her fingers turn the rotary wheel and it ticks back to its starting place.

"Yes," I admit.

"Where?"

I look up at her and say the only words I despise to hear, "England."